The PRESIDENT FACTOR

A City of Light Imprint

Blacklight Press
A City of Light Imprint

City of Light Publishing
266 Elmwood, Suite 407
Buffalo, New York 14222
info@CityofLightPublishing.com
www.CityofLightPublishing.com

Book design by Ana Cristina Ochoa

ISBN: 978-1-942483-86-1 (softcover)

10 9 8 7 6 5 4 3 2 1

The President Factor is dedicated to democracy,
a free press, and the right to vote.
and
My wonderful daughters,
Kristin, Jessica and Sarah
and my mother, Loretta Green,
whose love of reading started everything.

INTRODUCTION

The *President Factor* was first published in 2015, packed with political humor, irony, exaggeration and ridicule…and a mind-blowingly accurate view of the future.

Donald Trump had not yet descended his golden escalator onto the political stage when the author was crafting her characters. It's not about him. The rallies packed with shouting crowds of fervent, red-capped fans had not yet begun. Americans weren't yet calling other nationalists "terrorists" so readily. The U.S. president wasn't chatting up the president of Russia and nobody was manipulating footage to denigrate a presidential candidate. Yet…all these things, plus other we-never-thought-we'd-ever-see scenarios… are in these pages.

The author is no Nostradamus, has no crystal ball, and isn't a political pundit, yet she wrote a prescient political satire about the best and worst of politics with characters and situations that bear an uncanny resemblance to the mishegoss surrounding us today.

Prepare to laugh until you cry…and compare.

➳ ONE ➳

On May 20, standing on the floor of the U.S. Senate at precisely 12:05 p.m., Senator Adhemar Reyes (D-NY) shot himself in the foot.

Not like a Dick Cheney shot, which was a real shot (also with political reverberations), but a metaphorical *Oh shit, what did I just do?* shot. A year and a half later it would turn his run for office into more of a *hop* for office since one cannot run swiftly when shot in the foot. Even metaphorically. Especially when the office one runs for is the office of the President of the United States. The senator didn't even know he'd done it.

It was all captured on C-SPAN.

⇝ TWO ⇜

"I'm tired of the *I can see Russia from my porch* candidates," Adhemar shouted across the room to the senator from Tennessee. He timed his shout-out until he was far enough away that he couldn't be accused of hostility, but secure in the knowledge that his raised voice would demand attention. The debate was about the debt ceiling. No matter. Adhemar had the ability and the tendency to segue from any topic at hand to the presidential election a mere two years away. His target.

He strode back and forth on the blue rug with the gold pattern most of us recognize but probably wouldn't be able to identify, say, on a TV game show, even if it meant advancing to the next round. By the time the photo of the event appeared on the front page of *The Washington Post,* however, everyone knew exactly where the senator was when it was taken. His hand punching the air. Making his point. Months later, he would grimace in private, remembering his hubris, but that day he was very sure of himself.

He moved with a studied indifference to the C-SPAN cameras but was acutely aware of their presence. Like a dancer about to execute a *grand jeté* that would land right at the edge of the stage, Adhemar knew precisely how many steps to take before he stepped out of the range of one camera and forced the technical director—TD—in C-SPAN's control room to switch to another to pick him up. He never let that happen. He wasn't sure if anyone was actually in the C-SPAN control room at any given point, so he couldn't risk walking off the screen to become a disembodied voice from who knows where—like a conductor from the pit or that thing that happens when your Netflix stream freezes and the audio continues under a picture of something that was going on two minutes ago. No, he'd practiced these moves in his office. He had it down. He was a prepared man. Always.

The forty-three-year-old senator was engaging to watch even with the sound off. Handsome? Yes. Dark eyes. Ruffled black hair. Six-foot-one, trim and fit. Charismatic? Hell, yes. Animated, but never breaking a sweat.

Being a prominent Hispanic on the Hill placed him at all the DC parties. Being single placed him on a lot of women's watch list. Even on C-SPAN.

His status as a bachelor became fodder for hundreds of bloggers immediately after his fiancée, Maritza Soto, died in a freak accident three years earlier. He had just been voted the Politician Most Women Wanted To Be Sequestered With in a badly worded ad-hoc poll on a minor media website. The day the poll came out, Maritza was sitting at a sidewalk café in Adams Morgan, furiously emailing the article's link to all her friends from college when an SUV swerved to avoid a chipmunk zigzagging across the street. The SUV missed the tiny woodland creature but jumped the curb. It struck Maritza, killing her instantly.

Devastated, Adhemar moved through the next year in a proverbial fog, then snapped out of it one night when a rumor about a former vice-presidential candidate started to form, hinting at her running for president—yet again. Improbable as it was that this person would get the nomination, never mind be elected, the rumor started him thinking about the qualifications one needed to become president—and kick-started his plan to put himself in that exact office.

Which brought him to his C-SPAN moment.

"I'm tired of the *I can see Russia from my porch* candidates," Adhemar said, hitting it again. He paused to acknowledge a few *hear, hears* coming from his side of the aisle, then gave a slight nod for the support he was getting.

"I propose all candidates should be required to participate in a reality show to show how they handle themselves before we put them in the White House!"

Bang.

⇢ THREE ⇠

The folks who monitored C-SPAN got the word out to their bosses, who then passed it on to TV network bookers, who then bombarded Adhemar's office with requests. Entire networks of print and digital outlets ran the same drill. The resulting proliferation of information rivaled the best junior high tweetstorm when a girl from the uncool group shows up in homeroom with the quarterback's ring on her finger.

Gloria Rodriguez, Adhemar's press secretary and damage control maestro, was out to lunch when it all went down. More than fifty phone messages from Sunday morning talk shows, late night talk shows, and two very high-profile cable political satire programs welcomed her return, plus more from the major newspapers and the requisite glut of bloggers. Her inbox had stopped taking messages twenty minutes ago.

"What did he say?" Gloria drilled the intern whose only job was to monitor the Senator's activity on C-SPAN, note the time he said something, and give Gloria a heads-up if Adhemar did anything noteworthy or went off the rails—which he was apt to do.

"Ah. Something about a reality show?" the intern replied nonchalantly.

"You didn't think to call me?" she shrieked, now pacing back and forth behind the intern.

"You were out to lunch."

That stopped the pacing. "What about a reality show?"

"I don't remember."

Since interns are there to learn, this intern learned that he was now off C-SPAN monitoring and assigned to getting coffee for the senator's entire staff. And nothing else. It sucks to screw up in Washington DC.

Gloria was queuing up Adhemar's speech on the office DVR when he walked in.

"You said something about a reality show?" Gloria spat at him, furiously pressing buttons on the remote to get the blasted device to rewind faster. She kept hitting the wrong button, sending the TV into some other dimension—classic TV shows kept popping up on the screen. After *Mayberry RFD* and *I Dream Of Jeannie* played for the third time, Gloria threw the remote at the couch and spun to confront Adhemar. She thrust a crumpled list of requests at him. "What did you say?"

Adhemar watched the remote bounce off the cushions and land in a bowl of guacamole on the coffee table. He trod lightly. "Hi, Gloria. Had lunch yet?" he deflected, hoping the guac wasn't hers.

"What did you say that resulted in every fricking booking agent on this planet frothing at the mouth to get to you?"

"Something about a reality show," Adhemar replied with a boyish grin. Typical Adhemar. He smoothed out the list Gloria had compiled. "*Entertainment Now* wants me?"

"Senator, everyone wants you."

The next day, Adhemar headed to New York City for a round of TV appearances and interviews. His first stop was on BCD network's morning show, *Wake-Up America*. Wink Goodenoff, the host, had quite a bit of close-hand experience with politicos, having worked on the Hill in his senior year at

GW University. How he doglegged into morning TV with a major in poli-sci was always a topic of discussion at his parents' Thanksgiving gathering—the result of his dad being a former U.S. Senator. Wink therefore planned questions for Adhemar, whose answers could be quoted later that year if his dad went off on him again.

After the obligatory *Hello* and *How are you*, Wink dove in. "Let me start the morning, Senator Reyes, with this: I can't remember a time in American history when the voters were as disillusioned with the state of politics as they are now."

Adhemar was on alert. "Exactly, Wink. Can I call you Wink?" Ever charming.

"Of course, Senator."

"Well, Wink. That was the impetus for my suggestion of a reality show to test the mettle of the candidates."

"Senator Ryes, I'm looking at this thing a little differently. Are you trying to make your bones—if I can borrow from the mafia here—by killing off the other candidates? Before we even get to the nominations?"

"Wink, are you saying some politicians might not throw their hats into the ring if they think there is a chance, however remote, that my suggestion could become a reality?"

"Yes, that is exactly what I'm saying."

Adhemar hadn't been thinking of that at all and was impressed with Wink's evaluation of that possible consequence of his proposed show. His C-SPAN statement was pure hyperbole with just one purpose: to get enough press so when he did announce his candidacy, the majority of the American people would know who he was. And he certainly wasn't going to announce the next morning on Wink Goodenoff's show. He had an answer prepared, of course, if anyone ventured into his reasons for the attack on the *I can see Russia* politician.

"My goal, Wink, was to shine a light on what's been missing in American politics. An actual accounting *slash* wide-open book. Of how and what a candidate would do, of what resources they have, and what background they would bring to the Office of President of the United States." Adhemar flashed his perfect white teeth at Wink. He was not above rhetoric.

"Will you be one of those candidates, Senator?"

"I'm just a concerned citizen right now, Wink. Shining that light."

Deflected.

And on to another show.

Later that night, after an entertaining ten minutes on the number one late night talk show that included a bizarre routine with the host adlibbing topical humor to the tune of *H.M.S. Pinafore,* Adhemar headed downtown to the Meatpacking District to meet up with his college buddy Hank. They eventually settled at one of the tiny sidewalk tables of Jean-Georges' Spice Market, snacking on a selection of spicy appetizers and playing the newest game in town: taking a drink every time someone rode by on a bright blue Citibike. Adhemar and Hank had a line of tequila shots set up.

New Yorkers had embraced the bike-share program, modeled after those across Europe. Riding any bike by Spice Market was a bit of a feat, however, considering the restaurant was located on a cobblestone street and Citibikes were a bit clunky with puncture-resistant, nitrogen-filled tires.

"I never thought Bloomberg would pull it off," Adhemar said, watching a Citibiker navigating the cobblestones, fascinated with the dexterity necessary to keep from skidding sideways. "But I like his take-no-prisoners attitude. The guy had no fear. He never waivered from his quest to make New York greener and he got it done. He had a vision, Mike

Bloomberg did. I hope people will one day say that about me." Adhemar said all this with a casual tone.

"You're going to bring in more bikes?" Hank said. "How about jet skis? For the folks in Williamsburg to get over to Manhattan?"

Adhemar turned his attention to one of the appetizers, plucking a piece of black pepper shrimp with his chopsticks and deftly dragging it through the thick, spicy, dark brown sauce that gave the dish its name. He chewed for a moment, contemplating. He would have liked better circumstances than a drinking game to tell one of his oldest friends about his decision to run for president, but the opportunity presented itself. "Well, starting with no fear, I'm…"

"Bike!" Hank shouted, spotting one coming around the corner on 13th Street.

Adhemar paused to throw back another shot of Petron. "Why are there so many bikes here?"

"Dunno. What were you starting to say?"

"Oh. Right. I'm going to run for president," Adhemar finished.

"Oh. Right. Holy Christ!" Hank mocked.

Adhemar sat up straighter in his rattan chair. "It's a natural progression for me. And I have great faith."

"In yourself?" Hank said.

"In the American people."

"You've never lost your idealism, A. R."

"Is that something one loses as one gets older?" Adhemar said. "I'd like to think I've kept a little of that from our days together. Mixed with a dose of realism."

"Okay, if you do get elected president…" Hank started to say. Spotting another Citibike wobbling by, he grabbed a shot and threw it back. "Did I just say, *If you do get elected… president?* I think I'm hyperventilating here."

"*When* I get elected, you mean," Adhemar shot back.

"When you get elected p—p—president…" Hank pretended to stammer. "What'll be on your agenda? Minimum wage? Budget? Taxes?"

"My platform will reflect the times."

Hank threw up his hands. "Jeez. You're already talking like you have a speech writer."

"Nothing wrong with speech writers if they can get inside your head. But I am the only one inside my head at present." Adhemar suddenly pointed a chopstick at the Gansevoort Hotel across the street. "Ah. *¡Mira!* The reason for the glut of Citibikes on this street—there's a bike docking station over there." He slammed back the last shot on the table and jumped up. "Let's go! Before another bike comes by and we have to get another round."

Photos of their bike excursion showed up in all the papers the next morning. NY1's Pat Kiernan highlighted a few in his "In The Papers" segment. Holding up a photo from the *Times,* he said, "Senator Reyes jumped on Bloomberg's green agenda last night. Here he is biking around the Meatpacking District outside our studios. Looks a bit wobbly, though. The senator has been coy about a run for the White House, but my prediction? He'll be in it."

🐴 FOUR 🐘

Pat Kiernan was proven correct three months later when Adhemar announced his candidacy to a group of reporters on the F train platform at Broadway/ Lafayette.

"It just popped out," he told Larry Richman on Skype that evening. Larry was chair of the Democratic Committee, and protocol dictated he be given a heads-up if Adhemar was going to declare. Oops.

"How does something like that *pop out?*" Larry barked.

"Let me rephrase. The timing was right."

"How so?"

"I'd just come from a fitting at the Hugo Boss store on Greene Street and they saw me. Either I owned up to having custom suits, or I gave them something else to chew on."

"I buy that."

Adhemar nodded.

Larry leaned forward and shouted, "Not! Honestly, Adhemar. Couldn't you have picked another location? Something iconic? The Statue of Liberty? The Brooklyn Bridge? Macy's?"

"I'm a man of the people, Larry."

"With custom-made suits."

"My policies are simple, Larry."

"You realize the photos from today are disturbingly urban?"

Adhemar shrugged. "So be it. I represent all of New York State. I happen to live in Manhattan and ride the subway. Can we get past this?"

Larry calmed down. "Let's talk running mate."

Adhemar had an answer prepared. "ZeeBee St. George from Massachusetts."

"I know where she's from. She's Black."

"You're stating the obvious."

"She looks like Kerry Washington."

"That's a good thing. I did a little polling—"

"You *have* been busy."

Adhemar ignored the thinly veiled sarcasm. "I have. ZeeBee rises above sex, age, and race. Tests high with both men and women. Quite a feat when you consider the qualities one needs to get points in enemy camps—so to speak."

"Okay. She can be on the short list. What else did your clandestine poll say?"

"Her resemblance to Kerry Washington is an advantage for two reasons. The first being that both women are beautiful."

"Check."

"The second, because some folks thought she actually was the star of that political espionage show *Scandal*. Talk about blurring the line between reality and entertainment. That will work in a lot of key districts."

"I think you need a sit down with Ms. Washington."

Adhemar nodded. This was exactly what he planned. He was pleased Larry was on board with ZeeBee. So far, at least. "Agreed. Let's see how she thinks."

"Try to avoid the press. Don't want to cue any speculation popping up around her until you are sure you're on the same page."

"What? You don't think we should meet at the Lincoln Memorial?"

"Ha. Ha."

Married for five years, Senator Zeniba "ZeeBee" St. George met her husband, Sam Fischer, at a party on the Hill. Nothing surprising there, except he was the date of the Soviet ambassador's daughter. And undercover. CIA undercover. Sam was currently assigned to the White House to work with President Thatcher Cushing, a moderate Republican. Although ZeeBee and Sam both worked in DC, they kept their respective jobs separate and their personal life personal. A sexy senator and a Jewish spy. Quite a team.

Adhemar arranged for her to be invited to a small, select gathering at the office of New York State Congresswoman Nikia Southerland. The invitation read: *Bring something homemade to share.*

ZeeBee and Sam kicked around some options. "Chex Party Mix? Rice Krispy Treats?" Sam suggested.

"Very funny, Sam."

"Just keeping it all American."

ZeeBee tapped the invite on the kitchen counter. "It's odd, isn't it? Asking us to bring something homemade."

"Don't know. You've never been to one of these things. For all you know, the highlight might be someone's basement fermented wine."

"You think so?"

"No. How about those killer spicy sunflower seeds you make? That says accomplished. And earthy."

ZeeBee recoiled. "Earthy? Thanks. Not a description that brings anything remotely attractive to mind." She pulled out her recipe box and started rifling through the cards. "I'll bake. Something no one else would make." She snapped her fingers. "Blueberry Thing."

"Huh?"

"Blueberry Thing. You love my Blueberry Thing."

Sam raised his eyebrows. "I love a lot of your...*things*, Zee, but not sure which one is the blueberry. But I'd love to find out." He started gliding across the room in a Justin Timberlake move, arms outstretched.

ZeeBee swatted him away, laughing. "Blueberry Thing is what I call the dessert with the sweet crust with blueberries and sour cream on top."

"I love that thing!"

"I know."

"What's the real name?"

"I have no idea. That's why I call it Blueberry Thing."

"It doesn't bother you that you may have renamed something that might have pedigree? It could be called Aunt Whatever's Best Blueberry Dessert Ever. It might have won a bake-off somewhere."

"What's in a name?"

"The attribution. Or the blame."

"Ah! I forget you CIA types always need someone to blame."

"Everyone needs a scapegoat, ZeeBee."

"Nothing will deter me from making my Blueberry Thing. And I will take all the credit *slash* blame for it."

The next afternoon, ZeeBee walked into Congresswoman Southerland's office, swinging a cream-colored, triangle-shaped paper tote bag from Takashimaya. Inside was a matching cookie tin filled with Blueberry Thing. While the famed Japanese department store had closed its Fifth Avenue location years ago, it had been ZeeBee's favorite place to shop whenever in New York City—picking up the bulk of Sam's birthday gifts on the second floor, which showcased everything from hand-knit sweaters you'd picture on someone hiking across the Scottish moors to impeccably designed travel accessories. The floor was fittingly titled Jet Set. She'd frequently pick up a tin of their fabulous tea cookies from the Tea Box Café restaurant in the basement. She had also amassed a collection of Takashimaya's iconic three-sided shopping bags with black rope handles.

ZeeBee headed over to the Congresswoman's desk, where a diverse selection of goodies was laid out. As she popped open her Takashimaya tin, Adhemar suddenly appeared at her elbow.

"This has to be more than a coincidence," he said.

ZeeBee had spotted Adhemar when she first arrived and planned to work her way over and maybe strike up a conversation on—something. Anything. She believed he would come out on top at the convention and ultimately sweep the elections. *Wouldn't hurt to be on friendly terms with the president,* she thought. And now, he was right next to her, chatting her up! *Play it cool.*

She met his eyes. "Coincidence?"

Adhemar nodded and brought forth an identical tin. "Tea cookies from Takashimaya are one of life's most pleasant experiences."

ZeeBee gasped. "I'd have to agree. But if yours is filled with the same thing mine is, then that's a little creepy and I'm turning around and heading out the door."

"Watcha got?" Adhemar asked.

"Blueberry Thing."

"Obscure name, but I'm safe." Adhemar popped open his tin. "I made gingersnaps that no one should eat."

ZeeBee reached in and snagged one. "Oh don't be so modest. I'm sure they're great," she said, popping the cookie into her mouth, thinking, *How did I get so glib?*

Amused, Adhemar watched her chew and then quickly spit the cookie into the napkin in her hand.

"What did you put in these? Twigs?" she managed to croak.

Dipping his head in a boyish manner, Adhemar admitted, "I've been informed the recipe called for *ground* cloves. Not *whole* cloves. My bad."

"And yet you brought them."

"Didn't find out until I got here. You are not the first to chew on what you appropriately called a twig. But I did warn you."

"You did." She laughed.

"And you ignored me."

"I did."

"Is this a common occurrence? Ignoring what you must concede was spot-on advice."

"I thought you were…" She groped for the right word. "Teasing?"

"Not my style."

"So I'm learning."

Adhemar flashed a smile. "So, Senator St. George—"

"Call me ZeeBee."

"So, ZeeBee. Will you take my advice when you're my running mate?"

"Of course…*What*?" ZeeBee sputtered.

"Twigs aside, will you take my advice when you are my running mate? Or maybe I should say, *if* you were my running mate."

"For vice president?" Her voice cracked.

"What else!"

ZeeBee pulled herself together. "Baker of the year?"

Adhemar burst out laughing. "You have a sense of humor, ZeeBee. I like that."

"So do you," she said. "I thought your reality show idea was brilliantly absurd. In the right way, mind you—absurd."

"And so is this." Adhemar took out a mini iPad and pulled up a site. "Check it out."

ZeeBee tapped the window open. Shining brightly on the 3.1 million-pixel retina display was a cartoon-like replica of the *Russia from my porch* VP candidate decked out in one of her signature red suits. Someone with too much time on their hands had created an interactive game where the little figure could be moved to select spots on a U.S. map, including a stage at a NRA convention in Fairfax, Virginia, the back of a moose in Anchorage, Alaska, and the Oval Office in the White House.

"Oh. My. God," she said.

"Move her into the Oval Office."

ZeeBee moved the tiny cutout figure into the White House.

"Stand by!" Adhemar said.

On the screen, a giant sinkhole formed around the figure, then swallowed it and the entire White House. The sinkhole expanded until it reached the Capitol Building, and then—*glump*—the entire U.S. government was sucked into oblivion.

ZeeBee laughed. "Okay. That's really funny, but she's old news. Why now?"

"People believe she is going to run."

"No. They don't!"

"They do. That site is funny, satirical, and yet over the heads of millions of Americans. So, is my idea so farfetched?"

"Yes," ZeeBee said, laughing. "And your remarks are now part of the congressional record."

Adhemar nodded. "Well, there is that. But I wasn't being entirely serious. I took a bit of creative license to make my point."

He spotted Speaker of the House Trammel Washington heading their way. The dapper black man carried a platter piled high with what appeared to be old shoe leather. Adhemar waved him over. "Trammel. Two questions. One—what the heck are you carrying?"

Trammel shoved the platter at ZeeBee and Adhemar. "Bison jerky. Grass-fed bison jerky from my home state of Colorado. Try some. What's your second question?"

"What are you hearing about my reality show idea?"

Trammel thought for a moment. "People are talking about it. I might be able to get it by the House, but then the Senate would have to pass it. And the Senate hasn't passed anything even remotely resembling forward thinking in years."

Adhemar turned to ZeeBee. "The Speaker of the House says it's forward thinking." He picked up a piece of jerky and began to chew. "You made this in your kitchen, Trammel?"

"I opened the box in my kitchen."

"That counts."

Trammel eyed ZeeBee. Being one of the higher-ups in the Democratic Party, he was privy to the reason ZeeBee was at the gathering. "Senator St. George. What's your take on Adhemar's reality show proposal?"

"I think he made a good point. The American public should look good and hard at a candidate's experience. Question if they have the chops for the job. But a reality show? That's going too far."

Adhemar continued to gnaw on the jerky. "It'll die. We're just stuck in a slow news cycle. But keeping the dialog going will help move the idea of questioning credentials from C-SPAN to the kitchen table. And that's what I want to encourage."

"That's because you have an outstanding record, Adhemar," Trammel said. "Foreign Relations Committee. Multiple domestic committees. Your work on the Energy and Water…"

Adhemar waved his hand in a dismissive fashion. The discussion was veering towards *rah-rah Reyes*. "I'm sure ZeeBee is aware of my background."

"I am. But shouldn't every presidential candidate have a record like that?" ZeeBee said.

Adhemar smiled. "One would think."

"Then I agree—in theory a reality show would show up those deficiencies and how that would play out in a crisis. But in reality—not that I want to use this word—in reality, a reality show is not…realistic."

Adhemar grinned. He liked ZeeBee's reasoning and brashness.

The vetting was quick. ZeeBee's only vice was constantly snacking on Hale and Hearty oyster crackers. Not enough to keep her off the ticket.

But Adhemar was wrong about his reality show.

It didn't die.

FIVE

Fifteen months later, Dave Reynolds, the thinning-
on-top (but who cares?) blonde wunderkind host of
the political talk show TalkOut, patted the corner of
his mouth with a starched white napkin. He'd been
sitting on the show's set, gorging on the blini topped with crème
fraiche and caviar constructed for him before every show by
his personal chef. It was in his contract. Petrosian caviar, fresh
every Sunday, delivered in the signature blue coolers. Today it
was packed with Reserve Alverta, the glowing nobs the size of
cranberries. He'd left some on the plate.

Henry, the show's floor director, crouched in front of
him. "Whatta we have today, Davie?"

Dave passed him the last caviar-capped blini. "Alverta,
Henry. Briny. Buttery. Sweet."

Henry popped the goody into his mouth, tapped his
headset, and held up his hand, fingers outstretched. "Mmmm.
I agree. Here we go. In five, four…" He winked. "…briny,
buttery, sweet."

The red tally light came on over the middle camera. They
were LIVE. On the video wall behind Dave, the *TalkOut* logo
popped on in all its 3-D glory. It landed in the middle of the
screen, then pulsed, sending itty-bitty American flags flying
every which way. Dave had come up with the concept himself.

He put on his earnest *pay attention to what I am about to say* face. "Showdown. It's the time of the people with this heck of a political game of hot potato we're going to witness starting tomorrow night," he said, leaning towards the camera. "Good evening, I'm Dave Reynolds. As we all know by now, the growing revolt against our electoral system came to a head a year ago when, spearheaded by Senator Adhemar Reyes, Congress passed the sweeping election reforms now known as the *make it work* factor. These reforms empowered the Speaker of the House to construct a set of scenarios to test the two major party candidates running for president of the United States."

The *TalkOut* logo flew off the screen, replaced by video of two men obviously green-screened, standing side by side in what appeared to be cumulonimbus clouds. The cloud video came from a site the art director found that morning offering *free, naturalistic,* even *organic* background footage in HD, downloadable after answering a short quiz about how often the show needed/bought stock footage/images for use in broadcast/cable/web/other. Placing these two men, one of whom would be the next president of the United States, in this weird tableau was probably a result of the blinding headache he had after drinking the better part of two bottles of Cuervo the night before. This unfortunate choice would be talked about for days after someone tweeted: *Praise the Lord, our candidates are coming from God.*

On the left, Adhemar smiled broadly, his right eyebrow raised in what was now his iconic *trust me face.* Despite the cheesy cloud milieu, you'd want to meet him. Lower thirds on the screen identified him and his party affiliation: *Democrat.*

Next to Adhemar, wearing well his ex-college football frame even at fifty, Governor Beau Simpson—identified Republican—seemed to focus on some dot in the distance. Likely a goal post. He's the neighbor who plays in the street with the kids. His lopsided grin brought him down to the people's level. Yet he looked at home in the clouds thanks to echoes of him striding through fog-machine effects on the sideline at Cowboys games for years—a perk passed down to him from his maternal grandfather who won the right to be on the sidelines twenty-five years ago during a tobacco-spitting contest with the then Cowboys' head coach. It was the closest Beau would get to professional football, but even so, he savored it.

Dave swiveled in an Aeron chair and tilted his head to the video wall and the bigger-than-life presidential candidates behind him. "These guys will be bringing along their running mates to what is promising to be the mother of all reality shows—*The President Factor*. They'll face simulated crisis situations that could occur during their time in office. The way they handle themselves is expected to show who has the chops and the gravity—the *gravitas*—to be elected this November."

In *TalkOut*'s control room, the TD called for a WIDE SHOT and the camera pulled out to show the entire set. Next to Dave, Trammel Washington fiddled with the up and down lever on the right side of his Aeron chair. Wearing a black pinstripe suit, white shirt, and a Miró-inspired bright blue tie with red and white abstract squiggles, Trammel was country meets avant-garde. It worked.

Dave swiveled back to camera. "With me tonight is Speaker Washington, the man who had task of carving this turkey of a game show."

Like a carney ride, Washington's chair suddenly slammed to its lowest position. Without acknowledging the mishap, Trammel spun his now truncated seat to align with Dave and grinned. Nothing could faze him after falling off the podium behind the president the week before during the State of the Union. He had been leaning over to look around the back of the president's head to get a glimpse of the teleprompter after the President Cushing had gone off-book, targeting Adhemar with a reference to immigration reform, when he lost his balance and toppled off. Trammel wanted to see if someone had changed the speech passed out earlier in the day. They hadn't. The president had been riffing. A dangerous thing. Trammel sat up in the chair and nodded to Dave.

"It is my job, Dave," he drawled, flashing a smile. "It's an honor, actually."

Dave nodded back. "Yes. It certainly is. Let's take a quote, Mr. Speaker, of someone who's spoken out: former President Winston. As he said in *Time Magazine*, quote—these are his words—*If everyone who ran for president had to prove they knew what they were doing before anyone would vote for them, nobody would get elected.* Mr. Speaker, what are we stepping into?"

"No one wants a pig in a poke, Dave," Trammel said with emotion.

"That's a little strong, isn't it, Mr. Speaker? We've heard Senator Reyes and Governor Simpson's platforms. They've been running on them for at least six months."

"Platforms, smatforms. When push comes to shove, will they be able to see us through the next crisis?" Trammel was clearly worked up. He was flushed.

Dave leaned down and poked him on the knee. "America has never worried about that before. Is this really the time to make that change? Test those waters?"

Annoyed, Trammel poked him back. "Absolutely. We can't believe what candidates say. The American people demand proof."

"In prime time of course."

"Where else? Then they'll take that information to the polls in November."

"Can you give us a hint of some of the things we're going to see in the coming weeks as this plays out?"

Trammel closed his eyes. "Nope."

⬅ SIX ➡

he President Factor set designers had quite a task
on their hands. They needed to construct replicas
of select rooms in the real White House. The sets
had to be, to quote network president Buzz "B."
Billingsworthy, "Emmy award winning, for Christ sake."

The network decided to shoot at Silvercup Studios in
Queens, where a long list of feature films had been shot and
where *Blacklist, Person of Interest, Elementary, White Collar,
Sopranos, Sex and the City, 30 Rock,* and *Gossip Girl* had made
their home. Entirely nondescript on the outside—the Secret
Service loved that—except for the gigantic rooftop sign that
one could see from across the East River, the hulking building
was originally the Silvercup Bakery. Inside, it was like the back
lot at MGM, without the palm trees. The tax breaks New York
City had been offering for years made Silvercup a no-brainer.

When the story broke about the shooting location,
however, the folks inside the beltway made such a fuss about
spending money in New York that the network wound up
commandeering an abandoned airplane hanger next to the
National Airport for the show. This forced them to start from
the ground up since no studio in DC had enough space to
take it on. Ultimately, they trucked in what amounted to a
mini lumber company to construct the sets—never mind the

cost of building the lighting grids. It put them in the hole from the get-go. But the hole was in DC, not New York City, and to the politicos that was all that mattered.

A lot was riding on the show besides the November election.

Looking to make Buzz happy, the producers brought in cartoonist and fashion designer George Blunt as a consultant. Buzz had become a huge Blunt fan one summer long ago in the Hamptons when the only paper products in the house he and his college buddies rented were stacks and stacks of cocktail napkins decorated with Blunt's signature catfish. The blanket effect of hundreds of these napkins strewn everywhere triggered cries of *Ohmygod, I love that catfish!* from virtually every woman they brought home. Buzz cashed in on the warm feelings the design evoked and went so far as to buy a tee shirt with the catfish on it—which became his lucky shirt. When he became president of the network, he used the catfish design on his stationary.

George Blunt was a shoo-in for the gig. His design for the main set resulted in red walls on the right side and blue on the left with life-size cartoonish drawings of a donkey and elephant on their respective walls. Both animals looked suspiciously like Blunt's signature catfish, complete with wide, wide, bright blue open mouths. The room was intended to resemble the real Roosevelt Room in the White House, but the only thing close to looking like it could have belonged in that truly venerable place was an incongruous federal-style conference table that split the room in half. It was bare. A period light fixture hung above. Buzz loved it.

The President Factor control room was located half a football field away, down at the far end of the airplane hanger. It was designed for utility, comfort, and the *wow* factor, combining state-of-the-art equipment with a lounge/viewing area that bordered on the obscene. Exposure to hundreds if not thousands of hours of Bollywood movies by virtue of having a college roommate from New Delhi had had an effect on the interior designer's eye. Thus, the front of the control room resembled the Starship Enterprise—and the back, a scene from the *Jodhaa Akbar*.

At the front, thirty or so monitors filled the wall above a gigantic Grass Valley switcher, the piece of equipment that is the guts of all live production. The monitors showed the action on all of the sets from the different cameras in the rooms, along with the live feeds from the roaming camera crews. The largest monitor had an air sign hanging over it. The atmosphere brought to mind an airport control tower without the weird *niner, niner* language and cardboard coffee cups. *The President Factor* mugs were strategically placed on the consoles and in the lounge area. Marketing had done their job.

Sitting at the switcher was Bob Henderson, the show's director, wearing a headset clamped over a Yankee's cap. Behind him, reclining as best they could on bright red and gold-threaded plush hassocks and overstuffed chairs, a gaggle of network executives gathered to watch history in the making—at least the men did. The women were also there to watch Adhemar, though they weren't admitting it—including BCD TV VP of Programming, Makki Alden. Trim and fit at thirty-seven, with jet-black hair in a Cleopatra style, Makki was striking. One quarter Native American—Algonquin— she was named after her great-grandmother Makkitotosimew. At one point she sought to honor her heritage by changing her name back to the Native American version, but she dropped that plan after learning Makkitotosimew was Algonquin for *she who has large breasts*. Something Great-Grandma had also passed down.

Adhemar and Makki had met for the first time the week before at her office in midtown Manhattan. As programming VP, she'd brought home the bid to produce the show after spearheading five days of hard-nosed *I'm not going to provide coffee until you sign the damn contract* negotiations between BCD's lawyers and the federal government. It was on her head to make this show a success. She'd kept her distance from the two politicians until pretty much everything about the show was locked to prevent anyone from saying she was influenced one way or the other. The meeting was a formality: to meet the man who came up with the show. Nothing more.

Known in the trades as shrewd and successful, Makki intimidated most of the agents and a fair amount of the talent who made it all the way up to the 47th floor and past Jon, her assistant. Makki's office, almost as impressive as she was, provided a good setting for these power-positioning meetings. Showcasing ultra-modern Markus Johansson furniture and a Clyfford Still painting on an otherwise bare white wall behind her desk, it reflected her forward-looking sensibility. She'd bought the Swedish designer's signature *Walking Cabinet* after seeing it profiled by Design Milk. Then, falling in love with its bright red, wonky, twisted taking-off-to-go-somewhere design, she commissioned a desk to match. As a result, when you walked into her Spartan office, with the two pieces spotlighted as they were, you felt as though the desk just might move across the room and hurl itself over the edge of the right-hand floor-to-ceiling glass wall and the cabinet would go off toward the matching wall on the left. The escapist theme was also reflected in the Clyfford Still, with its little red splotch of color trying to escape the edge of the upper right corner of the ten-by-thirteen painting. The effect threw most people off.

Just what she wanted.

She'd done her own research on Adhemar, as she did on all her new stars. She knew about his fiancée's tragic death and perused the blogs about his bachelor status. Further research indicated he was not dating anyone. Not that it mattered; she'd been in *the biz* for years and had dated and dropped many an A-list celebrity. It was hard to knock her socks off.

Adhemar had also done research. He found photos of Makki and also read blogs. He learned about her intimidating presence. He considered himself prepared. It was his show. In his mind, she was riding on his coattails.

Neither, however, had anticipated their effect on the other. Jon would tweet that something literally sparked when he brought Adhemar into Makki's office.

The two froze, eyes locked like gunfighters. Adhemar broke first. "I'll bet they price these offices by the square inch," he said while thinking, *I'm starting to sweat*. He headed over to the north windows to put some distance between them. *Jesus, she's a giant magnet!* Looking out over Central Park, he watched a large bird circle. "That's quite a view, Ms. Alden. I think I spot a hawk."

"Call me Makki, Senator Reyes." *Did I remember to put on perfume? Why is he way over there?* "That hawk is named Brightmale and, yes, it is a fabulous view, but I don't think it compares to the one you will have next January," Makki said, regaining her composure.

"Taking sides are we, Makki?" Adhemar said smoothly.

Hearing Adhemar say her name with just a hint of a Spanish accent made Makki catch her breath. *Good Lord, he's sexy.* "Just stating the obvious, Senator."

"Please don't let that cloud your approach to this project. Beau and I must be on the same footing," Adhemar hastily added.

"Of course."

Still looking out the window, Adhemar put out a feeler. "But that shouldn't stop us from…say, meeting at the Bowery Hotel for some snacks later tonight, should it?"

Is he asking to meet me at a hotel? Good God! Makki pursed her lips. "Ah…"

Adhemar turned around and raised that right eyebrow. "I've been invited to a HappyRice food-tasting event. Asian food and specialty cocktails. I think most of the Iron Chefs will be there. Something about sea urchins? Anyway, the invitation is for two…" He trailed off with a boyish shrug.

Adhemar wasn't officially dating, but he wasn't blind either.

And Makki had remembered to put on perfume.

The HappyRice Festival crowd was a mix of hip tuned-in Asians and downtown funk. The Bowery Hotel was the perfect location. Its intimate bar with a mirrored ceiling and comfy faded rose velvet club chairs played off the exposed brick and threadbare—by design—rugs. A magnificent terrace reeked of old-world opulence. It was one of the must-go-to locations in Manhattan. If a hotel could have emotions, this one would: dark and moody.

The tasting was dazzling. Scattered stainless steel and minimalist glass prep stations offered extravagant Asian food from a smattering of the top chefs in New York City working overtime to outdo one another.

Adhemar and Makki refrained from gorging on the melt-in-your-mouth sea urchins, hand-prepared and served by a famous chef—eating just three—and headed for an array of Asian-inspired cocktails at the bar. After brushing hands numerous times, they gave in to their mutual attraction and moved to the terrace. The Secret Service melted into the shadows behind the bamboo. They had the corner to themselves.

"This is so unlike me," Adhemar said, leaning over to brush a firefly away from Makki's fourth Drunken Dragon's Milk, a drink made with Grey Goose vodka, young coconut puree, lime juice, pandam leaf syrup, Thai basil leaves, and homemade Macao five spice bitters. It was very potent. Adhemar was on his fifth Word Up cocktail, whose main ingredient was Bombay Sapphire East gin. He allowed his hand to land on Makki's shoulder.

"We have to maintain a professional relationship," Makki said, feeling the vodka. It came out *fessional*.

"Confessional? What, is my mother around here?" Adhemar joked, when he was really thinking, *Damn it, Makki, why are you so spot on?* He sobered up and leaned back. "You are correct. For *The President Factor* to succeed, it cannot have even the faintest whiff of bias."

"I don't know what your challenges will be, but someone will most likely think I do." Makki grinned. "Especially after you win."

They reluctantly pulled apart. And went no further. Adhemar headed back to Washington to prepare for the show. Makki took cold showers.

Now, in *The President Factor* control room, Makki wondered if Adhemar thought about her.

He did. Shaken by the feelings Makki brought on, Adhemar hoped he wouldn't run into her on set—and also hoped he would. Makki was the first woman he'd felt attracted to, or allowed himself to feel attracted to, since Maritza. He assumed she was watching the taping somewhere in the vast complex, which was a wee bit disconcerting and pleasing at the same time.

Adhemar strode onto the set, wearing a dark grey, one-button Hugo Boss suit with a yellow power tie. In that setting, he looked like an ad for *GQ*.

ZeeBee followed right behind in a tight, perfectly fitting black Calvin Klein suit that read *hip but relatable*, matching him stride for stride.

In George Blunt's politically correct Roosevelt Room, ZeeBee and Adhemar moved instinctively to the blue side. ZeeBee munched on her oyster crackers from a cellophane bag with a big red Hale and Hearty Oysterettes label.

"I'm a little bummed we're not shooting at Silvercup," Adhemar said, catching ZeeBee's eye.

"And why's that?" ZeeBee asked.

"I liked the idea of running into Robert De Niro or someone like that in the men's room. They shoot of lot of movies there, you know."

"In the men's room at Silvercup?"

"Funny."

"You really think about stuff like that?"

"Yep. I'm tired of only seeing only politicians at the urinals."

"TMI, Adhemar. TMI," ZeeBee said. Even after being interviewed ad nauseam about *The President Factor*, it wasn't until she was *in makeup* for the show, staring at herself in the mirror while Maxine, the makeup artist, slapped a truckload of foundation on her face, that she'd finally accepted that the show was actually going to take place. Throughout the preparations—even going back to the votes on the Hill—ZeeBee expected someone to call the whole thing off, but it never happened. And now, their every move was about to go viral. Agitated, she regarded Adhemar, who was annoyingly relaxed.

"You're responsible for this entire fiasco. You put it for a vote."

"You know I never thought they'd pass it," Adhemar replied. "And I had no choice."

ZeeBee knew he was right. "But that doesn't make this any easier. We're fucked."

"Equally fucked are Beau and Mike," Adhemar said calmly. "But we've got an edge."

"Which is?"

"We're smarter, ZeeBee. Plus, demanding proof of performance from the *I can see Russia from my porch* candidates is going to revolutionize elections in this country!" Adhemar stated with a hint of a fist bump, forgetting ZeeBee was his only audience at this point and the Russia line was starting to get stale.

"I'll be known as the father of modern politics," Adhemar said, ramping up.

ZeeBee sighed, recognizing Adhemar's poli-speak. "I can honestly say I don't want to be known as the mother of anything, but we've got to find a way to say that on camera."

Nodding, Adhemar came down from his soapbox. "Absolutely. You okay?"

"I look like a bad infomercial."

"The word *bad* is superfluous in that context, but you don't."

"I do."

"Honestly, you look terrific."

"Okay."

"I am sorry for throwing you into what you so graciously called a fucking fish bowl on *The Tonight Show*," Adhemar said quietly.

"That was unfortunate," ZeeBee said with true remorse.

"And bleeped out, but even my mother got it."

ZeeBee met Adhemar's mother, Marisol, a few weeks back at the White House Correspondents' Dinner. Marisol came as Adhemar's date for the evening and was a little overwhelmed by all the attention given to their table. Everyone who stopped by was introduced to her, of course. Meeting the journalists from the Sunday morning talks shows and all the network news she watched had impressed Marisol more than the politicians who stopped by.

Adhemar thought about Marisol's rigid glare when a contingent from Fox News snubbed their table.

"How's your mom? Come to terms with all of this?" ZeeBee said.

"Somewhat. I don't know if she is going to get this set, though."

"George never told me he was doing the sets."

"You know George Blunt?"

"Yep. Sam and I had brunch with him last week," ZeeBee replied casually. She never liked to make a big fuss over her connections to the high-profile people she had met when on the NEA board before entering politics.

"How's Sam?"

"The usual. Briefings, trips; underhand, clandestine CIA shit. You think he would have mentioned it."

"Sam?"

"No, George. How would Sam know?"

Adhemar deadpanned, "Underhand, clandestine CIA shit." He liked to tease ZeeBee about her husband's job.

"I walked into that, didn't I?"

He looked at the red and blue walls. "Do you really think this is necessary? I think the American people have the political color delineation stamped into their brains by now."

ZeeBee snorted. "They probably just needed a set, but I'm glad someone has taste. I was afraid they were going to ask us to wear red and blue tee shirts."

Adhemar took a step back and pointed to the cameras.

ZeeBee's eyes widened. Instinctively, her hand flew up to her throat in a gesture of *Ohmygod, what did I say?* Her crackers spilled out of the bag. "Are they on?" she blurted.

"Not yet."

"Thank God, or we just Plamed Sam."

ZeeBee's reference to the 2003 outing of CIA Agent Valerie Plame in Robert Novak's *Washington Post* column, for what a good portion of America categorized as political gain, reminded both of them of the reality of the situation: Politics was dirty and nasty, and now another part of it was going to be played out in front of millions of viewers.

"Didn't you read the rundown?" Adhemar whispered with a slight hiss. He had the show's rundown running methodically through his mind. He was little miffed ZeeBee was winging it, even if by his own calculations they had six minutes to go before the cameras turned on. Political paranoia was always present. *They could turn them on early just to screw with us.*

ZeeBee shrugged, not wanting to admit she never thought the show would get off the ground until an hour ago. "Waste of my time. I never believe TV people, especially producers. You think those open-mic disasters are accidents?"

"Well, once this thing starts, all cameras are recording. On all the sets."

"What about outside the studio?"

"Same thing. They said they'd be obvious, but I'd assume if someone from the show is with us, they've got a camera somewhere."

"Can we ask them to turn them off at any point?"

"Would defeat the entire purpose." Adhemar now sighed heavily and showed his annoyance. "Honestly, ZeeBee, you should have read the contract."

ZeeBee shrugged. "Wouldn't have made a difference. What would I do? Withdraw as your running mate?"

Good God, Adhemar thought, *don't even think that—let alone say it with cameras nearby.*

Adhemar's very healthy respect for TV cameras started when he was a mere thirteen years old. His high school soccer team, the Brooklyn Shooters, was invited to Peru to compete in a tournament with the top South American teams. The Shooters were a middle of the road team, but one of the parents on the booster club was from Lima and had connections. They wound up being the only American team in the competition. With Adhemar as their captain, they didn't do too poorly, coming in fifth after the local team in Argentina defaulted when half of their players came down with a bad case of dysentery. When they landed back in the States, *ESPN Deportes'* Ruben Santiago met them at the airport—heady stuff for a thirteen-year-old. Even at that age, Adhemar was a natural spokesperson.

As anyone who actually followed sports media celebrities knew, Ruben Santiago had an estranged son playing for the Buenos Aires Razors, the local team that defaulted to the Shooters. Santiago nonetheless eagerly addressed the U.S. team, happy to meet anyone who would have played with his son.

Adhemar blew it.

He gave what could only be a smart-ass, definitely non-PC remark: "They missed the game 'cause they were all sitting on the toilet. You'd think they'd have been used to the water, living in the Third World and all."

That evening, gathered around the TV with his mother, father, all the neighbors, and Andrea, a girl he desperately wanted to impress, Adhemar saw himself receiving a slap-down on national TV.

It went something like this: Ruben Santiago doing a stand-up at JFK. "New York's own Brooklyn Shooters came back winners and losers from their first international tournament tonight. Winners because they placed fifth in what is regarded as one of the most prestigious high school soccer tourneys in the world, and losers because of a callous and unsportsmanlike remark made by their team captain, Adhemar Reyes, regarding the Razors, the number one team from Argentina that had to drop out of the competition when four of their team members were hospitalized after eating a pastrami sandwich the Shooter's right guard shared with them. What a way to win? Right, Adhemar? And do your homework, gringo, Argentina is not a Third World country."

The lesson received that day knocked down Adhemar's ego, taught him to check facts, but most importantly shaped his respect for the power of the press and what to say and not say in front of rolling cameras.

Now, twenty years later, that lesson was about to pay off as he prepared to step into the diciest of all rolling-camera situations: a reality show. Squaring his shoulders, he stared at the door he'd walked through moments before—and just then noticed it was strategically placed for optimal camera angles, set into the wall like something from *Alice in Wonderland*. He expected it to bang open and spew forth the Mad Hatter.

Or Tweedle Dum and Tweedle Dee.

➤ SEVEN ➤

Almost.

Governor Beau Simpson and Congressman Mike Charleston strolled through an identical *Alice in Wonderland* door on the right side of the room. Both decked out in matching brown Pierre Cardin suits. The uniform look was Beau's idea. He thought they should appear to the American public as a united team. It wasn't enough that he'd pulled Mike to his breast right up there on the convention floor and gave him a big ole' Texas hug after declaring him his running mate; he was convinced that a constant visual reference of their partnership was needed to keep the public's perception from wandering. Or questioning. There *was* that platform break between the two of them on prayer in school, and he needed to remind folks that between them, they had all the Republican issues covered. After getting mobbed in college one day while wearing an official Cowboys uniform procured for him by his dad, he realized the average person was blind to face recognition and would jump to a conclusion faster than a blue jay.

Mike, on the other hand, wanted to remove himself a teensy bit from Beau, in case *we go down in a blaze of glory*—something he only talked about with his personal advisor, Vincent. Vincent had been with Mike since he tore up the election in his home state of Florida. Vincent suggested wearing his tie slightly undone. "It says you're flexible. Says you can compromise, Mike."

Although Mike would never compromise, he liked the idea of appearing to be someone who would compromise. He also added his personal touch to the Pierre Cardin ensemble— Bass Weejun loafers without socks—as homage to the Beach Boys, the only band he had loaded in his iTunes. His haircut mimicked the style of the band on the 1964 album cover framed in his office.

In lockstep, Beau and Mike stepped around the oyster crackers on the rug.

Adhemar boomed out a greeting: "Governor. Congressman." *Take control of the room*, Adhemar told himself.

Let the games begin.

All four sat on their respective side of the table and stared at each other. Despite the high-profile events each of the four had attended post-nomination, this marked the first time they had gathered in the same room. ZeeBee tossed the now empty cracker bag on the table.

Mike broke the ice. "Aren't those from…?"

"Hale and Hearty. New York," ZeeBee snapped.

"Made in Vermont," Adhemar added, not wanting to be left out, especially if someone had started taping early!

"My favorites too," Beau affirmed even though he had never heard of them, but if über-hip ZeeBee ate them, he figured he could score points with her crowd. But why the heck did she have them on the set in the first place? Had to be important. He mentally congratulated himself for adding the comment.

Mike's attention bounced off the crackers, however, and darted elsewhere. He started to sweat. The cartoonish drawings took him back to the walkway at Pirates Plantation, a long-demolished amusement park his parents took him to when he was twelve, and a near miss he had with a faux pirate ship, souring him on amusement parks to this day. A shame, really, since his kids had to enjoy Disney World every year without him.

He popped out of his chair and started pacing. Crunch. Crunch. Over the oyster crackers. Death to Hale and Hearty. Agitated. He whirled around and confronted Adhemar. "Anything to drink? This isn't going to be like *Survivor*, is it?"

"*Survivor in Chief*, you mean," Adhemar quipped.

Beau squinted at Adhemar as ZeeBee chuckled. Beau figured Adhemar had some secret information. This *was* his show, wasn't it? Despite being reassured by the producers that both teams were starting off on the same page, Beau believed Adhemar had some insider knowledge. Of something! He'd have arranged it if he'd been the one to come up with the game.

"Y'all have any idea what they're gonna ask us to do?" Beau asked with that lopsided grin.

Adhemar grinned back. "Not a clue."

After making a complete track around the room, Mike threw himself back into his chair. Still agitated. "How difficult can it be? I mean, letting Trammel Washington come up with the challenges?" he snorted. "Considering his—" He paused to look at the group, seeking approval. "Considering his constituents, this will be easier than meltin' an ice cream cone on a sidewalk on the Fourth of July."

Adhemar and ZeeBee recoiled. Did they hear correctly? Did Mike just insult Trammel with a racist comment? *No, couldn't be.*

Beau laughed. "In Memphis." The Republican team started snickering.

"Double scoop!" Mike threw back.

It was!

Before it could get any worse, their joke was interrupted by the stage manager, Josh Michaels, a trim twenty-five-year-old in a black *The President Factor* tee shirt, cargo pants, utility belt, and headset. He appeared from somewhere in front of the group—they couldn't see past the blinding studio lights. Josh came to this gig with a heap of reality show experience, moving up from key grip to stage manager on *The President Factor*. He was determined to keep to schedule. Presidential candidates or not, he had a job to do.

Josh clapped his hands. "Hello, hello, everyone. Please take out your phones and whatever else you might have with you that could make a sound. Then turn 'em off. Cameras are now rolling."

The group patted themselves down and complied with Josh's request. Mike blurted, "Are we live?"

"It's three o'clock, Mike. The show is on at nine tonight," Beau quickly said. "I believe we are taping right now."

Josh nodded. "That is correct, Governor. We're taping now. Then we'll edit the footage together for the show tonight."

"You can't edit the governor," Mike blustered.

ZeeBee leaned over to Adhemar and whispered, "Seriously?"

Beau came to Mike's rescue. "It's all good, Mike. These here boys know what they're doin'. Gotta make good TV. Right, Adhemar?"

Adhemar winked at ZeeBee. "You betcha."

The *Alice in Wonderland* door on the left sprang open. Trammel Washington marched in, carrying two thin folders. The same pinstripe suit worn on *TalkOut* coddled his frame, another Miró-inspired tie splashing color against the dark wool. The design this time: Miró's famous rooster crowing at the sky, with the red orb of a sun. *The President Factor* waking up America, Trammel imagined. Adhemar saw it as a nod to his, Adhemar's, Spanish heritage.

Trammel stopped at the head of the table and threw his shoulders back. He was not above playing to the cameras himself.

"This…" He paused for effect. "This is *The President Factor.*"

It appeared as though the four people sitting in front of Trammel didn't react, though if you were looking closely, you would see that everyone sat up straighter. But that was not enough of a reaction. Trammel's opening lines needed a stronger response. The studio was quiet.

Embarrassed silence in the control room.

Ohmygod, the show is tanking! Makki muttered, "We should have brought in an audience."

Then, to the amazement of everyone, ZeeBee blurted out, "Hurrah!" Adhemar turned and shook her hand, accepting the praise for all to see.

Folks in the control room burst into applause, and Trammel Washington moved on.

"Senator Reyes. Governor Simpson. Let's go over the ground rules. You each have a team comprised of a vice president, a chief of staff and another important member—a military leader—a chairman of the Joint Chiefs of Staff."

Mike broke in, "Ah, Trammel! Tell the folks at home how long we had to find that important member!"

Trammel chuckled. "Three days."

"Are you looking for someone or something to blame when you lose, Mike?" Adhemar said with a hint of mockery.

"Absolutely not. Just thought a little background would give the viewers some context," Mike blustered. Adhemar had hit it on the mark.

The call for a chairman of the Joint Chiefs of Staff to the game had been a last-minute surprise. Wanting to keep things fluid, Trammel thought it prudent to not give the candidates too much time to prepare. With the teams in the dark regarding the challenges, having a military component from the get-go might tip his hand to the first challenge. Better to keep everyone unbalanced, like in the real world. Consequently, a mere three days before they were to start taping the show, Trammel hand-delivered a note to each candidate, notifying them of the requirement to include a military leader. They were forced to scramble—first, to identify the man or woman with the real-life experience to advise them to victory, then to convince them to appear on a reality show!

Trammel continued with the game parameters. "In a few moments you will be given a scenario—a situation—that I have created. You have one week to solve it. A lifetime in a crisis situation. You will bring your solutions back here next Thursday night."

He paused to look from Adhemar to Beau. "Gentlemen, have you any questions?"

"Can we ask for help from anyone outside?" Mike said.

"You mean like a lifeline?"

"Yes."

"Nope. You are to solve this crisis with your teams and your teams alone. You will have full access to state-of-the-art military services for research."

"What about classified documents?" Adhemar asked.

"We actually wrestled with that, Senator Reyes. The president would and does have access to classified information, but allowing those documents to be seen in the light of the TV camera is not in the best interests of the nation. Despite what WikiLeaks says."

Trammel paused, allowing for more questions. ZeeBee leaned forward. "Now, I know you are taping, recording everything. Correct?"

"Correct."

"And you're going to follow us as we work out the solution, correct? How is this going to be used? When the show is on the air tonight, won't we see what the other team has planned? I know I for one don't want to share our plans with Beau. And I'm sure he feels the same."

"Exactly," Beau said. "Senator St. George has expressed my thoughts exactly."

The rest nodded in agreement.

"Good question. Everything we record is fair game for the show, but—and this is a big but—*but* we never air anything that would tip your hand to the other team. We have selected award-winning editors to put the shows and the commercials for the shows together. They are wizards at cutting video apart and putting it back together without giving away the punch lines."

"Of course!" Adhemar said. "You want people to tune in on Thursday to see how we came about our solutions."

"Yes, Senator, this is also about the business of TV."

Beau said, "And I thought it was just about electing a president."

Self-conscious laughter from everyone.

When they settled down, it was time to move to the meat of the show. Trammel held up the two folders he'd brought into the room. Slapping them on the table, he made eye contact with each of the players in turn. "Russia has amassed one hundred and forty divisions along the Finnish border," he said in a measured and properly somber tone. "Chatter has it they are about to invade."

Beau was the first to react, "Holy crap!"

"It's the game, Beau," Adhemar said with a slight hint of condescension in his voice. *Zing!*

"My God," Beau stammered.

Trammel threw him a withering glance.

Beau tried to save it. "I knew that," he said, looking across the table to Adhemar—challenging him to make a comment. *The bastard had to know this was coming,* he thought. *Why is he so calm?*

"Of course, he did," Mike quickly chimed in.

Adhemar, definitely *not* having inside knowledge of the game, was as stunned as Beau. He just had more presence to hide his astonishment. He did, however, think Trammel's info was sparse. He leaned forward.

"That's it? Russia is about to invade Finland?"

Trammel played it well. He slid the folders across the polished table to Beau and Adhemar. "The specifics are in your briefings. Your teams are waiting for you in your Oval Offices."

He motioned for the contestants to stand.

"We'll see you all back here on Thursday for *The President Factor,* where live on national television you'll present your solutions. Good luck," Trammel said crisply as they headed toward their respective doors.

🐴 EIGHT 🐘

Trammel had wrestled with letting the candidates select the décor for their respective Oval offices, as they ultimately would do if elected, but decided he wanted the focus to be on the contest rather than the setting. Instead, he reached back in history and recreated the Oval Offices of J.F.K. and G. W. Bush.

None of this was leaked. Even to the candidates.

J.F.K.'s sunny yellow color scheme looked great on camera. Reclining on one of the striped couches, facing each other in front of a replica Resolute desk, was Adhemar's future chief of staff, Harrison Zimmer, and his future chairman of the Joint Chiefs, General Pinkus "Pinky" Bauer. Harrison—*not Harry, thank you*—wore a crumpled Thom Browne suit, legs crossed. He'd been wearing Thom Browne for years. Looking and sometimes sounding as though scripted by Aaron Sorkin, and with the distinction of being a Rhodes Scholar, Harrison was well chosen.

General Pinkus "Pinky" Bauer, rigidly maintaining his military stance in full dress Army uniform complete with tour of duty metals, stood and began pacing behind the desk. He'd kept his West Point physique through twenty years of duty postings, including a recent extended tour in Afghanistan. While waiting for the candidates, he'd taken particular note of the front carvings on the desk: the eagle facing away from the olive branch in its right talon and towards its left talon with the thirteen arrows on the front. Away from peace and towards war. Knowing that throughout history this part of the desk had been changed a couple of times to suit the man who sat behind it both pleased and concerned him. Pleased because that meant he would have a role and concerned because he would have a role! He wondered how Trammel positioned the first challenge.

"Harrison. What do you think they'll give us? An international crisis, I'm guessing. At least one. They have to give us some international face time," Pinky barked.

"Who do you think they got to decorate this room, General Bauer?" Harrison said.

"Harrison—who the fuck cares?"

"It sends a message about who Adhemar is."

"Jesus Christ."

The door opened, Adhemar rushed in and stopped cold, blinded for moment by the blast of yellow and blue.

Confident he would win the election, Adhemar had already begun the clandestine design of his Oval Office with William Willams, a high-powered talent agent who dabbled in feng shui. Adhemar didn't know if having a double name was positive energy, but the guy's ideas sure made a difference. Adhemar now swore by the ancient Chinese art. Once he moved his bed to align with his bathtub as William suggested, his approval ratings went through the roof. When he added a waterfall to his office and realigned his desk, he won the nomination. With this track record William Williams was now more important to Adhemar than the pollsters who reported his edge.

This was not feng shui. As he took in the décor, he recognized the nod to J.F.K. It gave him pause. Would the press start comparing him to Kennedy? *Yikes!* Quickly regaining composure, he nodded to a cameraman who moved across the room with him. He knew the moment would set the tone for his actions on this show. Almost a pre-election state of the union speech.

He strode to the front of the Resolute desk and posed in his best presidential candidate pose. "When I proposed *The President Factor* to Congress, I had hopes both sides of the aisle would come together for the good of the country. They didn't let me down. I am privileged to be part of this groundbreaking change to our national political landscape. But I'm more proud to be the person who had the foresight and guts to challenge the status quo for the American people."

"I'd say you're the father of modern politics," Pinky piped.

Adhemar paused. On cue, the cameraman zoomed in for a close-up. "I *am* the father of modern politics," he pronounced, spreading his arms. "It starts here!"

"What'd they give us?" Pinky asked, ever so practical.

"It's a bitch, Pinky. Russia is about to invade Finland."

Pleased, Pinky slapped his hands on the desk. "Knew it."

"Finland? Finland?" Harrison said. He'd bought into the whole reality show idea, but damn, this challenge was far removed from reality. "Ukraine aside, Finland?"

"Play along," Pinky retorted.

Relaxed, Harrison stretched out his arms across the back of the couch. "Hi, Adhemar."

"Your future chief of staff is worried about the yellow walls," Pinky snapped.

"I didn't say that."

ZeeBee slowly walked in. She held another bag of crackers in one hand, the briefing in the other. She munched and read from the brief: "Helsinki wants two thousand troops in support." Surprised, she looked up. "Do you think this has to do with the Nord Stream?"

"Russia is about to invade Finland for some reason, and we're dragged along because…?" Harrison asked, still resisting the challenge's premise.

ZeeBee looked up with a fake, blinding smile. "Because they asked us. And they are part of NATO in the Partnership for Peace. And it's the game, remember?"

"This is nuts."

"This is also being recorded, Harrison. Please remember that?" she chided.

"Shit."

"Didn't you read the contract?" ZeeBee said with a nod to Adhemar.

Across the hall, Governor Beau Simpson was enormously pleased with his Oval Office. He recognized Bush's rug with the radiating shafts of beige coming from the center. He'd commissioned one for himself for his office in Austin. Copying G. W. was Beau's version of feng shui.

Once Beau bathed in the aura of his hero, he jumped behind his own Resolute desk. Staking claim. When he realized the cameraman had missed the action, he recreated it. Walking with confidence, he strode across the room, sat down, and opened the brief with an appropriate *let me take charge* expression.

Beau's future chief of staff, Yancey Smith, was settled on the arm of one of the couches. All five-foot-five of him. In a light blue suit with a dark blue shirt and red bow tie, he blended into the décor. Someone had once described Yancey as beige. Not one to work out or even enter a gym, Yancey screamed academia. False lead. An eclectic writer, Yancey had the wit and tenacity to consult for the *Huffington Post* when it was a start-up.

General Tim "Hawke" Warford wore a uniform that mirrored Pinky's with his own share of medals. He paced behind the desk until Beau swatted him away. Beau didn't want anything to detract from the image he had had in his mind since he was fifteen years old—which thanks to his opponent now would be seen by millions on TV. Beau Simpson: sitting at the president's desk. Alone. He believed this was political blunder on Adhemar's part.

Slightly miffed, Hawke circled around front. "I've been gearing up for this day ever since I came back from the Gulf War, Beau," Hawke said, excited.

"Glad I could *a-com-o-date* y'all, Hawke," Beau drawled.

"Did your mama know what she was doing when she gave you that nickname, General Warford?" Yancey asked.

With Trammel's sudden inclusion of a military man three days ago, Yancey had huddled with Beau and came up with Hawke in half a day, but he'd focused his search on General Warford's battle experience not his nickname or family history. And now he wondered about both.

Hawke chuckled. "Well now, gentlemen, my mama certainly knew what she was doing when she gave me my nickname. She certainly did. Military does run in my family. You could say we Warfords have been on many a planning mission throughout history." Hawke was prone to flowery speech.

"How 'bout on the peace side? 'Cause I think that's gonna come into play right here and now," Yancey pointed out. *Gotta position ourselves on both sides to the voters.* Yancey would make a good chief of staff.

Sensing a split in the ranks, Beau jumped up. "We have a war room, right? Gimme the layout of this cockamamie place."

Yancey rifled through the paperwork and pulled out a floor plan. He trotted it over to Beau. "It's called the Situation Room."

Beau spread the floor plan on the desk. Checked it and punched his finger on a spot. "Yep. Thank you, Yancey. The *Sit Room.*" He looked wildly around. A cameraman quickly rushed over and positioned himself for a better shot. Beau waited until he got in place, straightened up, and looked into the camera with a serious expression.

"Let's roll."

Thrusting his arm toward a recessed door as though he were leading the Light Brigade, he rushed over, flung open the door, then whipped out of the room just as Mike was waltzing in on the other side.

"I found the bathrooms," he called to Beau's retreating back.

NINE

Recognizing it wasn't a good idea to replicate the real Situation Room on the first floor of the West Wing—national security and all—the art director, set designer, and the now powerful Trammel took their decorating cues from the W Hotel in Manhattan and an upcoming disaster movie helmed by Ridley Scott. In reality the White House Sit Room was a working space with little charm. Replicating it certainly would not have done for this groundbreaking show anyway.

Both faux Sit Rooms were identical: chrome tables and low lighting and Breuer's iconic leather and chrome Wassily chair. The furniture was already available for sale on *The President Factor* website. The focus and the action, however, were on the high-tech TV screens lining the pale blue walls: maps of Russia and Finland overlaid with icons for tanks, people, missiles, and other assorted images that one would find associated with military action. Footage of troops milling about played in HD. The screens in both rooms ran the same images. The teams would quickly move into vastly divergent areas and call for different maps and feeds, but for the opening shots of the room, the producers knew they had to put something on the screens to make it look exciting. Trammel orchestrated everything. An even playing field.

In his Sit Room, Adhemar and his team worked on iPads the show had provided that were Bluetooth connected to the screens.

"It's another Seven Days To The River Rhine," Harrison said. A military buff, he was familiar with the chilling top-secret map uncovered and published at a Polish press conference in 2005, detailing a 1979 Soviet plan to drop nuclear bombs across Germany and Belgium. Hamburg—gone. Frankfurt—gone. Munich, Antwerp, Brussels—gone.

"That was pure military simulation," ZeeBee retorted. "Warsaw Pact war games."

"And what are we doing?" Harrison said.

"He's got a point," Pinky said.

Adhemar said, "The Russians wanted to position NATO so they'd would strike first, then the Russians would come back, blow up Germany, and then say, *Oops! My bad, we're here at the Rhine River, we'll accept a ceasefire... and now we'll just take it over* scenario. And this was right before they invaded Afghanistan. Now, with what we know following their action in the Ukraine, nothing is beyond the realm of possibility." He tapped the brief. "This is actually a good scenario. It's not like those guys hadn't thought about invading *slash* starting a war before. Nikita Khrushchev had plans to hit New York and said so in his memoirs."

"Should we be thinking about the *why* of the invasion?" ZeeBee asked, bringing the discussion back around.

"My initial concern is where to get troops to counter the attack. Put them on our side of the border. After that we can figure out the why, take it apart, and work on diplomacy," Adhemar answered. "And we have to think of the consequences. Someone, and I can't remember who, said, *War is a declaration of failure of diplomacy.* I don't like the shoot first and ask questions later approach."

Harrison stabbed his fingers at the screens. "This is awfully close to reality. It's so specific we can see the insignias on their hats. They must have a cast of thousands somewhere."

"That's not real, Harrison," Adhemar said, strutting up to a screen. He tapped on the image of a Russian soldier. "It's CGI. Just like in *Gnomeo and Juliet.*"

"That's a bizarre reference," ZeeBee said.

"What would you use?"

"*Avatar.*"

"Okay. You win on that one."

"Or *Gravity. Game of Thrones,*" ZeeBee continued.

Adhemar tilted his head up and yelled, "Can someone show Harrison how you did that, please?"

The screens flashed and a sequence was built from a background shot of the border being filled in with wire-frame soldiers multiplied hundreds of times. Their uniforms painted in.

"Very convincing," Harrison said, impressed.

"I'd hope so," ZeeBee chuckled. "They've probably got a cast of thousands—of animators."

Adhemar gestured to the screens. "And we have to take it at face value. Or what's the point of going through this? Come on now." He looked pointedly at Pinky. "What would we do if this were happening right now?"

"Two thousand troops? That's Afghanistan," Pinky said.

Adhemar instantly knew he'd been right in picking Pinky as the chairman of the Joint Chiefs. Harrison, through his family ties, had consulted West Point and put Pinky on their short list, but it was Pinky's recent posting that made him stand out to Adhemar.

Adhemar rushed over and pounded him on the back. "Here we go."

Pinky shook his head. "We're on a timeline there. Pull out too soon and… Let's just say that's out."

ZeeBee was whipping through searches on her iPad. "Chad," she shouted out like she was playing charades and Adhemar had just acted out…God knows what.

"No," Adhemar said.

"It's the only other place we can get them from," she insisted.

Adhemar shook his head. "No. We're the finger in the dike. We pull out and the Janjaweed will pour through. It took a year to convince the UN to let us go in to protect the Darfur refugees and now you want to deplete the only thing that is keeping genocide at bay? We'll have to find them somewhere else."

"Or not," Pinky said.

The group froze.

"Russia? I think we have their address and they know it. Anything happens and their country will be destroyed," Pinky continued.

"By whom?" ZeeBee asked.

"By us."

"So we—"

"Do nothing."

"Which is, in essence, an act of war," Adhemar said, shaking his head. "I don't think we want to go there."

"Then, we have to look at the Darfur situation," Pinky shot back.

Within seconds the producers filled the screens with scenes of refugee camps in Chad. American troops at checkpoints, standing ready. No CGI needed this time, this was reality.

ZeeBee stared at a heartbreaking shot of blank-eyed children leaning against their mothers. "It's *Sophie's Choice.*"

"Basically, it's not what would Jesus do. It's what would Meryl Streep do," Harrison commented.

Adhemar sat down and carefully watched the footage from Chad as though the answer were in the eyes of the children. This could be a watershed moment. People would mark him as a hawk or a dove on the basis of this exchange. How did he want to present himself?

"Pinky, do you think this is just sabre rattling by the Russians? Or are they serious?" Adhemar was pacing. He stopped. "Scratch that. No time for détente, we have only a week."

"We do have time," Pinky said.

"For what?"

Pinky pointed to the TV. "Road trip. There's boots on the ground there, let's hit the ground with 'em. You can't make a choice, Adhemar, unless we see it for ourselves."

Adhemar chewed his lip. He needed to show decisiveness even though in the real world he would have a much bigger team analyzing everything. *Damn, this really is up to me.* The rest waited, poised to take off.

"Always good to look 'em in the eye, Adhemar. They've given us access to the military and that includes aircraft," Pinky said.

A scene from the *Blues Brothers* flashed in Adhemar's head. He stood up. The cameraman ran over and positioned himself directly in front. Adhemar nodded, anticipating that this was going to be one of those shots that would wind up on YouTube later on. It would look best as a close-up.

"Call them up, Harrison. Tell 'em to get the choppers ready. We're heading out." He held back from saying, *We're on a mission from God.*

ZeeBee mouthed to Pinky: "Choppers?"

Adhemar lead them out of the room.

In Beau's Sit Room, the action of the TV screens was also mesmerizing the group. Beau squinted at one screen showing the faux Russian troops standing at the ready. "Didn't they do this once before?"

"Yep. 1918," Hawke said.

"So it's plausible," Mike put out.

"Any damn thing is plausible today, Mike," Hawke replied.

"Word."

Beau rolled his eyes. The campaign team had worked hard to drum out Mike's slang, but every once in a while he slipped. Mike came to the ticket with something Beau considered a serious handicap: he was a speech chameleon, collecting dialect/cadence and speech patterns from his audience as they took the campaign on the road. This worked well for him in his state race when he jumped on stage at a concert and rapped with a local group, but Beau worried that Mike would offend others if he threw in a fo'shizzle or a BFF somewhere.

"Cut it out," Beau said, poking Mike in the chest to reinforce the point. Realizing too late that he'd committed the political faux pas of correcting his running mate in front of TV cameras, Beau scrambled to bring the focus back to the game.

"Hawke, we're not sittin' round your mama's kitchen table eating grits here. I need a viable plan."

"Or at least one that will appear to be viable to the American people," Mike added, trying to get some credibility back.

Yancey cleared his throat and pointed to a camera.

"Are we being taped?" Mike whispered, but not low enough to escape the ultra-sensitive mics.

"Yep."

Beau grimaced. "Shit." He looked to the ceiling, thinking the producers were sitting somewhere up there. "Ah…can we delete that last part? We weren't ready."

"There are no do-overs in the real world, Beau. I think that's the point of the game," Yancey pointed out.

Mike needed to regroup. He slipped out of the room and made his way back to Beau's Oval Office. His mistakes in the Sit Room put him on edge. Normally he could banter back and forth with Beau until they came up with a plan. Then they'd rehearse their statements with their advisors, going over every conceivable question a reporter could put to them. And then they'd rehearse every conceivable reply that would support their position. But this? This reality show? This was inconceivable. He saw Beau's annoyance with his *viable plan* statement. Hell, they always talked about what would appear feasible to the American public. Wasn't that the name of the game? Direct everyone in one way and go in another if need be? But now this process was headed towards transparency, and he wasn't so sure it was a good objective. *Imagine letting your wife know what was going on in your head? Letting her in on your internal arguments. Good God. That would be catastrophic.*

Snapping himself back, Mike took in Beau's Oval Office. The view out the windows mimicked the view from the real Oval Office so precisely he'd almost believed he was at 1600 Pennsylvania Avenue when he had first walked into the space. He trotted up to the windows, wondering how they had put it together, smooshed his nose against the glass to peer through a crack between the wall and the framework and caught a glimpse of Adhemar et al. truckin' down the hallway. ZeeBee had her purse. They were leaving!

Ohmygod. Panicked, Mike dashed down the hall to his team.

Back in the Sit Room, Beau, Hawke and Yancey were intently reading the entry they'd pulled up on the main screen: *Wikipedia: Finland.*

"Hawke, it says here Russia *left* Finland in 1918," Beau pointed out.

"Yes, that's what I meant. They'd occupied it for almost a century," Hawke snapped back, trying to recover.

Mike burst through the door. "They left! They just took off," he shouted.

"Yes, that's what it says here, Mike. We're just figuring it out," Beau said.

"No. No. No. Adhemar and the others just left."

"All of them?" Beau said.

"I…" Mike wrestled with giving an indecisive answer. The group waited.

Screw it, Mike thought. *I've gotta carpe diem this!* He let out his breath. "Yep. All of them."

"Damn. Where'd they go?" Beau said.

Mike recognized this as a moment to display his ability to analyze, even though all he had to go on was ZeeBee's swinging Kate Spade bag. "To Helsinki. I'm sure they're going to Helsinki," he said with confidence.

"They'll beat us," Hawke said.

"To what? It's not like we were going there," Yancey said. "We weren't, were we?"

"They'll have a leg up on us if we stay here," Hawke snapped with alarm.

"A leg up on what? What exactly are we going to do in Helsinki? Tour the Olympic Stadium?" Yancey said, dripping sarcasm.

"We should be where the action is," Beau interjected.

Pleased that his announcement had galvanized the team, Mike took it further. "Do we need any shots?"

Beau shot Mike a withering look.

"Yancey—go find the producers or whoever can get us there, pronto. Try to appear like you know what you're doing. And while you're doing it, don't look for any of those—" Beau made scare quotes with his fingers—"*I'm gonna tell all* cameras where you can pour your little heart out to the TV audience, so they can edit it back in later when it turns out we got beat on this thing 'cause my chief of staff was sitting in the Situation Room with his head up his ass while the other team was on their way to a win."

Yancey took the critique well. He was used to Beau deflecting blame to him. It's what he was hired to do—be the fall guy. He just didn't realize it would start this soon and that it was going to show up on TV. He sighed and pointed to Hawke.

"Military strategy's his job, not mine." Yancey bowed to the group. "But I'll do your bidding, of course."

Realizing what he just made happen, Mike blurted out, "I don't like the idea of going into a war zone."

"It's not a war zone, for God's sakes," Beau shot back.

"Oh, really? Then what do you call that?" Mike pointed one of the TV screens, where Russian tanks were pulling up to the road.

Yancey was about to point out that the images were fake but thought it better for Beau to score the point.

"What do I call that? Bluffing. Puffing up like one of those bullfrogs in my daddy's pond," Beau said.

"Your daddy's pond is a run-off from a chemical plant," Mike snarked back.

Realizing Beau had also been fooled by the animation, Yancey started to jump in to save him but unfortunately paused for a moment to think: *Who has his head up his ass now?*

Beau snapped a reply, "Yes sir, it is. And this thing stinks just as bad." He scowled for a split second and then, lightning fast, straightened his shirt, turned, and spoke to the camera. "But I'm ready with a plan to drain that swamp of war mongers. I have a plan. I won't be zipping off without a plan like my opponent. No running off to God knows where…"

"You have a plan?" Mike said with surprise.

Beau winced. "Of course I have a plan."

"What—"

Beau interrupted Mike before he did more damage. "A presidential plan. Which I shall share with the American public at the appropriate moment."

With that Beau turned and ran out of the room before Mike could ask for details.

Confused, Mike looked to Hawke. "Where'd he get a plan?"

Hawke tapped his front temple. "Right here."

⇺ TEN ⇻

As he was heading off the set, Adhemar had pulled out his phone and turned it on. There was a text waiting for him from Makki: *Meet me by bay three.* As soon as she sent it, Makki realized she had left a word out. Her message read like something from a sci-fi movie where the crew is on a space station somewhere and the captain wants them to gather to map out strategies to fight the aliens. She then quickly sent another one: *Make that EDIT bay three.*

Amused, Adhemar swallowed a grin when he saw the second message pop up. Of course he would meet Makki! Turning, he collided with ZeeBee. More spilled Oysterettes. ZeeBee was leaving the trail of breadcrumbs to get out of the forest.

Adhemar regarded the crackers. "You seem a little frazzled, Zee."

"You're the one who stopped like a tourist. What's wrong?" she asked, pointing to his phone, concern in her voice.

"Huh? Oh nothing." Adhemar was flustered. "I just have something to take care of before we take off," he said, quickly shoving his phone back into his jacket.

"I'll come with you."

"No!" Adhemar said firmly. Seeing ZeeBee jump, he brought his attitude down a notch. "Go say goodbye to

Sam, and I'll meet you at the plane in the morning. Pinky's arranged everything. We can't get out until tomorrow." He put his hands on her shoulders and gave her a gentle nudge towards the exit.

ZeeBee wondered what was in the text, but if Adhemar didn't want to share it with her, she had to respect that the man needed some privacy. *It really was a fucking fishbowl.*

Being in the control room had its benefits. With cameras placed everywhere, Makki could find and follow Adhemar within *The President Factor* studios and parking lot. She had watched him pick up her messages and head back inside. Heart pounding, she hurried toward edit bay three. By the time she arrived, Adhemar was inside. He had loosened his tie and was casually leaning against the edit console facing the door. Another *GQ* moment. This time, the cover.

Oh, crap. What have I done? Makki thought, closing the door behind her.

Oh, crap. What am I doing? Adhemar thought, reaching out to her.

Oh, crap. What's going on in there? thought the Secret Service agents positioning themselves outside.

Nothing more than a kiss.

Any progress that might have occurred was interrupted when show footage started appearing on the screens behind Adhemar.

"Ohmygod." Makki stiffened. "Don't turn around, Adhemar," she whispered into his ear as she realized what fine, contract-binding line was about to be crossed. And it was her fault! "You have to get out of here before someone sees you and thinks you're trying to cheat!"

"I wouldn't do that."

"I know. But right now, I am looking at Beau and his team making plans…on a monitor directly behind you."

"Ohmygod! I'll call you," Adhemar said, bolting out the door and startling the Secret Service agents.

Agent Kraatz, the younger of the two, over-reacted. "Get down!" he shouted, pushing Adhemar to the floor and throwing himself on top. He had an Olympic silver medal in wrestling—one of the reasons he was chosen for the protection detail. The recruiters had seen him take down an opponent in seconds.

"What? Where?" Adhemar shouted back as best he could from under Agent Kraatz's armpit.

"Behind you, sir!"

Adhemar snarled, "There's no threat behind me, Agent Kraatz. Good Lord. But I do need to get out of here."

Agent Kraatz rolled off and in one fluid move was on his feet, offering a hand-up to Adhemar. Off they went.

As Adhemar hurried toward the exit, the reality hit home that he had been a head-turn away from compromising his integrity and reducing *The President Factor* to a punch line. *What were you thinking? Or rather what were you thinking* with? *You most definitely will not call her! Damn.*

"Everything all right, sir?" Agent Kraatz asked, keeping pace alongside the fast-moving senator.

"What makes you think otherwise, Agent Kraatz?" Adhemar said calmly.

"You look like you are in pain, sir," Agent Kraatz said, keeping his voice low enough not to be picked up on *The President Factor* microphones. "When I pushed you…"

Adhemar had not been hurt by the take down. "I'm fine, Agent Kraatz," Adhemar shot back, not addressing the real pain at all.

＊ ELEVEN ＊

Immediately after securing the production of *The President Factor* and way before meeting Adhemar, Makki had written a creative brief that set the guidelines for the editing of the show and, more importantly, how far the editors were to go in making the network commercials (aka promos) of the reality show a little less real. She directed the editing to be *provocative to the point of manipulation*. Someone at the network actually copied that into an email and sent it to the production team—which included Trammel Washington.

Trammel immediately printed it and dumped it into his safe deposit box. Insurance. He'd bring it out if anything went south and the voters took it out on him. If not, he was just going to pretend he didn't read it. As host he knew he had little to do with the actual editing/putting together of the show and had hoped to God there was no obvious misdirection by anyone.

Now it was showtime. And after all the hype, all the waiting and all the commentary, *The President Factor* finally hit the air. Trammel was nervous. Between the taping in the afternoon and the show's premier at nine o'clock, he'd poked around backstage in the edit rooms. He stumbled across one of the editors playing with the footage, putting a shot of a smirking Beau immediately after the clip where ZeeBee said, "It's *Sophie's Choice.*"

Instantly Trammel argued, "That can't go there. Beau wasn't even in the room with her." The editor just shrugged, pulled out Makki's memo, handed it to Trammel, and went back to being *provocative to the point of manipulation*.

Trammel stepped out of the edit room and never went back. There would be plenty of time for denial after everything aired—if in fact anyone protested, which wasn't likely. He figured neither party would cry foul this early in the game. Being in the dark on what was going on in the edit rooms would be best for him.

He pushed this all to the back of his mind and concentrated on a more immediate concern. He was about to ad lib on live TV, something the producers dumped on him an hour before announcing they didn't have enough footage to cover the first show. When he protested—after all, they had been taping both teams for at least three hours that afternoon—they said there wasn't enough *usable* footage. They explained that by design and Trammel's own words, they couldn't use any of the footage that would signpost where the teams were going. That would tip off the opposing camps to the other's strategy. They also insisted that what was left wasn't *compelling*. Trammel put up the argument that if that was the case, wasn't that what they were supposed to show?

He lost.

Now *The President Factor* was on the air and he was standing on Pennsylvania Avenue in front of the real White House, waiting to get a cue from the director that they were coming to him. Live. He was told he would need to riff for about ten minutes! *Good grief.*

To his left, a group of about twenty people sat on director's chairs, watching the show play on tricked-out iPads. Behind them loomed a block-long *The President Factor* bus with Beau and Adhemar's faces beaming in ten-foot, full-color decals.

Trammel nervously touched his IFB, the earpiece that kept him in touch with the show's director who was sitting in the trailer.

"Trammel. Stand by," the director cautioned.

Trammel was keeping an eye on a small monitor the cameraman had jury-rigged. It played the show. What the editors had put together, just as Trammel feared, was far removed from what had happened in real time.

On the screen:

Beau, learning that Adhemar and his team has left the building, was running out of the room.

Close-up of Mike: "Where'd he get a plan?"

The shot froze on Mike's confused face.

The editors had edited the show to look as though Mike was commenting on Adhemar, not on Beau.

The director barked in Trammel's ear, "You're up."

Trammel brought a mic, complete with T*he President Factor* mic flag, up to his mouth and jumped right in:

"Good evening again, *The President Factor* viewers. In case you don't recognize it…" He glanced over his shoulder at the White House. "I'm standing in front of the endgame for Governor Simpson and Senator Reyes. And we're live. Let's talk to some folks over here about their thoughts on tonight's premier. They've been watching along with you."

Said folks were a mixed bag of personal supporters, pundits, and ordinary Americans. Trammel had mentally mapped out his interview earlier and walked past two young men wearing *Reyes For President* baseball caps to stop next to a balding fifty-year-old male. It was Beau's brother, Benny, who apparently got the wardrobe notes, for he too was decked out in a brown Pierre Cardin suit.

The director quickly called for a lower third to be written onto the screen: *Benny Simpson, Candidate's brother.*

Trammel thrust his *PWH* mic at Benny. "Benny, how do you think the governor did tonight?"

Grabbing the mic, Benny leaned over and blocked Trammel out of the shot. Logging more than two hundred thousand miles on the campaign trail over the past six months with this brother had given him some skills. "I think Beau won tonight," he chirped and winked into the camera.

Annoyed, Trammel pulled the mic back. "Of course you do, but what can you point to that would indicate a win?"

"The plan. The president of the United States should always have a plan. Beau told us he has a plan."

Rubbed wrong by Benny's initial maneuvering with the camera, Trammel pressed. "But we don't know what his plan is. How can you say he won when we don't know what his plan is?" Trammel turned to camera with an incredulous look.

"It's simple. Beau has a plan. Adhemar doesn't," Benny said with authority.

Trammel shook his head. "I'm not so sure about that. Senator Reyes didn't announce he had a plan, but we heard him make arrangements to go somewhere. He must have a plan or he wouldn't just up and call for choppers."

"I didn't hear Reyes say, *I have a plan.* Words speak louder than actions, Mr. Speaker. Beau Simpson says he has a plan and that's better than actually acting on something. He said it, so he won tonight."

Trammel sighed. "Is it possible—"

Before he could finish, Benny grabbed the mic again. "It's a beautiful thing, to watch democracy in action," Benny said, starting to cry. "I love this country so—"

Trammel wrestled the mic back, spun around, and moved down the line to a stunning blonde with her legs thrown over the arm of another director's chair. Posing.

Trammel addressed the camera: "One Plan? Two plans? Who's really got a plan? Let's change gears for a bit and talk to Mary McCormic, political analyst for Political Salon, the hottest blog on the net today. Let's get her comment on an interaction we saw earlier."

He pointed to Mary's iPad. The producers threw up a pre-selected clip of Adhemar's Sit Room.

ZeeBee: "So we—"

Pinky interrupted: "Do nothing."

Adhemar: "Which is, in essence, an act of war."

The editors had deliberately cut off the end of Adhemar's sentence: *I don't think we want to go there.*

Trammel said, "Mary. What do you make of this exchange?"

Mary tossed her hair. "I'm concerned. History has shown talking about war is a prelude to war. There is no accidentally dropping that word into casual conversation. If Reyes is elected, he is going to take us to war."

"With Russia?"

"Not sure, but he will drag us into a war somewhere. He's heading someplace, isn't he? Lots of stuff happens around the world, Mr. Speaker. Lots of stuff."

"You got all that from that one line?"

"Mr. Speaker, the people of this country look to us, the political analysts, to interpret what the candidates say. The candidates themselves look to us to interpret what they say. Plus, I have to look beyond what is actually said in order to make a point."

Trammel visibly sagged but soldiered on. "Okay, then. America, thanks for watching tonight's premier of *The President Factor*. Tune in next week as we follow the teams to…? That's the big reveal."

Trammel's IFB came back to life. "We're out."

"Thank God," Trammel said, turning his back on an approaching Benny.

A hundred yards away, the gates opened and the presidential limo pulled onto the White House grounds. It stopped at the North Portico. Two Secret Service agents jumped out of a trailing black Land Rover and ran to the limo. One in front. One in back. Inside, CIA Operative, and ZeeBee's husband, Sam Fisher sat relaxed in the backseat, watching the closing animation of *The President Factor* on his iPad.

It's said that successful operatives blend in with their surroundings, and Sam was a master at his job. With his over-the-top priced suit and undone tie, he mirrored the man sitting next to him: President Thatcher Cushing.

The interior of the limo, however, was another story. Sam did not blend into the décor. It was pale pink, custom designed by Cushing. Pale pink leather seats. Pale pink leather door panels. Pale pink everything except the carpet. That was charcoal grey. The president had heard from a college friend in the film industry that a certain male actor insisted—had it in his contracts—that the walls of the rooms he would be shot in—in any film—be painted pale pink. And they were. The actor said it was the best color for his complexion. What the president's friend didn't know was that Cushing identified with the actor after seeing him in a flick years before that involved a slew of undersea animals and lots of angst. Never mind that three quarters of the movie was shot outdoors; if his favorite actor wanted to be seen against pink walls, then the president could at least have pink walls in his limo. It unnerved Sam when he first started working on the president's detail, but by this point in the game, nothing fazed him regarding his boss.

The president was also focused on Sam's iPad. The two had been watching the show on their way back from a performance of the dreadful modern opera *The Bar with No Name* at the Kennedy Center. Neither had any interest in avant-garde performances, but the president needed to make a pretense of not being interested in *The President Factor*, so he grabbed a random pair of the tickets always coming from everywhere it seemed, sent the Secret Service out to get the place swept—quickly—and headed over. The two had slipped out during intermission, driving around for almost an hour, watching *The President Factor* on Sam's iPad to complete the ruse.

"How much do you think this is costing these guys? Reality shows are supposed to be cheap to produce. This ain't cheap, Sam," the president said. "Reyes is heading off to some foreign country for God's sakes. It really irks me that they left out all the good stuff, but I suppose the teams could watch the show and figure out what the other is doing?"

"Very observant, sir. Simpson is heading somewhere too. That remark from Mike about getting shots? They're leaving the states for sure. But considering the stakes, the show's a bargain, Mr. President."

"Trammel didn't ask for my input!"

"Wouldn't have been appropriate," Sam said.

"You didn't get briefed?"

"Nope."

"Nothing from ZeeBee?" the president pressed. "No idea where they're heading?"

"Nope."

Sam abruptly touched his iPad off, leaned forward and reached for the door handle. He was accustomed to accompanying the president—being a sounding board—but like ZeeBee, he worked to keep his professional and personal lives separate. He'd always wondered why this president had insisted on his being around so much when Sam was a Democrat and the president was Republican until ZeeBee got tapped for the VP spot. Knowing how extensive the president's reach was thanks to all the post 9/11 wire tapping, phone listening, Twitter following, and all around Internet monitoring the government was still doing, Sam had no doubt the president knew Adhemar was going to name ZeeBee even before Adhemar knew it himself. Sam and the president were in a constant state of dancing around one other.

"We should be able to control it," the president muttered.

Sam fell back into the comfy pink leather seat with a sigh. *Here we go again.*

The president continued, "Isn't there some regulation we can cite that would keep them from scripting this any which way they want?"

"No. First Amendment," Sam replied with patience.

"National security?"

"That's stretching it, sir. But we might be able to make a case for a preemptive strike on later episodes. In case it goes off the deep end and actually winds up…"

"Affecting my approval rating?"

"I was thinking more along the lines of affecting the global economy."

"That too."

"Hmmmm." Sam stared out the window. He wasn't going to feed this.

"I need to find out what Reyes is planning," the president said.

"He has a plan?" Sam said innocently.

"Cut the crap, Sam. He's clearly got a plan."

"Pardon my being blunt, Mr. President. But why do you need to know?"

"So I can get out ahead of it, Sam."

"Nothing to do with the show?" Sam challenged.

"Of course not. That would be cheating," the president said as innocently as he could.

"That would be correct, sir."

"He's a clever son-of-a-bitch," the president spat out.

"That's what makes him the front runner, Mr. President." Sam hoped that would be the end of the discussion.

He was wrong.

"I need your help here, Sam."

Oh, crap. Sam tensed. "I'm not sure I like where this is heading."

"You know what I mean."

Sam was not playing. "No, Mr. President, I do not."

"Do I need to spell it out?" the president snapped.

"Yes, sir. If this is going to be another Watergate."

"No one said anything about wire tapping, Sam."

"Okay, then."

"Just wife-tapping."

"ZeeBee isn't home right now."

"When she is available then, Sam. Get me some intel."

"Jesus. It's just a game, Mr. President," Sam said a little harsher then he intended. This was the president after all. Even if he didn't vote him into office, he was sworn to obey him.

"Life's a game, Sam."

Back in *The President Factor* control room, they had broken out the champagne. People worked their mobile devices, nibbled on Brie and raspberries and ignored a forlorn curry quinoa salad on political grounds. They read blogs and tweets and shouted out the rave reviews coming in: *Political fire and brimstone! Inside the beltway to inside your living room with a bang!*

Buzz B., the network president, handed Makki a glass of Dom. "Another hit, Makki," he purred. Buzz was reclining alone on a bright pink and turquoise hassock that would seat four. None of the executives or the guests thought it appropriate to plop down next to him. He had that effect on people. Makki was on a smaller hassock next to him.

"Yes, sir," Makki said, keeping her answers short. She'd made the mistake of giving a lengthy answer early in her career and was sharply reprimanded by Buzz, who didn't even have time to pronounce his last name. "Billingsworthy? Too long," he was once quoted as saying in an interview with *Rolling Stone*. "Just call me Buzz B. Short and to the point. That's how I like it. You should be able to have a conversation with me in five words."

"Make sure *The President Factor* stays a hit," Buzz said, topping off Makki's glass. Buzz didn't apply the five-word rule to himself, of course.

Makki nodded vigorously, reserving three words for wherever Buzz went next, yet making sure he knew she was agreeing with him. With Buzz's five-word limit, BCD's entire executive wing had developed a nodding technique that resembled a trick horse going through a routine. A few people started studying sign language. It was exhausting at times.

"We're committed to the entire run, so the show's success is important to our bottom line," Buzz said with nonchalance. He started playing with the tassels on the hassock.

"Understood," she said, a bit confused. *Of course, the show's success was important.* But the bottom-line comment seemed a little over the top. She had dramas on the air that cost more to produce than *The President Factor*, even factoring in the cost of the set and the candidates jetting off to parts unknown—to the public, that is. She of course knew exactly where they were going to be at any given moment.

"Just keep 'em interested, Makki." Buzz rolled off the hassock, stood up and walked away, leaving Makki wondering why he felt he needed to say that. She sure would have liked to get more information from Buzz on why this show was so important, but only had two words left. She didn't think *why* should be one of them.

"Of course," she said to his retreating back.

᭐ TWELVE ᭐

Adhemar's mother, Marisol, lived in Brooklyn in a magnificent brownstone that hadn't changed since it had been erected in the 1890s. She'd inherited the property from her parents when she was in her twenties but never thought of moving. Nor did she rip out the woodwork and tin ceilings in the 1970s when everyone else on the block was jumping on the modernization bandwagon. It was now worth millions.

Marisol was the queen of retro but not by choice. She just hadn't redecorated. Ever. When Adhemar was a baby, she'd gone rogue and bought a slew of Eames chairs and a George Nelson Marshmallow sofa at a garage sale because she *just liked the way they looked*. Part of her living room resembled the MoMA with the rest securely anchored in her Mexican roots. Juxtaposed over the eighteen bright, round red and orange cushions that made up the Nelson sofa, which Marisol covered in plastic, of course, was a four-by-eight foot faux oil painting of Jesus. In one corner a life-size plaster Madonna, head encircled with bright red and orange plastic flowers, smiled down on two of the Eames chairs. Marisol had a theme going.

Somehow it worked.

Adhemar suffered for years when his friends stopped by and made fun of the sofa until one of them wound up at

FIT and saw most of Marisol's garage sale bargains in his design history class. Suddenly everyone started looking at the furniture, and by extension Marisol and Adhemar, with a new eye. Later on, Adhemar used the furniture as a benchmark when he brought women home. If they recognized the significance of the pieces, he'd keep going out with them. If they made a face, he dropped them. He used this litmus test on ZeeBee, who not only knew the names of the designers but also recognized the pieces as originals.

Adhemar sat on the edge of the Nelson sofa, which was a feat given that the seat was angled to throw one against the back; but he was not planning on getting too comfortable. It was 6:00 a.m. He'd let himself in. He knew Marisol *got up with the roosters*. Not only did she use that expression, she actually kept chickens and a raggedy old rooster on the roof of the brownstone—recent acquisitions once the mayor made it legal in the five boroughs to keep poultry. Her neighbors were not happy.

The rooster had crowed a few minutes ago, and Adhemar heard Marisol moving around upstairs.

"Mamá," he called.

"Adhemar? You're here?"

"Yes, Mamá."

"Did you hear Hector crowing?"

"Yes, Mamá."

"Such a strong voice. Just like your father's."

Hector was also Adhemar's father's name. Hector the plumber and part-time drummer died when Adhemar was in sixth grade, and his mother had been naming various pets after him ever since.

Marisol came down the stairs pulling a striped cotton robe tight over a knee-length nightgown. At sixty-seven, she was still in shape, walking everywhere, including a weekly two-mile hike to La Guadalupe Fruit & Vegetable to get her groceries. The neighborhood had changed, but Marisol's cooking hadn't.

"You're here? Not on that fancy set?"

"I gotta go out of the country, Mamá."

Marisol put her hand to her heart and sank down next to him. The plastic covering crackled. Adhemar smiled at the sound. And the drama.

"What did you do, Adhemar?"

"No, no, Mamá. I'm going to Africa—"

Marisol quickly made the sign of the cross. "Africa?" she said with a challenge.

"Africa, Mamá. It's for the show. I don't want you to worry."

She folded her arms, defensive.

Adhemar probed. "Didn't you watch last night?"

"I can't watch."

He frowned. She shrugged. "It goes too fast for me."

"Mamá."

"All the talk of war."

"You did watch."

Marisol conceded. "For a bit. You and ZeeBee…she's such a nice girl, Adhemar." She got up and went into the kitchen and tossed over her shoulder, "But such a mouth."

She grabbed a coffee capsule from a gleaming stainless steel revolving tower on the counter. It was studded with yellow, green and brown capsules hanging like chads on the sides. "Come have a cup of this fancy coffee you got me."

In truth, Marisol liked the fancy Nespresso maker Adhemar had bought. She'd become a home-barista, making espresso for her neighbors to counteract their feelings about Hector's morning wake-up call.

Adhemar poked his head into the kitchen. "I can't stay."

"You can make time for breakfast."

"I have a plane to catch."

"It'll wait."

"I'm not president yet, Mamá."

"It'll wait. You're on a plane to Africa? All of a sudden, you're on a plane to Africa?"

"Yes, Mamá."

"You're not flying commercial, then. That transport plane will wait. Sit."

Adhemar laughed and sat down in his spot at the white enamel-topped table with the red trim, absent-mindedly tapping out a song with his fingers.

Marisol pulled a tray of eggs and a cloth-covered plate from the refrigerator. Moved over to the counter. "Did you see that guy on the TV yesterday? Making the fake huevos rancheros?"

"It's happening, Mamá."

She ignored him. "It's not like it is so difficult to make real ones."

Adhemar continued, not getting sidetracked. "Hispanics in powerful positions. First, the Supreme Court, and now the nomination. Next, the White House." He paused for the punch line. "And not as a gardener."

No reaction. Marisol busied herself at the stove. Opening the oven, pulling out a cast iron skillet. All but slamming it on the stove, but pulling back, letting it hit the burner with a polite bump.

"Come on, Mamá. That's funny."

"Adhemar, you've got to let this go," she said, cracking an egg so hard the some shell flew into the pan. "They throw bricks, threaten. You have to watch for everything. They sent that powder—" Her voice cracked.

She picked the shards of shell out.

"It wasn't anthrax. It was ground up Pepto Bismol or something like that," Adhemar said in a calm voice. They'd gone down this road before.

"They meant it."

"I mean it too."

"That was just health care reform, Adhemar. Not putting a Latino in the White House. That's going to push them over the edge."

"I can't walk away from the people, Mamá."

"You shouldn't have gotten yourself in this place." She turned around and mocked, "*Esto es importante, Mamà.*" She picked up a small piece of eggshell between her thumb and forefinger and thrust it into Adhemar's face. She opened her fingers and let it fall.

"*Phhht.* That's how important it will be if they kill you."

"We agreed we were not going to go there again. And I have the Secret Service now, remember? They're outside. You want to make them some *huevos* too?" Adhemar said, trying to lighten the conversation.

"*You* agreed. I'm still saying novenas."

Ah. She was coming around. He got up and hugged her.

Marisol let herself be enveloped in his arms. She looked up at her son. "You always like being in charge."

"I do."

She pointed her finger at him. "You'll not be so much in charge when you're the president."

"Ah, Mamá. I'm going to change that."

Marisol bit her lips. Eyes filled with tears. Adhemar tightened his arms around her. Protecting.

"I promise, Mamá," he said into her hair. "*Esto es importante.*"

⊷ THIRTEEN ⊶

The Hôtel N'Djamena la Tchadienne was a typical French-style hotel. Worn out. Buildings whitewashed years ago. Requisite pool. The heat, staggering. Gnats swarmed. Some other kind of bug screeched like an air conditioner compressor when the belts were going.

The flight to Chad had taken a long twenty hours, but Adhemar and his team were able to sleep and arrived somewhat refreshed—if one could be refreshed in the sweltering 108-degree heat. It was 9 a.m. Adhemar and ZeeBee sat on low-slung, bright blue chairs under red striped umbrellas by the pool, eying the water and the incongruity of finding it crystal clear and inviting. ZeeBee—stunning in a one-piece white swimsuit à la Ester Williams. Adhemar lounged nearby, handsomely roguish in khaki shorts and a powder blue tee shirt with a hand-screened crude replication of the hotel on the front and La Tchadie boldly emblazoned across the shoulders. Ridiculous oversized cartoon-like character blow-ups bobbed in the water.

ZeeBee swatted at the gnats. "The next scenario cannot include a trip anywhere hotter than ninety-eight degrees."

"That leaves out DC," Adhemar said.

"Exactly." She leaned over and grabbed a bright green can of Deep Woods Off. "Imagine finding this here." She sprayed herself, then offered the can to Adhemar. He waved her off with a self-satisfied smile. He sighed.

"What?" ZeeBee said after a moment.

Adhemar was waiting for the cue. "This is so good. Imagine when this is over, we'll have the American people's backing on everything we do. They'll have watched us making decisions, weighing consequences. Thinking. Strong decisions. Good decisions. We'll be able to make real changes."

"What's prompting this?"

"This place. It looks like '80s Russian surplus."

"It is '80s Russian surplus."

"The idea of a country that told its people what to think, how to act, and took over every part of their life, being reduced to representing badly designed furniture in a godforsaken country that is the uppermost region of the deadly tsetse fly—"

"Here it comes," ZeeBee said. Adhemar was starting to believe his own hype. By the time he got on the plane that morning, he was deep into the raison d'être for *The President Factor* and the effect he figured it would have on the voters.

"The United States will never be that country," Adhemar said, stretching his arms wide. "This is the beginning of transparency. Good old accountability. Taking it to the kitchen table."

"I was just hoping to avoid another fiscal cliff. Your rhetoric is wasted on me, Adhemar," ZeeBee said, ever practical.

Adhemar was using the opportunity of being alone with ZeeBee to practice his shtick. Big, extraneous gestures were needed for TV. Unless the camera was zoomed in, facial nuances were not seen on standard definition, aka SD TV, and a lot of folks had not embraced HD yet. Or they had not figured out where their HD channels were and were watching an SD signal stretched and blurred out on their HD TV, wondering why it looked so bad.

Pausing for a moment, Adhemar turned to his running mate. "You ever dream about being in the White House, ZeeBee?"

"Literally dream?"

"Yeah. Like go to bed and wake up thinking you were there. Not as a tourist or a visitor, but that you belonged there. Had the right to walk around."

"Have you?"

"All the time."

ZeeBee bit her lip. "Well. I might as well tell you. And you can't tell Sam."

"Okay. But you're going to be hanging around there next January. I think the cat's out of the bag, Zee."

"Not this one," she twisted a piece of her hair, suddenly shy.

Hmmm. Adhemar had not seen this side of ZeeBee. *Is she blushing?* She was. *Oh, this is interesting.* "Come on. Tell me. You had a dream about being in the White House?"

"Not exactly *being* in the White House, although I was in the White House in the dream. The focus of the dream was—zooks, I can't believe I'm telling you this." She paused to collect her courage. "I was Obama's girlfriend in my dream."

Adhemar broke out laughing. "How did you know you were his girlfriend?"

"You know how dreams are. I had this gigantic ID badge around my neck. It had like an eight-by-ten photo on it, with glass…glass over the top and a metal frame."

"I'm picturing this."

"And the glass kept slipping out and my picture kept falling out and then the Secret Service pretended they didn't know me—"

"Of course not. You weren't Michelle."

"Funny. Then Obama saw me and waved me into the Oval. He came over and gave me a hug." The blushing continued.

"And?" Adhemar asked provocatively.

"And then I woke up."

"That's all?"

"Yep."

"Then how did you know you were his girlfriend?" Adhemar wasn't buying the and then I woke up.

"The hug. It wasn't a campaign trail hug. It was a—you know—girlfriend hug." ZeeBee pressed her lips together, unable to bring herself to say *sexual*.

"Was it a good hug? And where was Michelle?"

"I dunno. In my dream he was single. And, yes, it was good. That's almost blasphemous, isn't it?"

"I can see why you didn't share it. When did you have this dream?"

"Two weeks ago. Maybe I'm thinking about you being single in the White House and this was the only way it could be expressed. Obama. The hug. Not a friendly hug. Single man in the White House. Get it?"

"Hmmm. Maybe."

"You really should start dating, Adhemar."

A waiter in denim shorts, a yellow La Tchadie tee and huaraches walked up and handed Adhemar a bottle of Coke. "Monsieur?"

"How can you drink that in the morning?" ZeeBee said, shuddering.

"It may be morning in Chad, but my body says it's the middle of the night. Did you get any francs?" Adhemar asked.

"No. Where would I have done that and why?"

"To take care of stuff like this," Adhemar said matter-of-factly, not registering that he could have done the same thing. "They have currency exchanges at the airports."

"*The President Factor* should be taking care of stuff like this," ZeeBee shot back. "And we flew out of Dover."

"Right." Adhemar squinted at the waiter. "How many American dollars? Ah, *combien*? *Combien* American dollar?"

The waiter took out a calculator, punched in a bunch of numbers. "*Cinq.*"

"*Cinq*? That's five, right?"

Blank look from the waiter.

"How much? *Combien*?"

The waiter punched in more numbers. "*Sept.*"

"Six? Six?"

The waiter punched in the numbers again. "*Huit.*"

ZeeBee jumped in, "This is like the national debt! It keeps going up. Stop him, Adhemar."

Adhemar handed the waiter a five-dollar bill. "I'm going with his first answer."

"Why are we at this hotel?" ZeeBee said, waving her hand at the spread-out buildings behind her. She pulled out her iPhone and read from a link she had saved from TripTips. "If it weren't so blasted hot, I would have preferred to sleep in the street. They must have put in the pool after this review, although we haven't really explored inside yet. I get skeeved from yucky showers. And I hear there are lizards in the rooms."

"I thought there wasn't any Wi-Fi."

"It popped in for thirty seconds a few minutes ago. International service, my ass. Maybe if we could have connected with the State Department's warnings before we were dumped here, Pinky wouldn't have gotten shot at when he was taking pictures of Cameroon across the river."

"They did tell us not to go outside the gate, ZeeBee."

"This is like the Newark airport! Here's more—"

Harrison came up behind her and read over her shoulder. "Do not stay here unless you're under siege. Are we? Where's the TV crew?"

"At the bar. Can we suspend the *don't let anyone take your picture with a beer in your hand* rule after the drive by?" ZeeBee asked Adhemar.

"No. How's Pinky?" Adhemar asked Harrison.

Harrison plopped down in another of the bright blue lounge chairs. "Sweating. He's trying to get our escorts here sooner."

"Where are they? Why aren't they here already?" Adhemar said. He didn't like wasting time. He knew very little about General Sykes, the man they were heading into the bush to meet, except that Sykes was chosen by the Pentagon to lead the mission a year ago. Adhemar preferred to have time to size up his opponents.

"They had us down to arrive this afternoon," Harrison informed him.

"Shit."

A Mirage fighter jet screamed by overhead, low—its jet blast whipped up the water in the pool. Startled, ZeeBee screamed and dove in. She surfaced, checked the skies. All clear. She swam to the pool's edge. "What the hell was that?"

"Crazy French pilots. Flying to Mali," Adhemar explained, watching the jet disappear.

"Why? Are we okay?"

"We're fine. The fighting is far from us."

"How many wars are going on in this country?"

"No wars per se. Military action."

"Okay, how much military action?"

"Let's see. The UN, France, and the U.S. are maintaining the refugee camp along the Darfur border. The French are helping Mali repel the advance of al-Qaeda-linked armed groups following a coup."

"Jesus."

"Nothing right near us, though."

"That should be reassuring, but I'll feel better when the Army gets here."

"Yep."

Grabbing an inflated animal that resembled a rat, ZeeBee paddled to the middle of the pool.

The door to the hotel banged open. A fully uniformed Pinky trotted out and made a beeline for the group. He tucked in under an umbrella and snorted when he saw ZeeBee in the pool. "Is that a rat? Who's on strike?" he barked. *Rat-ta-tat.* He was drenched in sweat. "Jesus Christ, it's hot. Where'd you get the suit, ZeeBee?"

"Vending machine in the lobby," ZeeBee sang out. "Thought you'd be used to this from Iraq."

"You never get used to this."

"What's the scoop on our escorts?"

"U.S. Army is on the way. Couple of hours. Three tops. We won't have to spend the night here."

Harrison said, "Thank God. It's too hot to sleep in the street. I read on TripTips—"

Adhemar shook his head. "Come on, guys. People live here."

Harrison deadpanned, "The people I'm worried about do not live right here."

ZeeBee dog-paddled her giant inflated rat around the pool. After accepting the nomination, she'd had scant downtime and three hours in this pool was as close as she was going to get to a vacation anytime soon. She watched Adhemar, Harrison, and Pinky through half-closed eyelids.

"We knew what we were getting into," Adhemar said. Now that he knew the Army couldn't get there for a bit, he started to relax. He watched ZeeBee paddle around.

"How bad can it be in a place that has a pool?"

"With rats," Harrison said.

ZeeBee laughed. "Ha. Pinky—gut feeling. Is Chad going to be our solution?"

"Redeploying troops is always a political hot potato."

"It's just theoretical, though," Harrison added.

Adhemar quickly took control. "Hold on. We're asking the military to consider moving two thousand troops elsewhere. Whether it's theoretical or not, the information— the answer we get from General Sykes—will be made public. Something to be taken seriously."

He spotted the camera crew shooting out the bar window. He waved. They waved back. He jumped up.

"Come on. Let's get ourselves some suits."

Harrison shuddered. "They'll probably be Speedos."

Not deterred, Adhemar looked for an ally. "Pinky?"

"Why the hell not," Pinky snorted.

Moving out of the shade, Adhemar and Pinky hustled towards the hotel. Halfway across the blinding hot concrete, Adhemar shouted back, "I'll get you a green one. Harrison."

Harrison waved his hand.

Adhemar continued, "To match your eyes."

Pinky slowed down. He wanted to have a sidebar with Adhemar outside of the camera's range—and it had better happen before they hit the lobby, what with the camera crew camped right around the corner in the bar. "Adhemar. This is something of a security risk."

"He's not the Green Lantern. I'm not outing him."

Pinky stepped off the path and gave him a hard look.

"Oh." Adhemar breathed in sharply. "You think discussing everything in the open, showing an insight into how our military leaders think, is a security risk?"

"Yes."

"And you don't think it's worth it?"

"Depends on the outcome, Adhemar."

"We can't control that, Pinky. And we're showing how the future leader of the free world thinks. And that is *definitely* worth it. Do you have a handle on Sykes? He's U.S. Army, and that should put him on our side."

"Yes, but you're going to ask him to give up some of his men, Adhemar. I'd take some time to slide into that conversation."

"Agreed. That's why I'm itching to get to the refugee camp. It's like five hours away, isn't it, Pinky?"

"Yes, sir."

"Let's hope our escorts get here soon, then. I'm wasting time getting a tan."

FOURTEEN

FINLAND

Three thousand miles and light years away, Yancey sat in the back of a black van sandwiched between two cameramen racing along Hammarskjoldsvagen Street in Helsinki. He caught snatches of "Good Vibrations" coming from Mike's earbuds two seats up. The cameramen kept flipping their cameras on and off to record out the windows.

Yancey never thought Beau would take him literally when he spoke of beating the other team to the Olympic Stadium, but there they were whipping along at around 128 km. The speed had startled him when he glanced at the dashboard a few moments ago until he realized it was in kilometers. *But that was still eighty miles per hour! Did he want to die for the darned game?* Absolutely not. But he couldn't risk asking the driver to slow down with the camera guys there. He didn't want to hear *Simpson's team takes a slow ride to solving the crisis* bounced around the cable talkies in the morning.

Beau and Hawke pored over a map of the city as though they personally needed to give the driver directions. The map was in Finnish. They had no idea what it said but had agreed on the plane to present a better image on camera after being caught flat-footed when Adhemar's team got a jumpstart. They reasoned that map reading showed leadership. It wasn't working. They had the map upside down.

Yancey spotted the Olympic stadium and its iconic tower through the windshield and seconds later, the van screeched to the curb. The Secret Service jumped out, followed by the cameramen, who trained their cameras on the van's doors. Beau acknowledged them as he emerged, then pulled Mike to the rear of the van out of camera range. Yancey wasn't the only one not taking chances.

"Quit askin' me about the plan," Beau hissed at Mike, exasperated with his constant questioning. He hated how he sounded, but needed to nip this behavior in the bud.

"I—"

"Quit. It."

Realizing their quarry had moved off, one of the cameramen spotted the two. Beau broke out in a big smile and motioned for him to come over. He was done chastising Mike and figured the crew, like everyone else who maneuvered themselves close to the candidates, were political junkies. His experience with the folks who showed up early to fundraising events and backstage at the speeches was that they liked to feel they were getting inside information, or at the very least were hearing something before it was made public. And sometimes that happened. If he played this right, he thought, he could have the entire crew on his side in no time. His assessment, however, didn't take into consideration that this wasn't a junket, but a TV show and the sheer economics of the union paycheck for the camera crew was the only reason they were there.

So Beau continued under the delusion that he was about to bring the cameraman into the inner circle. *Reel them in, then ask a favor.* The political machine grinds on.

He motioned the cameraman closer and whispered, "I'll have an exclusive for you guys later."

The cameraman took a step back. Beau read that as an indication he was overcome with emotion at this blessing. *Time for the ask.* The cameraman, however, was thinking, *What is he talking about? Everything we shoot will be an exclusive.*

In the same hush-hush tone Beau continued, "Y'all see the other team?"

The cameraman was prepared for this. He'd been prepped by Trammel. He didn't whisper. He spoke loud enough for Yancey and Pinky, hovering over on the sidewalk, to hear distinctly:

"Governor, we've been instructed not to interact with you. Plus, the viewer isn't supposed to know we're here."

Beau was taken aback. "That's ridiculous. Who do they think is recording everything?"

"It's the fourth wall, sir."

Mike blustered, "Those Ruskies! They built a wall here too?"

The cameraman started to explain, "The fourth wall—"

Sensing the cameraman's irritation, Beau quickly said, "I'll take care of this, son." He needed to keep the cameraman on his side, somehow.

"Thank you, sir. We're just here to record and observe."

Beau tried another tactic. "Did y'all observe the other team anywhere near here?"

With that, the cameraman hoisted his camera to his shoulder and turned it on. Overhearing the exchange, Yancey diverted him to the Olympic Tower. "Let's get back to the game, shall we?"

Mike craned his neck to get a better look at the cylindrical tower rising above the stadium. "If this thing were to really happen, it would be so *déjà vu.*"

"Like how?" Yancey challenged.

"Like in the 1940 Olympics—they were going to be held here but got cancelled because of the start of World War II."

"And it's *déjà vu* because…?" Yancey braced himself for the answer.

"Because…because it happened once before. And this could be the start of World War III."

"Oh. My. God." Yancey muttered.

"What?"

"You can't anticipate *déjà vu*, Mike. It's an illusion of having previously experienced something."

"Right."

"Right, how? You'd need to have been here to experience something that throws you back to 1940."

"Exactly."

Rattled, Yancey walked away, concerned that this absurd exchange would make it through the edit process and the voters might figure out how disconnected Mike was from—well—the basics of linear thought.

While Mike and Yancey were discussing the broad strokes of *déjà vu*, Beau had been scrutinizing the tower. He suddenly started hopping from foot to foot and danced over to the cameraman. "I got it! I got it! I got it!"

Oh God, now what? Yancey thought and hurried over to step between Beau and the camera. "What the governor is trying to say is that now is the time to unveil his plan."

Part of Yancey's job was also to translate what Beau was saying or at least an approximation of what Beau thought he was saying.

Beau nodded. "Correct. This is the proper place to unveil part of my plan."

Breaths held.

Beau waited until both cameras were focused on him.

"We shuttle everyone into the stadium and then send busses to pick 'em up and take 'em out of town before the invading army gets here!" He slapped his hands together. Done!

"Oh. My. God," Yancey said. This time loud enough to be picked up by the mics.

Hawke had the presence to counter Beau's statement. "Crackers, Beau. That's not gonna make it out of the coop." He whipped his hands around over his head. "Shit. You can't just circle in the air with a chopper, land by the levee, and expect the world to rise up and applaud."

He strutted off. "We need a battle plan. Let's get to the top of this here tower."

The rest reluctantly followed. Yancey spun his hand over his head like a helicopter. "Whoop. Whoop."

They considered walking up the twenty-four stories for about ten seconds, then took the elevator. Out on the observation deck, the city of Helsinki spread before them. A magnificent view of the waterways snug up against the historic city.

Beau split off.

"Let's divide up and then y'all report back to me," Beau said as he tore away.

Yancey, Mike and Hawke moved to the railing and looked down on the bright green grass of the stadium. One of the cameramen hung over the railing a bit to get a shot.

"What exactly are we looking for?" Yancey asked Mike, gripping the railing a little tighter as a gust of wind came up and the tower swayed a bit. They could hear snatches of music drifting up from somewhere below.

"Dunno. You were the one who wanted to beat Reyes to the Olympic Stadium," Mike said. He was struggling to keep up with the game's premise as it was, never mind trying to follow Beau's cloaked clues. If you could call them that.

Yancey shook his head. "Oh no. You're not blaming this on me. You said the other team was heading to Helsinki. I was being sarcastic. Has Beau given you a hint?"

"No. But I'm confident he has a plan."

Beau's plan at the moment was to look as though he had a plan—or was about to hurl himself off the tower. Hard to tell which way he was leaning. He cursed Yancey under his breath for his comment on camera about the friggin' tower back on *The President Factor* set. Now, 238 feet in the air, looking towards Helsinki Harbor, he was desperate. He admitted to himself that he—not Yancey—had forced the trip and the next installment of *The President Factor* would no doubt show that. He had to get something out of it or look foolish to millions of viewers and possibly lose the election.

What to do?

A quick decision. An energetic call across the platform to Mike brought him running, trailed by the cameramen.

Grabbing Mike by the shoulder, Beau turned him towards the sea beyond and made wide, sweeping gestures, pointing at nothing in particular. Mike whispered, "What are you pointing at, Beau?"

"Pretend we're going over that battle plan Hawke mentioned."

"What battle plan?"

"The operational word here is *pretend*, Mike," Beau hissed. Mike nodded and pointed alongside Beau. This he understood.

The cameras rolled.

ꔰ FIFTEEN ꔰ

Meanwhile in Chad, Pinky and Adhemar tinkered with the large vending machine, reminiscent of a 1930s automat, in the hotel lobby. They were still wearing their sunglasses. It was bright. Too bright. Lunchroom cafeteria bright.

Pinky spun a knob. Stacks of vividly colored bathing suits rotated by. All the men's were Speedos. Adhemar turned his back on the display to watch an old Sony TV that was balanced on a metal cabinet across the lobby. Rabbit ears.

Shaking his head at the selection, Pinky said, "This is depressing. I say screw it. Forget swimming. Let's join the camera crew in the bar. Even they abandoned us for the AC."

Adhemar abruptly whipped his sunglasses off and trotted across the lobby, eyes fixed on the TV. "Pinky. Look at this! What's going on?"

Pulled by the tone in Adhemar's voice, Pinky stopped perusing the offerings and snapped his head towards the TV. It was tuned to France 24.

On the screen:

A reporter stood in front of a map of the U.S. A bull's-eye was slapped over Kansas.

When Adhemar reached the set, his first instinct was to make the sign of the cross. He was still at the stage where he didn't censure all his actions and what he was seeing looked catastrophic.

Reporter: "Le fongus, UG99 s'étend maintenant a travers l'État du Kansas, le plus important producteur de blé des États Unis.."

Pinky yelled, "What's he saying?"

As Adhemar watched, the TV shot changed from the map behind the reporter to images of wheat fields.

Not wanting to move, just in case by some miracle English was going to appear in subtitles, Adhemar yelled back, "I don't really speak French. All I know is a few things like *Please, How much?* and *Where is the bathroom?* Which until now, was all I needed."

Like a horror show, the shot of the wheat fields changed to a close-up of a shaft of wheat. Black fungus grew up the stem.

Pinky sprinted over. "What the hell is that?"

Suddenly, the shot froze.

Adhemar and Pinky screamed, "Noooooo!"

They waited. It stayed frozen. They ran over to the desk, startling the desk clerk. Adhemar, his voice going up a notch, yelled, "The TV? *Le* television? *Kaput?*"

"That's German," Pinky said.

"Right."

Desperate, Adhemar pointed to the TV. "*Que—? Que—?* Shit!" He slammed his hand on the desk.

"I speak small English," the desk clerk stammered.

"Great. What happened to the TV?" Adhemar said, as though it were the clerk's fault.

"Not…okay."

Pinky leaned into the clerk's face, intense, "We see that. Can you fix it?"

The clerk pulled back.

Thinking the guy was about to bolt into that back room all desk clerks seem to hang out in when you are standing at the counter wanting to check out, Adhemar pulled his hand across his neck in the universal gesture that says *stop talking!* He directed it at Pinky. Pinky nodded, not in the least offended.

Adhemar calmed himself down and spoke slowly. "Repair? Make okay?" He made a motion like screwing in a light bulb.

"Perhaps," the clerk ventured.

"Good," Adhemar said, relieved.

"Good." The clerk smiled at them but remained behind the desk. Adhemar extended his hand. The desk clerk shook it and repeated, "Good."

Stalemate. Frozen smiles.

Not wanting to toss a pebble into this pond, Pinky whispered, "Adhemar. Ya gotta say something else. In French!"

The only thing remotely French going through Adhemar's head at that moment was the song "Alouette" and a bizarre rendition from his childhood that involved an out-of-tune piano that his next-door neighbor constantly played while making up his own verses and pointing out body parts that Adhemar instinctively knew, even at six, were not in the real nursery song. Finding out as an adult that the man was a drag performer in the Village, Adhemar wasn't going to use anything from that memory here.

He was circling the drain. He gestured to the TV. "Ah… *s'il vous plaît?*"

"*Oui.*"

Pinky quipped, "That one I know."

The desk clerk marched to the TV and slammed his hand on the side.

It went black.

Merde.

Two hours later, the Army rolled in. They couldn't get the TV to work either and hadn't seen the news story. This comforted Adhemar. If the Army didn't know, then he reckoned the U.S. wasn't under attack. Mobile phone reception was still elusive. He was sure this was a typical overblown story about a truck tipping over, spilling something or other on the roadway.

They headed out.

ZeeBee, still in her Ester Williams suit to the delight of the other occupants, climbed into a transport with Harrison. About to jump in after her, Adhemar was stopped. "Have to ride in separate transports," a burly sergeant told him. "Don't want both of you gone if we get attacked."

Harrison, spooked, ducked as though bullets already flew overhead. He remembered the potshots taken at Pinky outside the gate. ZeeBee scrambled to put on a pair of shorts and a shirt.

"You update your will, Adhemar?" ZeeBee asked as she whizzed by.

"Actually I did," Adhemar shouted after her.

"Good idea, Senator," Agent Kraatz said, tucking into the transport beside him. "The first time I went into a war zone, I had to do that and my wife kinda freaked."

"Exactly," Adhemar said.

"Sometimes it's best not to tell them. Not bringing it to mind, you know what I mean?"

As they rolled through the countryside, Adhemar was silent, thinking about his updated will. Maritza had been included in his old one and he hadn't updated it for…well, who knows…sentimental reasons? As soon as they declared they were going to take a trip to Chad, *The President Factor* attorneys came in and asked if his papers were in order.

It was sobering to be forty-three years old and realize that the only person you can name in your will is your mother.

Bumping along a very dusty road in a Godforsaken country, Adhemar took stock. Maybe it was the Godforsaken country but most likely it was a combination of ZeeBee's White House dream and the heavily armed Rangers guarding the back of the transport that got him thinking about being single and dying alone. He pulled out his phone and stared at it, even though he knew he wouldn't, couldn't, call Makki. He didn't get this far to blow it with a phone call. Saying *I'll call you* was the clichéd ending to many an encounter so it just popped out of his mouth back at edit bay three. *No one really thought the other person was going to call. Right?* It was like saying how are you? You really didn't want an answer. *Makki had to know that.* Their kiss, however, was a promise. That he would contact her after the game was over. Surely she got that.

But he still looked at his phone.

As they bumped their way along heavily rutted roads, the cameraman across from Adhemar tried to frame a shot. Banging his head on a crossbar after one cavernous rut, Adhemar exclaimed, "Christ, these things drive like a…right!"

Bump. Bump. Dodge the craters in the road.

The sergeant across from Adhemar leaned across the aisle. "Senator, I was instructed to brief you on a situation at the camp."

Adhemar tensed up. *Great, they have a situation.* He nodded. *Go ahead.*

"The Janjaweed took a run at the camp last night. See, it's not like the camp is enclosed behind any kind of fence or barbed wire, sir. There is an official entrance where we're taking you, of course, but with folks arriving every day, the camp keeps spreading out like spilled shoe polish."

"How do you keep control?"

"The folks in the camp? They're not going anywhere. I'm not authorized to give you the specs on our surveillance, but we saw the Janjaweed coming. They did a drive by and took some potshots."

"Anyone hurt?"

"No, sir, but the general wanted you to know. He can go into more detail on the what and why when you arrive, sir."

Another three hours and four Motrin later they popped out of the brush to rows upon rows of dusty beige tents housing thousands of Darfur refugees spread across a flat plain. A handful of scrub trees provided shade for a few camels hobbled nearby. A UN truck rumbled past, kicking up more dust. A U.S. Humvee with an American flag attached to the antenna followed.

General Jonathan Sykes, silver-haired, in fatigues with four shiny stars tacked across each shoulder, was sitting in an open Jeep at the edge of the camp. That he considered this a farce showed on his face. He didn't have the time or the inclination to entertain anyone—even presidential candidates. He wanted to give a quick tour and get them the hell out and back to the relative safety of the capital before the sun set. When he heard about the visit, he calculated how much the cameras and equipment would be worth on the black market and figured there was already a buzz in the bush, making night travel exponentially more dangerous.

Adhemar took a measure of the general's demeanor as the transport bounced to a stop. He waited for the dust to settle, then hopped out waving off the cameras and moved directly to Sykes, hand outstretched.

"General. Thank you for accommodating us. Would it be okay with you if the cameras powered up?" Adhemar asked, shrugging his shoulders as if in apology for even thinking of invading the general's privacy—never mind wanting to point a camera in his face.

Charisma won.

The truncated tour took two hours. They drove past lines of families snaking here and there, the men and women in brightly colored long robes. Some of the women wore *lafai*, a fifteen-foot scarf wrapped around their bodies. People queued for water. Food. Medical treatment. Goats ran about.

Controlled chaos. A group of women sat on the ground around a square box filled with grain, measuring rations with coffee cans with precision. Everyone sagged under the weight of his or her plight. Even the children.

Tea and biscuits were waiting for them back at the main tent—a holdover from the Brits and Irish NATO troops. Camp chairs and tea. It was almost civilized.

Adhemar blew across a tin cup of Bewley's breakfast blend after adding a splash of the tinned evaporated milk Sykes offered. "I'm hooked on this stuff," the general said with a shrug.

It was good. They sipped tea and munched biscuits, looking back at the camp and the sun that was mercifully settling.

"I understand there was a situation here last night," Adhemar said.

Sykes took a moment to pop the last of a McVities digestive biscuit into his mouth. "Yes, sir. The Janjaweed are getting bolder. And that makes them more dangerous than they were six months ago."

"What's changed?"

"Some of these folks are poised to go home."

"Is it safe?"

"Depends on how you define safe. We came in under Chapter Seven of the UN charter when they started to exterminate in Darfur. The people fled here. Chad had and still does have an open-door policy for refugees. We rolled over here when the Janjaweed followed the people across the border. Now the people are poised to return to their lands, and the Arabs sure as hell don't want to see that happen. They want to keep what they took over."

"And the refugees?"

"Think about it. This place sucks, but at least you aren't being raped and murdered in your bed. But if the government says you can have your lands back—might you go home?

I think the Janjaweed want to make sure no one takes the government up on that offer."

ZeeBee jumped in. "The Janjaweed *are* the government, yes?"

"Publicly, the government says they do not support them, but there is evidence to the contrary."

"So this is about land?" ZeeBee asked.

"Nothing is ever simple in Africa."

Pinky asked, "What's the troop count?"

"The EU mission has forty-five hundred. The UN by themselves has around five hundred. We've got close to six thousand deployed across the entire country."

As Adhemar listened to the general rattle off the statistics, his conversation with Pinky regarding making public everything they discussed weighed heavily. He chose his words carefully. "And if we deployed them elsewhere?"

"In Chad?"

"No. Elsewhere."

"Now why would I do that?" Tea and biscuits aside, Sykes gave his shoulders a clear *don't mess with me* roll.

Adhemar took a more conversational tone. "You wouldn't exactly— but theoretically or rather hypothetically… could we deploy troops elsewhere?"

"Hypothetically?"

"Hypothetically."

"Even hypothetically, it would not be advisable."

"What about downsizing? Say by two thousand," Adhemar proposed.

"What are you asking me?"

Time to lay it out. "General. Can you afford to lose two thousand troops?"

"These people can't afford to have me lose even one soldier, Senator Reyes." Sykes was hitting his stride. "I'd sure as hell like to go into attack mode and blow those emmer-effers off the face of the earth." He looked Adhemar straight in the eye. "But we're never gonna do that again, are we? No more…" Sykes made quote signs…. "*mission accomplished?*"

Ever conscious of the camera, Adhemar exaggerated a headshake. "Don't count America out, General. I'm not going into this election with a *sins of my father* mantel. There is no presidential bloodline here."

"Interesting how you phrased that, Senator. You'd be the first Hispanic president. Is that a bloodline you think about?"

"I can't escape who I am, General, nor would I want to. But—"

"But?"

Adhemar rose and moved toward an American flag hanging against a white mess tent behind them, making sure a cameraman stayed with him.

"But…I am not running as "the Hispanic candidate," but as the man who can lead his country and restore the faith the American people once had in their leaders." He stopped next to the flag. ZeeBee suddenly appeared with a small Sudanese child around two years old. She passed the child to Adhemar. They hadn't coordinated anything, but ZeeBee had been standing off to the side, chatting with some of the mothers and children while Adhemar and the general talked. After hearing Adhemar throw out the running as the Hispanic candidate line, she was jerked back to why they were there: To win the election. And this was a baby-kissing moment.

Adhemar continued, speaking in sound bites now. "My parents came to America for a better life, and I will bring a better life to all Americans." He nodded to the child.

"Ah, Senator. That child is not American," Sykes pointed out.

"Someday, General, with God's blessing, he may be," Adhemar said with forced emotion, half expecting to hear applause. From someone.

Harrison elbowed Pinky. "That-a-boy."

Sykes was annoyed. "Oh, good grief. Why are you here, Senator? They tell me this is all a what-if type of thing. Not a real situation. Just for TV. Right?"

"Yes, sir."

"What's the *if?*"

"Russia invading Finland," Adhemar said sheepishly, realizing how ridiculous that sounded.

Sykes burst out laughing. Hearing the scenario put him at ease. Even though Adhemar's visit was pitched to him as inconsequential to his assignment, he didn't trust anyone. He'd thought they might have been testing his readiness for battle. Not now. This really was for TV.

"Holy corn-fuckers. Who came up with that one?"

"Damned if I know."

"Ain't never gonna happen."

"Isn't that what they said about another Rwanda, General? Yet, here we are," Adhemar said. Now back on firm ground.

"So it's us or them," Sykes said. He'd play along.

Adhemar nodded.

"Which way you leaning, Senator?"

"You'll have to watch on Thursday with the rest of the world, General," Adhemar said, hoping the producers would glom on to this sound bite, turn it into a promo for *The President Factor* and run the heck out of it to keep viewers hooked. His face all over the TV without having to dip into his campaign chest to pay for it.

"I'm Adhemar Reyes." *And I approve this message...* he added silently to himself.

SIXTEEN

After *The President Factor's* premier, Makki had returned to New York City and became a phone watcher. And hated herself for it. A watcher and a checker. Yes, her phone was working. No, Adhemar hadn't called. Or texted. *He's thousands of miles away. In Africa,* she told herself, permitting an excuse. *They have phones in Africa,* her practical side spoke. *Yes, but maybe he doesn't have service! Damn it. The man makes me feel like a teenager.*

Back and forth, ad infinitum.

Adhemar thought she got the throwaway aspect of *I'll call you*. She hadn't.

It was now Tuesday. Makki was at Morimoto's on 10th Avenue, having a late lunch with her assistant. Even though she was feasting on delicious toro tartare and assorted sushi rolls, she was in a glum mood, sinking fast.

"What?" Jon said after she checked her phone for the tenth time in an hour. "Are you looking for a notice of the big bonus Buzz is certainly giving you for the great numbers we got with *The President Factor?*" He scraped a bit of the toro tartare off the glass board with a little silver shovel-like utensil and dipped it into a line of nori paste, sour cream, and little rice crackers. It was one of the restaurant's signature appetizers. "Ohmygod. This is fantastic. I'm so glad you finally decided to start eating Japanese."

"Jon, what time is it in Chad?" Makki asked.

Jon, of course, knew things like this, having been Makki's personal assistant for ten years, taking care of just about anything she wanted and adroitly anticipating her needs.

"They are 6,420 miles away and five hours ahead, so it's eight o'clock."

"Hmmm."

"Hmmm? Why hmmm?"

"Nothing, just hmmm."

"Sweetie, you don't just hmmm. What's up?" He pulled out his phone and started to scroll through his contact list. "You want me to get the team in Chad on the phone?"

To his amazement, she smacked his hand with her chopsticks. "Put that away."

Jon scowled back. "They probably don't have service there anyway."

"You think so?" she said perking up.

"Does it matter?"

"Yes."

"*Pourquoi?*"

"*Parce que,*" she said, deftly lifting a thin slice of shaved ginger with her chopsticks and draping it across a piece of spicy tuna roll. "Just because."

"Do you want me to check to see if they have service? Or not?"

"No. Yes. I don't know," she whined.

Jon had never heard Makki whine. It unnerved him so much that he accidently dragged his next shaving of tartare across a humongous blob of wasabi and shoved it into his mouth without looking. After an embarrassing few minutes of choking and massive amounts of tearing, Jon was able to continue his probe of his boss's demeanor. And finally got it out of her.

He wasn't that shocked. He'd been wondering about that last minute HappyRice outing anyway.

"I just wish I knew if he is deliberately not calling or can't call. It that too much to ask?" Makki said, after pretty much telling him everything but delicately leaving out the meeting in the edit bay. She trusted Jon, but the integrity of the show was at stake.

"Yes," Jon said, straight-faced.

"Stop it," Makki said, picking up her phone again and staring at it once more.

"Why should you be any different than any of us who have sat by the phone," Jon sniffed. "You're not going to see anything there unless he's got FaceTime turned on and doesn't know it. Or you've placed a listening device…" Jon trailed off watching Makki's eye's widen. "Oh no, you didn't!"

"Of course not. But, thank you for the suggestion. I have the next best thing."

"You've joined NASA."

"Funny. See if you can guess. What came in from the crews in the field this morning?"

"The stuff from Chad."

"Exactly. I'm going to screen it to see if any of it shows Adhemar using a working cell phone!" she said smugly in an *Aren't I clever?* way.

Jon threw back a look: *Who are you?* He refrained from putting that into words and didn't comment.

Makki stiffened at his look, then suddenly realized this was not one of her girlfriends she was spilling to, but her assistant! Makki quickly deflected his attention. She nodded at the toro tartare. "You really made a mess of that wasabi."

Oh thank God, she's back! Jon thought. He gratefully turned the conversation to neutral ground. "You'll make a mess of the show if you start second-guessing the editors at this stage. That's why you have an executive producer, remember?"

"I'm not going to give direction. I just want to see how things are shaping up. Anyway, it's my ass if the show tanks."

"That is true. It is sweeps."

It was no coincidence that *The President Factor* was airing during a sweeps period. Sweeps, in TV language, are the months when the ratings—the information that indicates who is watching what, in whatever numbers they are watching—get churned out by the big machine that is Nielson. Ratings are used to set advertising prices. February, May, and November are sweeps months. New shows premiere, and new episodes of ongoing shows run during those months—not repeats because reruns are not going to get the ratings.

Compelling teases of upcoming shows generate audiences. Large audiences mean good ratings. Network careers hang on ratings.

Half an hour after leaving Jon at Morimoto's to finish off the last of the toro tartare, Makki was back at work two floors down from her office, peeking through the glass door to the edit suite manned by C. J., the network's top editor. With the emphasis Buzz was piling on *The President Factor*, she figured C. J. would be putting together the show and the promos. Taking a deep breath, she pushed the door open and went in.

"Hi, C. J.," she said, all business. "Did we get any footage back from Chad and Helsinki?"

"Just Chad so far. They sent us a bunch."

Makki smiled. She was right. C. J. had the footage! "Mind if I take a look?" she asked, knowing full well C. J. couldn't refuse.

"Knock yourself out. There's hours of stuff. I've got the raws from all the cameras, plus the footage from the studio. Anything in particular you're looking for?"

Careful, Makki thought.

"I was in the control room when we shot the studio stuff so I'm just looking to see what came in from the field. Buzz is all fired up over this show, so I'd like to stay on top of everything," she said with a nervous laugh.

"Right. I can set you up on one of the extra computers in the corner."

Moments later, Makki grabbed a couple of Twizzlers from the requisite candy jar that resides in every Manhattan edit room and started with a clip marked N'Djamena.

SEVENTEEN

t Dell's Diner in Boise, Idaho, the dinner crowd was hanging on. It was 7:30 p.m. Access time in TV language. The hour before prime time when entertainment shows are king. In the corner, a fifty-inch HD TV was tuned to *Entertainment Now*, a magazine-style program on BCD, the same network as *The President Factor*. Seconds ago the show open teased they had an insider's look at *The President Factor* with a *we've got something no one else has* tone. The place was hushed, watching. The cooks were watching. Servers stood between the booths, plates in hand, watching. A young couple with a screaming toddler had just been escorted out the door. *The President Factor* was serious business.

On the TV, with de rigueur TV-host long, black hair brushing her shoulders, Samantha Hellman, thirty, sat at the command desk next to her co-host, Jim Nathanson. Jim wore charcoal grey. Calvin Klein. They looked grand. Behind them, a video wall showed a close-up of Adhemar with an Exclusive graphic flashing.

Samantha flipped her hair. This was her moment—no one would forget the face of the woman who doled out *The President Factor* treats.

Samantha: *"We know we're going to hear from the network on this, but heck, we've got some bootleg footage that will be shown on this Thursday's THE PRESIDENT FACTOR. We'll let our lawyers battle it out tomorrow, but tonight, we're going to show it to you."*

Jim, throwing her a sharp, questioning look: *"I don't think we'll be in any trouble, Samantha. We're on the same network as THE PRESIDENT FACTOR. Plus we're news—"*

Samantha: *"We are?"*

She didn't want to be known as a news…anything. The word anchor escaped her at that moment. News people get whacked, she figured, thinking of Ann and Katie. She kept a perfect smile on her perfect face.

Jim: *"We're news and we're protected under the first amendment or something like that. So we can show the footage."*

Samantha, chirping: *"We're entertainment."*

Jim carried on: *"We're entertainment news and by golly, THE PRESIDENT FACTOR is a cross over! The footage we obtained needs to be shown tonight so that the American public can form an opinion before they see show itself. It's the American way."*

Irked by his lengthy airtime buttering up the viewers, Samantha snapped: *"Just read the prompter."*

Jim took the hint. *"We'll start with a clip of Senator Reyes."*

On the video wall: *A clip of Adhemar in Chad played. Adhemar was saying, "…There is no presidential bloodline here."*

Then the video went still.

Samantha: *"That's it?"*

"Yep."

"We don't have the beginning of the bite?"

"Nope."

"Just the end? A snippet?"

"Yep."

"Did they say where he was? Any hint?" Samantha was pumping Jim for info. Why did he get to be in control? She fumed.

"Nope."

"Hmmm. Anything from the other team?"

Ticked that she kept questioning him, Jim needed to regain his position.

"Yes, Samantha. It's another snippet. Again. This time it's of Governor Simpson," he said, dripping sarcasm.

Watching this exchange across America, *Entertainment Now* fans were perplexed. Never before had their favorite hosts shown anything other than happy banter, even when they were exposing some rock star's drug demise. All was usually upbeat. Can't have anything serious invade the entertainment world. *What's happening here? The President Factor* was already having an effect on national TV.

A snippet played on the video wall. A clip from Helsinki, outside the stadium:

Beau: *"This is the proper place to unveil part of my plan."*

Knowing Samantha was going to jump all over him again, Jim quickly said, *"Let's take a break."*

They went to commercial.

In Dell's Diner, Jimmy, one of the servers who had been watching the TV, shook his head in appreciation for Beau's statement. He'd been riveted to the screen, holding two plates of Dell's nightly special: braised Snake River Farms Kurobuta pork short ribs with sweet potato, apple, and bacon hash. He came to and slid the plates in front of Rick and Ann, two fifty-year-olds in matching denim shirts.

Jimmy snorted. "I knew it. Beau has a plan and that wetback has no business running for president."

Ann nodded. "Just confirms what Rick and I already thought. Reyes just said there is no presidential bloodline. He admitted there is no way he thinks he can win!"

Rick grabbed a rib. "That is just what he said. Why is he wasting the taxpayers—my—money with this ridiculous campaign then? No presidential bloodline! Nothing to connect him to the White House. Agreed." Rick pounded the table for emphasis causing the wooden ducks, forever frozen in flight on the wall next to him, to shake. "Did you notice some of those people in the background? They were blacks. I don't know where he is, but he's taking his campaign to the minorities. Typical Democrat."

"You gonna watch on Thursday?" Jimmy prodded.

Rick nodded vigorously. "Wouldn't miss it. I usually can't ever figure out what the heck these po-lit-it-cal folks are yammering about on TV. But now, after watching *The President Factor*, I'm startin' to see both candidates clearly. I sure did enjoy that first show. Why, I was so proud to be an American with this new way of peeling back the layers of our candidates."

Ann reached across the table and patted Rick's hand.

"You sure have a way with words, honey."

"I was so proud. I was so proud. I—I—" Rick struggled to his feet and saluted the TV with his pork rib. "Mighty powerful television."

☙ EIGHTEEN ☙

I t was midnight. Beau's group had left the Olympic Stadium and staggered over to the Hotel Potkaista, a landmark neo-classical luxury hotel in the heart of the city where high-profile visitors stayed when in town. They'd checked in and regrouped in the Potkaista Bar, a popular place to see and be seen. *The President Factor* team had done well in their hotel selection. Hawke, however, was more impressed that he was getting Starwood points than he was with sparkly chandeliers and opulent surroundings. The waiters whispered by.

Beau was hunched over a *croque-monsieur*, a combo of warm ham and cheese, grilled open-face to a crispy golden brown. He examined the surface as though he were going to see in the melted cheese the face of the Madonna or a symbol of something—anything—that would jump-start an idea. The camera crew were in the corner, flirting with the waitress, and Mike and Yancey were at the other end of the bar, arguing about the merits of the local beers while mock-racing two of the hotel's trademark red rubber ducks found in their bathrooms. The Secret Service were hidden somewhere.

After biting off the corner of his *croque-monsieur,* effectively ruining what he had finally deduced was a pretty good replica of the map of Texas, Beau considered inviting Yancey and Mike to join him for a brainstorming session, but the memory of the lackluster results from the last one he tried to get off the ground with the two men gave him pause.

Beau took a pull on his gin and tonic and shuddered as he remembered how Yancey and Mike went off the deep end. It happened after his advisors suggested Mike Charleston as a running mate and Beau invited him to a get-together in the great state of Texas. Austin, Texas. His hometown. His great-grandma had a saying, "You can't take anyone out to hunt till you've chewed possum with 'em." Grandma repeated that homily *ad nauseam* at every Simpson clan gathering, so Beau couldn't forget it if he tried.

With a nod to Granny, Beau planned a face-to-face with Mike at the Outback Steakhouse on Lamar Boulevard, avoiding the hip-happening and music-playing downtown area where the press would spot them. Avoiding the governor's mansion too. Scores of news vehicles and satellite trucks were parked every which way outside the mansion since Beau had made his announcement to run. There was no way he could sneak Mike in there without him becoming the topic of the day/week for all the networks and bloggers. Beau sought to avoid that. He was going to make his decision without the media making it for him, *goldarnit!* Hence his choice of breaking bread with Mike at a chain restaurant in a city that boasts some of the best beef and barbecue anywhere.

Outback had no possums on the menu, but they did have a few specialized items. After scarfing down half of a Bloomin' Onion, Mike took Beau by surprise by starting to riff on the fancy *aussie-tizer.*

"Your down-home politics are like this onion, Beau. A delicious surprise. And everyone likes to peel away," he said, dipping a piece into the spicy signature sauce. "Which has got me thinking. You know, Beau, if you became president, you'd peel away the rotten parts of Washington."

Mike paused for a moment, a well-dipped piece of onion halfway to his mouth as if to take in what he had just said, then caught Beau's eye.

Beau's eye was hopeful.

"That's it! You can be called the Peeler!" Mike shouted, throwing his hands in the air and letting go of the dripping piece of onion. It flew over two tables to come down on the head of Jeremy Long, a twenty-two-year-old rocker who had stopped in to get fueled-up before his performance later that evening at the Dirty Cat, a club on Guadalupe Street. Luckily Jeremy had well-lacquered hair and the dip-covered onion sliver bounced off into the aisle without him even noticing.

Caught up in the excitement of food fireworks, Beau blurted, "Mike, y'all should join me in the peeling!"

There was no going back.

The next day, Beau completed his dream team with Yancey and the following week he brought the group together at the W Hotel in the heart of the 2nd Street District. Beau chose the W because he felt guilty about Jeremy Long after he walked past the singer on the way out of Outback. The remains of some signature sauce were imbedded in his hair. Not that patronizing the hotel would put money into Jeremy's pocket; it was the Dirty Cat's proximity to the W—a block away—that gave Beau the connection. He equated this type of thinking to fuzzy logic and would say so to the press in the upcoming months, not realizing that fuzzy logic is a legitimate mathematic process, not a way to justify his fuzzy thinking.

When Mike and Yancey walked into the room at the W, Beau was on his third whiff off a little metal canister of H2O that he had found in the suite's Munchie Box. He took another hit and marched over to the panoramic windows.

"Com-ere. You can see Dirty Cat from here," he proclaimed, pointing to the street.

Yancey drifted over and peered out. Not having been briefed on the Jeremy Long connection (and why should he be?), he had no idea what he was looking for. He spotted a woman below. Her position on the corner and her attire, or lack thereof, set off alarm bells. *Ohmygod! She's a hooker!*

He recoiled and quickly ducked away from the window.

"Jesus Christ, Beau. Is this why we're meeting here instead of at the gov's mansion? Because of Dirty Cat down there?" he squeaked, his voice going up an octave.

Beau beamed at Yancey. "Why yes, it is," Beau said, pounding him on the back thinking, *By golly, Yancey sure is intuitive—he got the connection!* He ambled over to the Munchie Box and pulled out a bag of spicy nuts nestled next to a humongous bear-shaped jar of gummy bears.

"Is she…um…coming up here?" Yancey forced out.

"What do you mean, *she?*" Beau asked, struggling with the bag of nuts. "Dirty Cat is a *what,* not a she!"

The bag suddenly split, sending spicy cashews bouncing across the pristine white three hundred-thread-count duvet.

"Shit!" Beau said.

At that moment, Yancey realized he had just accused the man who might be the next president of the United States of betraying his wife and consorting with prostitutes. And Beau's answer plainly showed he was wrong to do so.

He quickly recovered.

"Just kidding, Beau, I spotted an alley cat on the garage roof and I was just pulling your leg." He whipped across the room to help Beau sweep the nuts off the duvet and prayed the woman on the corner had either found a john or moved away so Beau didn't clue in to what would have surely removed Yancey from the dream team before he'd even loosened his tie!

Beau, thankfully, was easily distracted. He was also extremely clear-headed after his H2O boosts and suddenly wanted to use his newfound energy—somewhere.

"I'm gonna head down to the pool on four and do a drive by. There are some pretty big spenders in this place, and I might as well add to my war chest."

Yancey couldn't get him to the door quick enough.

"While I'm gone, maybe you two can get together and pick a campaign song?" Beau threw over his shoulder.

Whether it was the lack of real food in the Munchie Box or the sheer ridiculousness of planning any part of a presidential campaign on the tiny squares of the white note cards with the cut-out W the hotel provided in an ever-so-fabulous leather box (which they were forced to use, having forgotten to bring any writing supplies and resisting paying for the in-house Wi-Fi that would have at least allowed them to do some research) Mike and Yancey's suggestion of the Beatles' "Taxman" as a campaign song was *sooooo* off base that Beau didn't even want to hear their rationale for the darned thing.

Now, months later, sitting at the Potkaista Bar, Beau realized he wasn't up for another "Taxman" moment with Yancey and Mike. Especially in front of the cameramen.

He decided to call his brother, Benny.

At one time, Benny had run a successful lawn maintenance company with undocumented Mexicans in his hometown of Dallas. Based on that, Beau figured Benny would have some kind of connections somewhere and would be able to get a person inside the studio to poke around to see what was being sent back from the Reyes team—wherever the heck they were. Plus Benny was always playing the angles, and Beau wanted to get his input on what they might be able to salvage from the trip to Helsinki. The sticky part was that Trammel asked the teams to keep their whereabouts secret to build up an audience for the next show. Something about the producers wanting to create a bunch of promos and teases to play out on the network leading up to Thursday nights, but Beau figured he could tell his brother that he was in Helsinki so that Benny could find his passport real quick in case he had to fly here to rescue him from something. Right?

Having talked himself into breaking the rules, Beau relaxed and ordered another gin and tonic, took a quick covert look around the bar and ever so casually pulled out his phone. Then it hit him—Mike had the only international phone. He couldn't drag Mike into this, and Yancey had talked him out of adding Skype to his iPad.

Crap! The camera crew was wrapping it up with the waitress and heading his way.

Double crap. He couldn't call anyone now. And he still didn't have a plan.

⇒ NINETEEN ⇐

After eating three quarters of a large Mel Cooley veggie pizza with pesto that she had ordered around ten o'clock from Two Boots (best crust in New York City) and drinking five of those little cans of ginger ale (that she always bought because she didn't want to drink a big can, which didn't matter in this case because, heck, she had just drank five of them), Makki fell into a post-binge stupor in the corner of the edit room. It was 1:00 a.m. She'd been scrolling through hours and hours of footage from Chad from every freaking camera and not once did she see Adhemar with his cell phone, other than in one shot taken from inside the transport. Even then, she really couldn't make out what he was doing because the footage was too shaky. Was that a cell phone in his hand or a box of Junior Mints? She finally concluded that Junior Mints would be melting all over the place, since they were in Africa, so it had to be his phone. But even so, she couldn't tell if he had it to his ear or if it had simply been flung there by the ridiculous bouncing of the transport. *Didn't they give the cameramen Steadicams?*

She was slightly slumped over in her chair, but still awake when Buzz buzzed into the room. His entrance electrified C. J. who quickly queued up the spot he'd been working on.

Buzz didn't notice Makki in the corner—thankfully, because *why the heck am in here?* she screamed to herself, watching her career flash before her eyes. Especially at one in the morning? Hold on. *Why was Buzz in here at one in the morning?* Makki held her breath.

Buzz barked at C. J., "Let's see what you did with that footage from Helsinki, buddy."

Makki perked up. *We got footage from Helsinki?* Even though her main focus was Adhemar, Makki's TV executive mode kicked in. She really hadn't been paying attention to anything C. J. had been doing for the past nine hours, except to notice that every once in a while he played music that sounded like the opening to the Super Bowl.

She maneuvered her chair to get a better view of C. J.'s screen. A title slate came up, indicating it was a thirty-second spot for *The President Factor*.

The spot opened with a shot of Beau in front of the Olympic Stadium:

Beau: *"This is the proper place to unveil part of my plan."*

C. J. stopped the playback. "That bite has gone viral, sir. Ever since we fed it to *Entertainment Now.* Good call on that."

Buzz nodded, accepting the praise as a matter of course. Makki was stunned. Not just about Buzz's involvement in deciding which clips got released or by C. J.'s sucking up, but with the fact that C. J. used more than five words. She started to wonder if Buzz only played mind games with the executives.

C. J. played the rest of the spot:

Hawke: *"Let's get to the top of this here tower."*

The sports music started. Sped-up shots of Beau and the team heading into the stadium were followed by a slam cut to the team running out of the elevator. Then shots of Beau and Mike pointing to the sea…at nothing of course, but in the context of the spot, Beau appeared to be pointing out a battle plan. The fast cutting and the sports music projected a picture of Beau as the quarterback he once was, directing his team to victory. In control. Dynamic.

Next came footage of Yancey taken outside the stadium before the group went inside. It was his reaction to Beau's absurd statement about the busses and shuttling folks out. C. J. had deliberately left Beau's statement out.

He also used a technique called rotoscoping to replace the background behind Yancey. Only the best designers/editors can rotoscope and have the results look believable. C. J. was one of the best. It took five hours to accomplish but when he was done, C. J. made Yancey magically appear on the platform at the top of the tower next to Beau and Mike saying, "Ohmygod!" as Beau and Mike pointed to the sea. By taking the bite out of context and manipulating the footage, Yancey now appeared to be impressed with something Beau was saying. Completely the opposite of what had truly happened.

The announcer came on: *"Does Senator Reyes also have an ohmygod plan?"*

Next C. J. had placed a shot of Adhemar drinking tea and eating biscuits with General Sykes.

The announcer: *"Maybe not!"*

This was followed by a shot of Beau and Mike inside the van looking over the map. C. J. had also managed to turn the map right side up. *Atta boy!*

The announcer ended: *"Can Senator Reyes catch up to the governor? Find out on the next The President Factor."*

Makki winced. *Dammit, we're going to have to recut it and take out the obvious bias for Beau and downright gross misuse of footage. Jesus, what a colossal waste of time. And money.* Thinking it would be embarrassing for C. J. to be reamed out in front of her, she slunk down further in her chair.

To Makki's total surprise, Buzz did the opposite. He slapped C. J. on the back. "Nice job! You can feed it. Got another one?"

C. J. beamed. "No sir, it took me hours to rotoscope that shot of Yancey and replace the background and then to turn the map..."

Buzz squeezed C. J.'s shoulder, "Let's not go over the details, son."

The door to the edit room suddenly banged open and a delivery guy from the corner deli was there with a bag full of Junior Mints. *Oh crap*, thought Makki. *I forgot that I ordered those. Hours ago.*

The delivery guy looked around. "Delivery for Makki?"

Busted.

Buzz spotted her. "Makki? What are you doing here?"

Sensing the tension, the delivery guy shoved the bag at Buzz and quickly left.

Okay, five words. "Sleeping," she lied, which got a *What the heck is she saying?* look from C. J.

Buzz tightened his grip on C. J'.s shoulder. Frowned.

What the hell? Makki threw the five-word limit to the wind. "I hate to admit it, sir, but I fell asleep a few hours ago."

"Ah, that is correct," C. J. stammered, following her lead. He had no idea why she was lying, but it was obviously not good for him or his shoulder that she was in there.

Makki piled it on. She scratched her head in a what's-going-on gesture. For good measure she added, "Are you screening something? What time is it?"

Buzz relaxed his grip on C. J. "Well, good morning, sunshine. C. J. was just letting me know the footage from

Helsinki arrived, and I thought I might take a look. But on second thought, I'll just leave it in his capable hands." Grabbing a box of Junior Mints out of the bag, Buzz ambled out the door.

C. J. and Makki eyed each other. Was she going to grill him? She certainly had lots of questions, the least of which was *Who told you to make Beau look good? And to trash Adhemar?*

Self-preservation took over. She didn't want to know if it was Buzz. Like Trammel, Makki decided what went on in the edit room stayed in the edit room. She stood up and stretched, knowing C. J. would almost certainly be looking at her body. She made her way to his chair, reached across him, breasts right in his face, and grabbed the bag from the deli. "I'm done screening. Think I'll head home."

C. J. nodded, visions of intimate moments with Makki flashing through his mind.

"Shall I leave you some Junior Mints?" she purred.

⇜ TWENTY ⇝

CHAD

The sun had set. Clusters of people lined the road, making everyone in the convoy of four U.S. military Humvees nervous. They streaked toward a group of low, spread-out, nondescript buildings two miles ahead: the airport. General Sykes wanted a safer mode of return transportation for Adhemar than the transports they arrived in. The general was right. The buzz was on. But whether it was a benevolent buzz as in *Let's go see if we can catch a glimpse of the guy running for president of the United States* or a *Let's run into the road and stop the convoy and then rob them* crowd no one knew. The drivers weren't slowing down to ask.

In the second Hummer, Adhemar and Harrison were squashed in the back seat next to a case of MREs (Meal Ready To-Eats). Pinky had muscled his way into the front next to Agent Kraatz, leaving room in the other vehicle for ZeeBee to stretch out.

Although he had discounted it at the time, Adhemar was curious about the story he'd seen on TV in the hotel lobby. Reception inside the Hummer was sketchy, so he cranked open his window as soon as they got underway and stuck out his iPhone, hoping for a signal. He quickly abandoned that when Agent Kraatz pointed out that the glass was bulletproof. Lowering it, he said, was: "Something you might not want to do, sir." *Okay.*

Banging his elbow on the box next to him, Harrison whined, "What's with the MREs? Are we taking the long way back?" He strained his neck to look out the slit of a back window. "What's in ZeeBee's Hummer? Canned peaches? If we wind up in a prison camp, they always seem to have canned peaches. Are they trying to tell us something?"

"I'm not going to answer that," Adhemar said tersely, now moving his phone around inside, eyes glued to the screen. "Come on." Suddenly little blue bars popped up. "Here we go!"

Pinky leaned over the seat as best he could in the cramped quarters. "Anything on that bull's-eye over Kansas?"

"Maybe it was just the French version of the *Wizard of Oz*," Adhemar tossed out. He waved the phone a little. "I'm trying to get an answer."

Adhemar entered *Kansas* in the search box. After scrolling past a slew of official state sites, a Wikipedia reference and at least fifteen hits related to the band Kansas, he came upon a YouTube posting: The White House comes to Topeka. It had that day's date. He tapped the screen and a video clip came up: A square-jawed, black-haired reporter stood on the White House lawn. On the bright orange bar across the bottom of the screen he was identified as Alan Smithee.

"Am I reading that right? The guy's name is Alan Smithee?" Harrison said.

"Yep."

"That's really funny."

"How so?" Pinky said.

"Alan Smithee is the official pseudonym you saw in film credits used by directors who wished to disown a project. Like when someone else takes over and your vision is crushed and nothing resembles what you wanted to do," Adhemar explained.

"Kinda like what happens to a bill in the Senate," Harrison added.

"Exactly," Adhemar said. "Maybe we should consider adapting that. Headline in the *Post* would read: Neither side could come to an agreement on the Alan Smithee Medicaid provision."

"So it's not a real name?" Pinky asked.

"It may very well be someone's name somewhere, but no journalist would keep it. Too much baggage even though they stopped using it in the late '60s, I believe. The great part was that in order to use the name, the director agreed not to discuss why they wanted to hide their involvement. No one was going to let out that the lead actor sucked. Worked for everyone."

"If you look it up on IMDB?" Pinky asked.

"You'll see a slew of movies directed by a bunch of different people all credited to Alan Smithee." Adhemar peered at the screen. "Do you also notice this guy's uncanny resemblance to Guy Smiley from *Sesame Street*?" He hit the little *play* triangle on his phone.

The video started: *Smithee waved his mic around.*

"Like something from a horror movie, this morning's announcement coming from the White House paints wheat products as the last thing you'd want to feed your kids. Here's Sydney Chase with the report," he said with an overabundance of frowning.

The shot changed to a young woman standing in a grammar school cafeteria dwarfed by a line of giant papier-mâché cookies, cupcakes and loaves of bread behind her. Some were covered with black Xs. A few were painted black. One chocolate cupcake appeared to be constructed from mold. Nothing resembled anything you'd eat. Sydney tossed her already tossed hair and smiled at the camera. *"John, the fourth graders at PS 25 here in Topeka have embraced the President's message that anything containing wheat is bad. They've constructed these papier-mâché…"*

She gestured wildly at a gigantic greenish beige cookie looming over her head. *"…things to help spread the word, under the guidance of a team of White House staffers who flew here bright and early…actually they were here at sunrise…to kick off the initiative."*

Adhemar snorted. "Embraced my ass. You couldn't get me to give up Chips Ahoy at that age for anything. Smithee, Smiley, and now this. That's strike three. It's a hoax." He pushed the video off the screen.

The Humvees caught up to a troop transport, lumbering along. The driver tooted his horn and the soldiers waved as the Humvees blazed by.

Harrison waved back. "We're not taking them, are we? I mean theoretically, they are not the solution," he said to the group.

"That is correct," Adhemar said.

"Now what?"

"I'll figure something out."

"We're running out of time, Adhemar."

"I'll figure something out," Adhemar repeated with conviction. "One way or another, we will have a solution to present on Thursday night." He opened the Flipboard app and went to the cover stories.

"Anything in there about where Beau is going?" Pinky wanted to know.

"No, but he is quoted as saying he had a plan."

"Think he does?"

"I'm sure he has a plan for something, but that might not have anything to do with solving the crisis."

Pinky snorted. "Well, I sure as hell am not taking notes from Beau Simpson."

"Amen to that," Harrison added. "What else you got?"

Adhemar flipped by a seemingly endless parade of articles about *The President Factor*, including a story about NY1 News using chia pet heads of him and Beau to predict the front runner—more sprouts meant more votes. He came across a link to the blog Boing Boing with a cover photo of a pop-up-book-like art installation with the White House in the middle, both *PWH* teams in various stages of popping up or sliding out from beneath a glorious rendition of a savanna. *Where did these guys get their info? They were nowhere near a savanna. Was Beau? Hmmm.* Adhemar's paper proxy was flattering and Beau's seemed to be wearing football shoulder pads.

"You going to open any of those stories and see what they're saying about us?" Harrison asked.

"Nope. They're mostly conjecture, positioning, and crap."

"Certainly not all of them?"

"No, of course not. But my one rule is never read an article about myself written by anyone I've never given or would never give an interview to. And anyway, outside of those chia pets on NY1, I'm not interested in any of these."

He pushed the pop-up-book art thing off and the next article showed ZeeBee standing in front of the Helsinki Olympic Tower. "See. Photoshopped."

"That's really good," Harrison said in appreciation.

"Yes, it is. And that's why *The President Factor*…the show, mind you, not this crap…is so important. It can't be manipulated."

"Sure it can."

"What are they going to do? Cut me out from Chad and place me in Helsinki? I didn't see a giant green screen behind me anywhere. No place to insert any different background footage."

"Maybe, Adhemar. Just maybe," Harrison joked.

"No. *The President Factor* is different."

"God, I hope so," Harrison said soberly.

"Look, I met the woman who is in charge and—" Adhemar started blushing. "And she isn't green-screening anyone."

Adhemar moved on to the BBC News section and paused on a photo from the *London Daily Telegraph* of a group of protesters holding black posters with pieces of printer-sized white paper pasted in the middle. Underneath each paper was a skull and crossbones.

"Ha!" Adhemar let out. At that, the cameraman hoisted up his camera and started shooting.

Harrison squinted at the photo. "You know what that's about?"

"I sure do. They're so far ahead of us it's embarrassing."

"I need a little more that that, please."

"Paper milling and water pollution," Adhemar said, putting a finger on the image of the piece of white paper. "This roughly translates to white paper killing the water supply."

"Yikes."

"Yikes, indeed. But it gives me an idea." He tapped the Flipboard off just as the convoy halted in front of a small building with a nondescript sign: N'Djamena Airport. It was noisy, windy and still blazing hot even though the sun had gone down hours earlier. On the runway next to the building, an Air France jet idled, door open, stairway down. Two armed Rangers jumped out of the first Humvee, double-stepped over to the vehicle and whipped open the doors.

Adhemar grinned at the Rangers. "We're taking a detour."

"Are we joining the protesters?" Harrison asked as he tumbled out the door past the K rations.

"In one sense, yes, we are." Adhemar replied.

"I guess you figured something out."

Adhemar slapped him on the back. "I guess I did."

TWENTY-ONE

Two minutes before *TalkOut* went live, Dave Reynolds was just finishing his caviar ritual. On the silver tray in front of him: a loaf of black bread, Russian Ossetra caviar, and Carelian caviar piled high atop mounds of sour cream. And as usual he'd shared his spread with his floor director, Henry.

"Davie, what's with the black bread?" Henry said, ripping a piece off the unsliced loaf.

"My homage to *The President Factor*. Black bread… Russia. Get it?"

"Nice. Nice." Henry popped some into his mouth, chewed. "It's terrific. What's in it?"

"Fennel. It's imported, of course. Don't want to run afoul of the White House and be seen enjoying any wheat product made in the U.S."

"What's up with that?"

"I'm looking into it, but most likely it's some senator in the Midwest wanting to jack up the wheat prices. God, I wish we had a mic in the Oval Office sometimes." Dave hung his head in mock embarrassment. "Did I just say that? Ha ha." He picked up the Carelian caviar tin. "And these beauties come from the beautiful lake-filled Savonia region of Finland. I'm immersing myself in the show's cachet."

"Uh-ha. Whatta ya gonna do if the next challenge takes them to Ethiopia? Starve?"

"Christ, Henry. That's offensive."

"Yes, it is," Henry mumbled, stuffing more bread into his mouth. He held up his hand and counted Dave into the show. "Coming to you in five, four..."

Dave shook off the thought that someone in the control room had recorded the Ethiopia comment; he'd likely have to do damage control later that evening, when it no doubt would wind up on some pseudo-news site attributed to him. *God, I hate these so-called journalists*, he thought. *If one of them actually went to a breaking news event and sent an honest-to-god report back instead of ripping off The New York Times, then I might have some respect.*

Dave removed the scowl from his face as the tally light went on. "Countdown to the second installment, or shall we say second episode, of *The President Factor*," he spat out, ramping up. "The country is buzzing. What are the teams doing? Where are they now?"

The screen behind Dave flashed, showing Adhemar climbing into the Air France jet, and then changed to footage of Beau and his team leaning over the Olympic Tower railing.

"This game has been kept under some very tight wraps," Dave chuckled. "This is worse than the last episode of *Seinfeld!* Or for those of you too young to be witness to that reference, think the finale of *Mad Men*."

He leaned into the camera, earnest. "Which is what these teams might be right now!"

Getting caught up in the moment, he grabbed the last piece of black bread absentmindedly and gnawed at it. "We'll talk strategy with presidential advisors from the current administration. On the table: Are both teams running down the same path?"

In Helsinki, having left the bar en mass to go up to Beau's suite, which was off-limits to the cameramen, the team was tearing through a fruit platter and watching *TalkOut* with Finnish subtitles on a ridiculously large plasma TV. It was 2:00 a.m. in Finland, but Beau insisted they stay up to catch the show, knowing Reynolds would lead off with *The President Factor* and hoping he might get some hint of what Reynolds thought Reyes might be doing—anything to help him with his own plan. Dave Reynolds was more than a political talk show host; he had been the press secretary for the last Democratic president and, boy, could he get inside the heads of just about anyone.

Mike snorted, "Going down the same path? Ha! We fooled them!" He squinted at the screen. "Is Dave Reynolds eating bread?"

Yancey said, "We fooled ourselves. Reyes is not here. Hasn't been here and isn't going to show up here. There isn't time."

"That doesn't make us wrong to be here," Hawke retorted. "Where the hell did Reyes go?"

On the TV, Reynolds was back from the commercial break. Two men had joined him. One was in full military uniform.

"*With me tonight is former White House Chief of Staff Jim Gordon and one of the former heads of the Joint Chiefs of Staff, General Billy O'Donnell. Gentlemen. Where did Senator Reyes go?*"

Hawke slapped his leg. Beamed. "I just said that. I should be on that show!"

"And you will be, Hawke. And you will be," Beau said, slapping him on the back. "Now, shush and listen." Beau got up and stood in front of the TV as if to put himself right on the *TalkOut* set.

Reynolds started off the discussion with the clip from *Entertainment Now* of Adhemar in some sort of bushland.

"Gentlemen, where in the world is Senator Ryes? General, does that landscape look familiar? I think I caught a glimpse of an Army vehicle in the background. And the people there with the senator, I'm assuming aren't props. They live there, wherever there is. What does that look like to you? And are those canned peaches they're carrying?"

"Dave, I think he's in Africa."

"Well, that's obvious."

Beau's face screwed up. That was not obvious.

"Where in Africa?" Reynolds continued.

"We have military bases in a lot of places."

"What's he doing visiting our military bases?" Reynolds got worked up as he always did. *"Raiding the troops? Well here we go again! What's he aiming—"*

ZZZZT—ZZZZT—

Just as the general opened his mouth to answer, the channel suddenly reverted to the hotel's in-house feed. Pictures of the lobby popped on. Light jazz filled the room. Beau swore and spun around, furious. "Who has the fucking remote?"

The other three stared back at him.

"Ah, Beau, you have it." Yancey pointed to the remote wrapped fiercely in his fingers. "You're gripping it so tight, you must have changed the channel."

"Christ!" Beau rapidly scrolled through all the offerings the hotel provided until he came back to international TV and found *TalkOut*. He turned it back on.

Reynolds: *"Up next, more intelligence leaks rock the FBI. What is the definition of treason and does it apply here? We'll be right back."*

"Shit, shit, shit!" Beau said under his breath. He didn't want his team to know he was floating downstream. "Well, that was enlightening—*not!* No matter, boys. Our superior cognitive powers put us out front. If I were to wager on this phase of the game, I would be smart to put money on us." He snorted. "Africa?"

Mike grabbed a grape from the tray, popped it in his mouth and slapped his leg. Delighted. "Now, Beau. You know you can't do that," he snickered. "That would be insider trading. Like Martha Stewart."

"So you do have a plan then? Beau?" Yancey asked.

Beau nodded and put his hand out to Mike. "Gimme your phone."

"Where's yours?"

Beau snapped his fingers. "Do I have to explain everything?"

Mike frantically patted his pockets. "I…lost it?"

"Mary, Mother of God, Mike! You had the only international one," Beau sputtered. "I can't trust the hotel phones. Someone could be listening in!"

"I think I left it on the bar," Mike said, jumping up. He ran out of the room.

"Who you gonna call?" Yancey said.

"The president," Beau said and then sat down, arms folded. The president was the next best thing to talking to Benny, and Trammel surely couldn't restrict him from talking to the president! *The man had advisors. He figured he could get some hints about Reyes from them, for sure.*

"This president?" Yancey didn't share Beau's opinion of the current administration. He had never seen the need to meet with or consult with his counterpart at the White House and wondered what Beau thought he was going to get from such a chat. That man didn't have an original thought. "Why?"

Beau took his time answering.

"It's a good thing."

While Beau was quoting Martha Stewart, Adhemar and his team were relaxing in first class on an Air France flight headed to London.

Back in coach, the other passengers were watching a news update from BCD News. After the international weather report, the Buzz-approved *The President Factor* spot popped on. Drink service stopped as the flight attendants stood in the aisles and watched along with their one hundred and twenty economy class *guests*. When it was over, there was a noticeable buzz in the cabin. Although first class was separated from the rest of the plane, a lot of the passengers had seen Adhemar and his entourage get on.

"What is he doing going to England?" the passenger in seat 25B asked his seatmate. "Chasin' after Beau?"

"Beau is in Helsinki. I recognized the Olympic Tower."

"You saw what I saw. They say he doesn't have a plan."

"Shame," the passenger across the aisle chimed in. "Couldn't help overhearing y'all."

Passenger 25B started to unbuckle his seat belt. "I'm gonna go talk to him."

His seatmate grabbed his arm. "What, are you crazy? Besides the air marshals, there are a slew of Secret Service agents up there."

Passenger 25B froze, and then popped his head into the aisle to peer towards first class. "You think so?"

"Where do you live? In a yurt? Of course they are up there. They'll throw you to the ground and cuff you."

"I just wanted to find out what he's doing going to England."

The guy across the aisle leaned over. "Getting a connecting fight to Helsinki, no doubt. He probably saw that commercial before we did and got an idea from it. Wish I were home right now. Then I could rewind it and see where Governor Simpson was pointing. Betcha I could figure out Beau's plan if I slowed it down. Betcha Reyes did that. Slowed it down so he could copy Beau's plan."

"Yeah! You could also read that map they were looking at if you could freeze the picture. That would show where they were heading," Passenger 25B agreed.

"I don't want to know," a flight attendant said, breaking into the conversation. She'd been hanging back a row, listening. She passed out their drinks. "I kinda like getting surprised by reality shows. Don't want to know who is getting booted off the island ahead of time."

"I think it is pretty obvious who that's going to be," Passenger 25C said, downing his Jack and water. "Every winner of any reality show worth its salt had a plan. Uh-huh."

Up in first class, Adhemar and his team, with individual iPads stocked with a slew of new release movies, were oblivious to the promo that had just run in coach. Adhemar popped a chocolate-dipped strawberry into his mouth and tipped an empty wine glass toward ZeeBee. The flight attendant appeared with another bottle of champagne and quickly refilled everyone's glass.

"Here's to traveling with *The President Factor,*" Harrison said, rising up, glass in hand, ready to toast the camera crew a few rows back in business class, but they were asleep. They'd been schlepping gear for hours in the hundred-plus degree heat and blazed through two bottles of champagne themselves once the captain informed them they couldn't power up their cameras while in flight. They were officially off duty.

Harrison snorted, nodded to the Secret Service agents in the row behind Adhemar, ZeeBee and Pinky. They were awake and sipping water. Getting up, he crouched down in the aisle next to Adhemar. "Now can you tell us why we're heading to London? It has something to do with those protesters, right?"

"Yep," Adhemar said. "One of the paper companies in the U.S. is about to build a plant outside London. Europe has led the world in healthy and sustainable paper milling, and the demonstrators don't want our dirty practices rearing their ugly heads in their backyard."

"What's not healthy about the regular paper milling in the U.S.?" ZeeBee asked.

"The process. In England, they use oxygen. Which is good. U.S. companies can use a form of chlorine. Lots of water and chlorine. That can turn into dioxins."

"Ouch!"

"Yep. Bleaching paper is the second-largest known source of dioxins. Happens when chlorine mixes with the natural chemicals in wood pulp. Pump that back into the streams and you can get dead fish and a slew of other environmental and physical ramifications. The cow downstream is drinking the water… You can follow the rest. It hits the entire food chain."

"Why are we still doing it?"

"Our current laws do not deal with it."

"Holy crap!" Harrison spat out.

Adhemar grabbed another strawberry. "Indeed. It also gets spread as sludge on farmland, gets into the air from paper sludge incinerators—picture that."

In unison, they looked at the chocolate-dipped strawberry in Adhemar's hand.

"That's gross," Harrison said with disgust.

Ever so vigilant, the flight attendant read Harrison's expression and rushed over. "Something wrong with your strawberries, Senator? I can bring you something else." She slid a silver tray forward.

"Not at all," Adhemar replied. "We were thinking of moving on to the warm nuts anyway." He dropped the strawberry on the tray.

Relieved that the airline had not poisoned the man she was planning on voting for, the flight attendant whisked the offending fruit away.

"Can we have some warm cookies now too?" ZeeBee called after her. "I love the warm cookies."

"That's a better picture," Harrison said. "Who are we meeting in London?"

"The prime minister," Adhemar said, settling into his comfy leather seat.

"This will help us?"

"It will," Adhemar said with conviction. "If we respect other countries and acknowledge that we Americans are part of this planet—forget the American exceptionalism argument that says we are different, that the rules don't apply to us, which seems to plague our leaders—it most certainly will help us. And maybe, just maybe, this little excursion in the name of *The President Factor* will effect change in and of itself. Can't ask for anything better than that."

Listening to Adhemar, ZeeBee finally understood why they were on the show. Adhemar had just presented not a policy or a platform, not something scripted to say at a rally, but something organic that came out of a real situation, or a kind-of real situation. An honest moment nevertheless. Adhemar had releaved what was in his heart and why *The President Factor* was so important to him, the American people, and the world.

Adhemar truly did have a plan.

Beau, on the other hand, had a plan to get a plan.

He was pacing, as best he could, in his suite's bathroom. Although his team knew he was calling President Cushing, he went into the bathroom to make the call in private. Sometimes the White House operator pretended not to recognize his name and he wasn't up to faking a phone call in front of them. He was too antsy to stand still, but the bathtub was freestanding smack in the middle of the room and maneuvering around it was taxing. Eying the extra long, gleaming, marble-encased bathtub, which took up the better part of the space, he considered pacing inside it, but thoughts of slipping and falling and making headlines kept him walking around it instead.

Not overly superstitious, Beau nevertheless subscribed to the rule of threes, and along with his pacing, he was chanting, "Good things come in threes. Good things come in threes. Good things come in threes."

He was two in.

His first *good thing* was Mike finding his phone, sitting unmolested on the bar where he had left it. It crossed Beau's mind that a nefarious someone could have placed a bug inside, so he sent Mike back down to the bar to inquire if anyone had come near it. No one had, so he placed the call to the White House.

The second *good thing* was when the White House operator put him through!

The third *good thing* he anticipated would come from the commander and chief.

"Stand by for the President," said the operator who had suddenly come on the line.

Beau put a smile on his face and purred into the phone in his most earnest voice, "Mr. President. Being as you are such a talented and successful politician and seer of the future—"

"Cut to the chase, Beau," the president barked.

Okay. So much for buttering him up.

Beau took a deep breath. "Well, sir. I'm having a little difficulty with this challenge."

"You have a plan?"

"Of course I have a plan," Beau answered too quickly.

"Then why do you need me?"

"I—" Beau blubbered.

"You are floundering. Correct?" The president was clearly annoyed.

Beau heard his lifeline fading away. "Yes, sir."

"I don't know why I should help you."

Beau winced. It was down to this moment. He played his last card. "Sir, may I remind you that I represent the glorious Republican Party. The very party you belong to? The party that needs to be in the White House—in power in the White House to continue your glorious legacy?" Beau knew when to lay it on. He'd seen a journalist get unlimited access to the president's personal notes on healthcare once with the same *carry on your legacy* speech.

The president sighed. "You know Reyes is in Africa?"

This put Beau in a pickle. If he asked, "Where in Africa," he'd look uniformed and the president had very little patience with uninformed people. He depended on those around him to be informed so he could stay *un*informed. This was going to be tricky. Beau cleared his throat. Icy sweat ran down his back. *What if the president asked him to comment on Reyes's plans? Damn that remote*! "Ahem. Of course I know he is in Africa."

"Okay, then what do you need from me?"

Whew! "Just a couple—say, three—ideas that can take me to a win on this damned show," Beau answered a little too aggressively. He waited. Had he overplayed his hand?

The president parsed his words carefully. "Do you think that's cheating, Beau?" If this got out, he wanted to blame it on Beau, of course.

"No, sir! It is our obligation to the American people to put another Republican in the White House."

"Continuity," the president said.

"Continuity is very important, sir," Beau echoed, even though he hadn't a clue what he would be continuing since the current president had no obvious agenda for him to latch on to.

"I'll see what I can come up with."

"Thank you, sir," Beau gushed. He stopped pacing and started vigorous fist pumping. Over and over.

"You cannot—I repeat, you cannot mention my help, Beau. I'll figure something out and get a message to you somehow," the president cautioned. "And no more phone calls, please?"

Beau panted. "Absolutely not, sir." His overzealous fist pumping had winded him.

"You okay, Beau?" The president heard the distress in Beau's voice. "What's going on?"

"I'm fine, sir," Beau reassured him, mind spinning to come up with something that would make sense. "Just doing a little…jogging in place, sir. Keeping in shape."

"Excellent."

Beau ended the call and flopped into the bathtub, exhausted. He called out, "Yancey!"

"Yup?" came the voice though the door.

"Pack us up, we're heading home."

"Home?"

"That's the plan."

⇜ TWENTY-TWO ⇝

Meanwhile, across the U.S., it was pretty much BAU—business as usual—with an added dose of *The President Factor* and political posturing. In Lawrence, Kansas, fifteen or twenty folks milled around the parking lot of Bang-Bang, a basketball-themed bar/restaurant, waiting for a table. They clutched basketball-shaped pagers that would flash and play the Harlem Globe Trotters theme song, "Sweet Georgia Brown," when their table was ready. Inside, the décor was over-the-top with regulation-size hoops mounted to the walls over orange and beige, properly dimpled, leather booths. The middle booths were even equipped with rims and backboards suspended from the ceiling.

The über-popular restaurant almost didn't open thanks to a video of the uproar that occurred when the owner's application for a zoning variance came up for a vote during what was normally a boring city council meeting. It amassed more than three thousand views in two hours on Lawrence—Your City, the local on-demand cable channel. The city council members were super entertaining when, en mass, they agreed that they didn't want a stripper bar in their city, citing statute after statute pertaining to local schools, churches and ice cream parlors. Full of posturing and raised voices, it was a performance akin to a filibuster.

They were wrong in their knee-jerk reaction and did an about face once the restaurant's owner explained that *bang-bang* was what the NBA players said when they hit a long three pointer—although no one believed him until he pulled out his iPhone and showed them proof right on the ESPN website.

Bang-Bang was *dope*! Its most popular entrée was the Spalding, a mass of fried chicken wings held together with sticky, orange barbecue sauce, then wrapped in bright orange foil to resemble—what else?—a basketball. The Spalding was served at Bang-Bang with pizzazz. A minimum of three servers would weave back and forth, passing the entrée. Once they got about ten feet from the table, one of them would shoot it through the hoop hanging over the table. The Spalding then fell into a custom-designed ceramic dish in the shape of two hands cupped together. Besides the massive cleanup that would be necessary if the shooter missed, there was another incentive for the server to make the shot. Every time someone scored a Spalding shot, a giant scoreboard hanging in the middle of the restaurant registered two points. The goal every evening was to reach a hundred points, after which the bar would donate a dollar a point to the local children's hospital. After the initial one hundred dollars was met, the bar's donation ratcheted up to two dollars a point. Bang-Bang hired a slew of college basketball players as servers. In the three years the bar had been open, there had not been one missed shot.

Until the night the cable talk networks started to cover *The President Factor*.

While BCD network had the corner on *The President Factor* footage, they did not have the corner on speculation. Nothing could stop the other networks from commenting on the premiere of the show, the "leaked footage" on *Entertainment Now* and the subsequent promos BCD had produced. And why would BCD want to stop the talk? Free publicity!

When *The President Factor* hit the scene, the cable talk shows were searching for something to sink their teeth into. Without a murder trial happening anywhere in the world that they could talk about inccssantly with analysts, profilers, re-enactors and the cadre of doctors and lawyers and other folk they had on retainer to spew out theories, they were losing viewers. The host (read sharks) regarded everything from the show itself to *The President Factor* snippets as chum and tore into it.

Besides the décor of baskets, scoreboards, and leather booths, Bang-Bang had that most basic requirement of a sports-themed bar: lots and lots of big screen TVs. That night, instead of being tuned to sports programming, they were all tuned to one of the cable talk shows known for its far right-leaning positions. On all the screens, like a scene from any of the plethora of TV shows set in the future, a toothy blonde beamed into the camera. She had the entire restaurant's attention. Hell, it would have been un-American not to pay attention!

In the little over-the-shoulder box next to her perfectly coiffed head was a map of Africa with *The President Factor* logo next to it.

Toothy blonde licked her lips, and then rattled off: *"I said to myself when I saw the footage of Senator Reyes next to those indigenous people: Why isn't he working this crisis situation out with Americans? On American soil? Why did he need to go back to his roots to get an answer?*

"Yes, America, I said his roots. You may think Senator Reyes is American, but we have a source that questions his birth certificate. We know his parents are from Mexico and Spain, a combination that quite frankly, is a little suspicious. Why, the Mexicans hate the Spaniards! I don't see how these folks got together, and yet we are to believe that they did—here in the United States of America? Got married on this soil and then his mother gave birth to him in New York City?"

She snorted.

A screen shot of Adhemar in Chad popped into the over the shoulder space.

She continued, *"This photo tells more than any certification the senator can come up with. General Billy O'Donnell himself identified the location as Africa. Based on that, we've asked Senator Reyes's campaign to provide proof of his birth, but they have yet to call us back. Now, just look at his dark skin. We believe he was born in Africa and is not qualified to run for president.*

"Today, Congressman Josiah Smith from the great state of Arkansas will ask for a congressional hearing into the question of Adhemar Reyes's birth."

The entire bar erupted in applause and cheers.

George Benson, a senior on a basketball scholarship at the University of Kansas was in the middle of his third Spalding shot of the night when the section of people in front of him jumped to their feet spontaneously, cheering even louder. He missed. Splat. The orange foil orb hit the wall and split open. Glazed wings splattered on Molly Wallace, the unfortunate who had ordered the appetizer.

Uh-oh. Sudden silence. Necks craned. Did George really miss? No! It can't be! It had been a source of civic pride that the UK basketball players had such good game.

"I don't think that counted, George," Bang-Bang's manager shouted from across the room.

"That's right, George," one of his fellow servers concurred.

"I second that," Molly Wallace said with an incongruous grin, her bare shoulders covered with chicken wings making her look like Wilma Flintstone. "You get a do-over, George. We spooked you."

When George got back on campus that night, he told his roommate, Glen, about the incident. "The whole place scared the shit out of me. Yeah, they spooked me and I missed my shot, but they scared me even more because of why they were cheering." George said in earnest. "I know this city—hell, this state—is a hotbed of conservative thinking, and I wasn't sure I could come down here and keep my politics to myself since my family are active members of MoveOn, but I've been quiet for too long. Hell, how can we get a do-over on that?"

"We vote," Glen replied. "Bang-bang."

⚖ TWENTY-THREE ⚖

While Beau was lying in the Hotel Potkaista bathtub, regaining his strength after his phone call with the President, Yancey organized their exit. Shortly thereafter, the group was rolling their suitcases past the magnificent ten-foot sculpture in the lobby, through the glass doors into the waiting limos outside. *Zip. Zip. Zip.*

Unfortunately, Beau's plan to boogie back to the U.S. without delay was derailed at the airport. No flights left Helsinki at 3:00 a.m. After milling around the terminal for forty-five minutes, it dawned on them: They were three men short. In their haste to get outta Dodge, they'd left the camera crew back at the hotel. The Secret Service were with them only because one of the agents was stationed outside Beau's hotel room.

"Let's just get that charter plane we were supposed to be on at noon powered up now," Hawke said, leaning against a pillar. He was exhausted.

"Perfect," Yancey agreed. "Who has their number?" He looked to Beau.

Beau shook his head.

"Oh shit," Yancey said.

"Shhh," Beau hissed. "Don't want to bring our escorts over."

Yancey moved next to Beau. Intrigued. *Why didn't Beau want to talk to the Secret Service?*

"Why?" he whispered.

"They don't need to poke their noses into our who, what, where, when and why," Beau said, casually walking towards a newsstand. A futile gesture since it was shuttered, but it took him farther away from the agents.

"Huh?" Confused, Yancey followed. "It's their job to know the who, what, where, when and why of our plans. Isn't it?"

Beau was in a pickle. He didn't have the phone numbers of any of *The President Factor* cameramen or any of the producers back in the States, all of whom, no doubt, would have info on the charter. He knew the Secret Service agents could and would be able to get anything he needed, but to do that, they would need to work with the real White House and then it might reach the president that he was—yet again— looking to DC for help. This would piss off the president. Plus, he couldn't risk taking the president's focus off the task at hand—coming up with a plan.

"I'd rather pretend we wanted to get here earlier. The agents might have lose lips and we don't want this on tape," Beau whispered.

"I think they are trained not to talk about their charges," Yancey said.

"Talk is one thing, lip flap is another," Beau shot back. "Sometimes one does not know one is spilling the beans until they're on the floor. You get what I'm talkin' about, Yancey?"

"No, but I'm sure you do."

When the camera crew woke up, they were understandably irate. Assuming Beau had had the audacity to leave them behind, they took their time gathering their gear and heading out to the airport. Since *they* had called the charter plane, they knew it wasn't scrambling a crew to fly Beau and his posse anywhere.

By the time they arrived, the Secret Service had moved the group into the first class lounge. Breakfast was being served. Yancey was piling herring on top of his scrambled eggs. He'd embraced the culture. Meanwhile Mike had embraced an annoying verbal tick: *joo*, a Finnish expression that roughly translated to *yeah*. He tossed it everywhere.

"*Joo!*" he said when he saw the camera crew, giving them a thumbs-up. Benny Goldstein, one of the photogs, bristled every time he heard it. After Helsinki, Benny would deliberately frame Mike half-off the screen for most shots, which resulted in his winning an award from IFP for his conceptual technique, interpreted as a comment on Mike's less-than-cerebral statements or his on-the-fence political stance on prayer in school.

An uneasy feeling developed between the crew and the team during the wait-time, but once they landed back in DC, Beau relaxed a bit and hustled everyone into the black-windowed Ford Explorers waiting dutifully at the curb. The time difference between DC and Helsinki had them landing around the same time they left. Lunch or dinner, didn't matter, the group was hungry again. Until he heard back from the president, Beau felt it best to avoid *The President Factor* set. Being in his Sit Room or Oval Office with the cameras rolling on them, just looking at each other, wasn't an image he wanted projected to the world, so he asked the drivers for a lunch recommendation.

"We want to go somewhere no one will recognize us," he added.

"Then we should go back to Helsinki," chirped Yancey.

After a few back and forths between the drivers and the convoy rolled up to YoGo Pizza, an out-of-the-way restaurant on the fringe of Dupont Circle. Beau et. al climbed out into the blazing DC heat in front of a brick townhouse on a block recently rezoned for business. The cameramen hoisted their cameras to their shoulders, ever ready.

Playing to camera, Beau took charge. "Nothing like pizza to cure jet lag, boys," he quipped, leading the way inside.

The restaurant's designer had just come off a six-month project for a daycare center in Crystal City and was still in a playful mood when she took the job. The design was an odd mixture of a 1950s comic book and *The Onion*. Giant cutouts of politicians lined the walls. Slapped on each was a specialty pizza title and a list of ingredients.

The President Factor group was alone in the place. They walked around, reading the menus off the cutouts.

"I'm going to throw up," Yancey said, stopping at the Bill Clinton cutout. He read the description. "The Billy. A fast-moving pie, smothered with French fries and hamburger. Barf!" He moved to a cutout of a smiling Jack Kennedy. "The J.F.K. A traditional white pizza with extra mushrooms. Hmmmm. Must be a reference to the Bay of Pigs," he said, leaning in to read the fine print on the bottom. "Yep! Ham slices optional. Love it."

Across the room, Hawke was focused on the Teddy Roosevelt cutout. Mindful of the crew hovering nearby, cameras rolling, he saluted the cutout. "The Square Deal. Pan pizza. Red sauce with all the meat you can handle," he read to the group. Moving to the adjacent cutout of F.D.R. he continued, "The Nothing To Fear Pie. Deep dish topped with jalapeño peppers, anchovies and a surprise ingredient." He shook his head and chuckled. "Nope, don't want to risk that one."

They made their way to a booth and slid in. Yancey suddenly noticed the empty tables. "I'm exhausted. Why are we the only ones in here?"

Beau shrugged. "Beat the crowd, I guess."

"It's noon on the Hill and this place is deserted? Did anyone see a Department of Health poster anywhere?" Yancey asked. He got up, staggered over to the counter and peered into the kitchen. "Hello?"

Not concerned with the empty restaurant, Mike was content to enjoy the décor. He reached across the table and poked Beau. "I wonder what they'll make for you when we win."

Beau had been thinking the same thing and had a ready answer. He puffed out his chest. "The Reality Pie, gentleman. To honor this here show that is going to take us to a win!" He high-fived Mike.

Still at the counter, Yancey spotted someone in the back. "Can we get some service out here?" he yelled.

A server strolled out with a quizzical expression. No pad. No pencil. He did a double-take when he saw Beau and the gang sitting at one of the booths. "Aren't you Governor Simpson from *The President Factor*?" he yelled across the room.

Despite wanting to keep a low profile, Beau was pleased with the recognition. "I am."

The server hurried over. "Sir, we don't have any flour."

"I am also the Republican candidate for president, son," Beau said with a little shake of his head. *God, he felt good.*

"Yes, sir. But we still don't have any flour."

Ignoring the server's response, Beau continued, "Before we order, I have a question for you."

"Governor Simpson—" the server tried again.

Cutting him off, Beau gestured to the cutouts lining the walls, nodding and winking to the team, sure that he'd get another great anecdote to tell his autobiographer. "Son, what do you think they'll call my pizza?"

The server shot back, "The Clueless."

TWENTY-FOUR

As Beau was being insulted, Adhemar and his team were at Dulles Airport baggage claim. They'd opted to fly back to DC directly from their meeting at 10 Downing Street despite numerous dinner invitations. Bug-eyed, still sunburned from Chad and rumpled from a combined thirty-nine hours of flying over the past three days, they stood patiently awaiting their baggage to pop out at carousel three.

"Do you think that's for real?" Pinky asked, breaking eye contact with an innocuous beige box stamped Caution: Human Organs that was the only thing left on the adjacent carousel. It had gone by four times.

"I hope not," Harrison said. "What happened to its escort? Imagine if it got on the wrong flight?"

They watched it circle by.

Barnk, barnk. With that annoying sound that bought travelers' attention, the belt on carousel three started up. First class baggage came out…first. Adhemar pulled a shiny silver-wheeled case festooned with World Wildlife Fund, Doctors Without Borders and Amnesty International stickers off the moving belt.

ZeeBee reached over and snagged a camouflage backpack with an Operation Chad patch and an American flag on the front. She slung it over her shoulder. It looked incongruous against her black Calvin Klein dress, as wrinkled as it was.

"What the heck is that?" Harrison said, pointing to the backpack.

ZeeBee twirled around. "Like it? I'm collecting souvenirs to sell on eBay if we blow it and I need money."

"Nice thought," Harrison replied. "Did you get one for me?"

"Nope."

Adhemar waved his two Secret Service agents over. "Guys, we've gotta do something about that box of human organs."

"Come again, sir?" Agent Kraatz said. *Did Adhemar just say, human organs?*

Adhemar spun them about to the adjoining carousel. The box had disappeared around the pillar. They waited. Around it came.

"Holy God," they said in unison. They cautiously approached: *Was this an abandoned package? Did they need to evacuate the terminal?*

Watching the agents move sideways to the box, Harrison grabbed his luggage off the belt and hissed to the team, "Let's get outta here before they lock this place down."

"Can't leave without our escorts," Adhemar reminded him.

"Crap."

Thirty minutes later, after contacting the courier service supposedly traveling with the organ box—they'd missed the flight after getting lost in the Heathrow duty-free shops trying to find some sausage to bring home—a futile gesture since U.S. customs would have confiscated it anyway—the Secret Service retrieved the box, passed it off and were on their way to customs. By that point the press had picked up on the incident and were waiting outside to cap the story already showing on the TV monitors in the airport.

Adhemar nudged Harrison. CNN showed footage of the human organ box being wheeled out of the terminal. They already had graphic going complete with his face and the title: Reyes and team save a life.

"Gimme a break," Adhemar said, reacting to the headline.

Poor choice of words when one is handing a passport to a customs agent.

After a flurry of messages into their walkies with mucho glances in his direction, two customs agents pulled Adhemar out of line. As he waited for whomever was going to do god-knows-what, Adhemar waved his group on ahead. No sense keeping everyone from their families.

Grateful for the pass, ZeeBee took off and within half an hour was struggling her luggage through the door of her two-hundred-year-old row house in Georgetown. She and Sam had bought the property when he was assigned to White House special duty. The building didn't distinguish itself from its neighbors on the outside, but inside! Inside was littered with every shape, size and type of art. An eclectic collector from the time she was in college, ZeeBee favored everything. Photos juxtaposed with oils, with collages, sculptures and weavings.

Her camouflage backpack got caught on a piece she'd picked up in New York City's Chelsea art district the previous winter. It was created by two artists who had aimed a shotgun at a three-by-five piece of stainless steel, blasted away, then threw the Swiss-cheesed metal into a fire to soften and bend it into shape. They listed it in the catalog of the 19th Street showroom as "a protest against the industrialization of America" and titled it *Blasted 34*, a nod to the start of what they considered "the downfall of true American life." Shiny, sharp and beautiful, it personified ZeeBee. Her favorite piece, she placed it in the front hall despite the protruding jagged surfaces that constantly snagged her clothes and now had trapped her *proud I took the trip* backpack.

Barking.

A golden retriever flew down the hall stairs. Ricocheting off the wall, Yipper landed in front of ZeeBee. He abruptly sat down and was rewarded with a vigorous scratch behind the ears.

"Zee?" Sam clattered down behind Yipper and grabbed ZeeBee in a tight embrace. "God, I missed you."

ZeeBee leaned into him. With their filled-up political dance cards—hers with the election and his, as always, with anything and everything the president could possibly conceive he might need a CIA officer for, they rarely had time together, but both knew what it meant to be Adhemar's running mate. ZeeBee had considered turning it down. She and Sam had been talking about starting a family when Adhemar came calling. They went from *oh-yeah* elation to *maybe-not* reality when they did the math and recognized Adhemar's presidency could span two terms. ZeeBee didn't want to be a forty-five-year-old former vice president running to rounds of fertility treatments. What cinched it was Adhemar's matter-of-fact take on the situation. "You don't need to put it off. We'll just get you a good nanny."

Now, after six months of campaigning across America, their relocation to Washington for *The President Factor* meant stolen moments with Sam, who was already seeing more and more of the inside of 1600 Pennsylvania Avenue than he cared to.

Still in ZeeBee's tight embrace, Sam looked over her shoulder and spotted the camouflage backpack caught on *Blasted 34*. "Operation Chad? You actually went to Chad?"

"We went to Chad."

"The press was saying you were in Africa. Huh. They had it right," Sam said with surprise. "Chad has a PX?"

"The entire country, no."

"Ha. Ha."

Seeing the backpack reminded Sam that the President wanted info on the trip. "Then you were on an Army base. Hmmm."

ZeeBee picked up on his thought process. "Hmmm? Why hmmm?"

"Nothing, just that you've been gone for a while." He shuddered. Feeling guilty about what he was asked to do but knowing he would have to do it, Sam reacted with his typical response to stress: sex. He picked ZeeBee up and headed towards the stairs to the bedroom.

"Hold it, big boy, I have to get back to the set," ZeeBee said with little enthusiasm.

Trained to spot weakness, Sam ignored her protest and continued up the stairs.

⊷ TWENTY-FIVE ⊷

After her marathon *Can he or can't he use his phone?* edit-room viewing session and the subsequent encounter with Buzz, Makki pulled herself together and snapped back into TV executive mode. Now back in her office, she put the experience to the back of her mind and blitzed through a stack of proposals for new reality shows from dozens of agents and various folks who somehow had gained access to her inbox. As she was flipping through a proposal for yet another *extreme celebrity putting himself into yet another absurd situation* show, she heard her door open.

"Hiya, Makki."

She looked up from a photo of Danny Bonaduce on the back of a camel to see Buzz coming at her. Jon was right behind him, making a *sorry* face.

"Hey, Buzz," she said cautiously.

Buzz walked to the windows on the north side, pulled out his phone, scrolled a bit and then the little whooshing sound happened, signaling he had sent an email. "I just sent you a link to the latest promo for *The President Factor*."

"Do you want me to approve it?"

"Not necessarily. But I figured since you have such a vested interest in the show, you might want to see it before we air it."

"Can I make any changes?" she said. *Might as well meet this head-on.*

"No. I approved it. It's already been fed." Buzz circled over to stand right in front of Makki's desk. She recognized the power position. Leaning back in her chair, she relaxed, not above playing with body language either.

Buzz picked up a pencil from her desk and distractedly tapped it on the photo of Bonaduce. "You realize *The President Factor* is not a documentary film, don't you? This isn't *Nanook of the North* here. We're allowed to manipulate things."

"Of course," Makki said choosing her words carefully. "Within reason." She thought about her memo: *Be provocative to the point of manipulation.* But this was manipulating to the point of provocation! Hmmm. How did she feel about that?

"Great. Just so we're in agreement," Buzz snapped out. He looked at the photo he'd been tapping. "Is that the guy from the *Partridge Family*?"

"It is."

"You get all the fun stuff, don't you?" He spun around. "This is the best office in the company, you know."

"I like to think so," Makki said. *Where is he going with this?*

Buzz paused as he reached the door, "I'd hate to see you on a lower floor."

Zing.

And out he went.

Makki immediately opened her email and watched the latest *The President Factor* spot Buzz had already let loose on the viewers. After she finished, she knew why Buzz had stopped by. He was showing his hand. The spot favored Beau again. *Why is the network blatantly backing him?* she wondered. *Should Adhemar be warned?*

She picked up her phone and put it down. *Damn you, Adhemar. If I call you to tell you about this, you will think I am just trying find an excuse to talk to you.*

This at least was partially true.

TWENTY-SIX

It took two hours for Adhemar to clear customs at Dulles, having dodged a strip-search only by the grace of God. After an undercover reporter exposed a slew of elected officials getting preferential treatment at the airport—pissing off all the weary travelers who are routinely held up—Dulles officials were not going to let Adhemar through after his remark without doing due diligence. Now even more exhausted, he trudged towards the exit, stopping for a moment to pull himself together before facing the gaggle of press ahead.

His phone buzzed with an incoming text from his agent, William Williams: *I have a car waiting 4 U*. Energized, Adhemar hurried towards the exit.

The car was a black 1964 Mercedes Benz Roadster tricked out with a mini refrigerator tucked in the corner of the back seat and stocked with mini bottles of prosecco. These were no ordinary bottles of prosecco. William had them specially bottled at a winery in the foothills of the Alps. They bore his signature W. W. label. Mounted to the side of the refrigerator was a coiled, rope-shaped something-or-other William had found on Etsy. He had filled it with black- and white-striped paper straws—perfect for sipping the bubbly wine.

The Benz whipped to the curb as Adhemar made a dash through the press, dodging microphones and cameras to jump into the back. Two minutes into the ride, he was strawed-up, sipping away and heading towards the William Williams Agency in Georgetown.

Occupying the top floor of a warehouse, William's space showcased authentic urban industrial design repurposed to perfection. The flooring was a combination of natural oak planks and polished circular metal plates where long-gone machinery had been bolted to the floor. At the far end humongous arched windows framed a magnificent view of the Capitol. In the center, two gigantic steel Ws hung from airplane wires. The view was the clichéd shot of TV opens and post cards, but it never failed to impress a guest.

Adhemar headed to the dangling letters and dropped onto a black leather chaise lounge, threw back his head and closed his eyes. The tableau was straight out of *Architectural Digest*.

William sauntered in, straight shoulder-length blond hair swinging. Trailing behind him like Canada geese, a string of assistants carried trays piled with precisely folded shirts, jackets, toys and assorted tchotchkes.

Adhemar forced his eyes open. "I apologize, William. This trip took more out of me than I anticipated."

William patted his hand. "No worries, Senator. Whenever you are ready." William's demeanor resonated with his high-profile clients because he had the ability to tune into their moods. If they were antsy, he talked quickly. Tired, he slowed down. It was as if he were feng sui-ing the conversations.

Despite the marathon travel and the prosecco, Adhemar rallied. "Whatcha got?" He nodded to the piles of swag and sellables.

"Everything you can think of. Plus a few W. W. specials." He nodded to the group standing the ready.

On cue, the assistants begin to disassemble their tableaux, shaking out a slew of high-end, designed shirts and jackets. *Here look at this blazer. Touch this belt. Feel the Egyptian cotton.* Each item was prominently branded with *The President Factor* logo along with a celebratory phrase:

Winner: Senator Adhemar Reyes.

The men and women draped shirts here and there. In well-rehearsed moves they casually flung jackets into piles on either side of Adhemar. Casual posing.

"This is nice," Adhemar said, grabbing a shirt with his posterized face silk-screened on the front.

"Shepard Fairey," William boasted. It was a close copy of the Obama *Hope* poster.

Seeing the future, Adhemar thought, nodding in approval. He grabbed a black sleeping mask with *The President Factor* affixed upside down on the front.

William had ripped off the upside-down design from the Standard Hotel. He knew the rep the New York City location had from guests brazenly standing naked in the floor-to-ceiling windows, flashing unsuspecting tourists strolling by on the High Line below. *Would Adhemar make the connection? How would that play in Peoria?*

Having stayed at the hotel's Sunset Boulevard location years before, Adhemar did indeed recognize the design and of course knew about the flashings. It amused him. As the Senator from New York he reveled in New York City's absurdities, outrageous behavior and bravado—even identified with it.

"And you jumped off the Standard, I see," he said, dropping the *Hotel* as folks who have either stayed or partied there were apt to do. He also recognized that legions of players or wanna-be players around the country would donate to his campaign to get the hip mask. *Nice touch, William.* He slipped the mask onto his forehead with a wink.

Now on firmer ground, William brought an arm to his face and spoke into his cuff, "Go."

After his first encounter with Adhemar's Secret Service protection unit, William became obsessed with everything about the agency—watching a marathon of movies that had any reference, however fleeting, to the Secret Service. As an homage to Adhemar's status, he went so far as to equip himself with a miniature mic and transmitter to wear on his wrist. It also gave him the opportunity to brag to everyone that he had a presidential candidate as a client when they inquired about the device.

Moments after William's terse message into his sleeve, wisps of smoke began creeping across the floor. It was planned. William knew a good presentation could sell a bad concept. The concept he was about to unveil to Adhemar, however, was solid, but the added drama of the smoke would catapult it to outstanding. William owned a mass of smoke machines that could create everything from a low-lying mist to pea soup.

Adhemar observed the smoke curl with amusement. *William must have told the Secret Service about this or they'd be grabbing me and hustling me down the fire escape! Wait? Was that...?*

Yes, it was.

Ever so softly "Hail to the Chief" was being piped in. Nice touch, William!

Two W. W. assistants melted in from the smoke, each gripping one end of a long glass shelf suspended from the ceiling by clear cables. In the middle sat a three-foot high replica of the White House, appearing to float across the room to Adhemar at eye level.

He was transfixed.

Hanging from the miniature portico, *The President Factor* bunting gently swung as though a breeze were blowing in from

Pennsylvania Avenue. William had rehearsed this presentation a dozen times; adjusting the fishing line that held the bunting in place until the desired amount of sway was achieved when pulling up short in front of Adhemar.

The effect was not lost. With a quick intake of breath, Adhemar leaned forward and peered through the tiny window to the Oval Office. Inside, seated at the tiny presidential desk, was a tiny Adhemar figurine. The resemblance was striking.

"It's a kit," William said. "Macy's has already placed an order. A substantial order."

Adhemar pictured a window display at the flagship store on 34th Street. Hundreds of people funneling by as they did for the holiday displays. His ego soared; his voice dipped with emotion. "This truly is special, William."

"Thank you, Senator, but there's more." William spoke into his wrist again. "Go."

Like a ship's figurehead slicing through the mist in a *Pirates of the Caribbean* movie, a stunning model glided across the room to strike a pose in front of Adhemar. She wore a skin-tight black tee shirt. Small white letters marched across her chest: *Here we go!—Adhemar Reyes, Father of Modern Politics.*

"I'm sure you'll say many more quotable things as the game goes on," William gushed.

Adhemar stretched his arm towards the model as though she were wearing the Shroud of Turin. "It's perfect," he whispered.

"You did create *The President Factor*, Senator," William whispered back, not wanting to break the spell.

"Yes, indeed, I did."

William shooed the others out of the room. "I am so honored you chose us to rep you, Senator. The show…it's such a brilliant idea."

Adhemar smiled and shrugged. *Aw, shucks.*

"I mean. What *could* go wrong," William continued.

Even jet-lagged as he was, Adhemar snapped to attention. "Go wrong? What could go wrong?" he spat out.

"That's what I was saying," William quickly replied.

"No. You were questioning what could go wrong," Adhemar said, agitated.

Holy God! William saw his White House connection drifting away.

"No, I was stating that nothing could go wrong by saying *what could go wrong.*" William explained. "It's just an expression. I put a period at the end. Not a question mark."

Knowing instinctively this was one of those moments that could flip towards paranoia or confidence, Adhemar took the high road. He stood up, smiling benevolently at William, who by this time was in the middle of a full-blown, gut-churning panic attack.

"You're right, William, I'm tired. I took it the wrong way." Adhemar then added a pragmatic request to cover the tiny bit of superstition he carried with him, courtesy of Marisol. "Just don't voice that again."

William unclenched his buttocks. "Copy that."

Adhemar frowned.

Oh shit, now what? William felt his stomach churn anew. *I just said...what? Copy that?*

Then it dawned. "Sorry. We rep Kiefer," he explained.

Adhemar laughed. "That's perfect."

"Do you want to take a few things with you, Senator?" William said, quickly steering the conversation to safer waters.

"No, don't want to get too cocky," Adhemar said. In reality he wanted to strip naked and, in front of the White House replica, roll around in the luxurious shirts and jackets. He allowed himself a small sigh of regret that did not go unnoticed by William.

"You sure?"

"Well, maybe one?" Adhemar capitulated and picked up a tee shirt.

As soon as the elevator doors closed on Adhemar, William scooted across the floor on shaky adrenaline legs and collapsed on the recliner. Also a pragmatist, he knew from the close encounter he had just had, he now needed to create the next iteration of *The President Factor* swag for the Senator or risk losing him as a client. He pulled out his iPad mini, tapped open Flipboard and searched for inspiration. In Top Stories, William found Buzz's new promo for *The President Factor* and tapped the little triangle to watch.

The President Factor signature animation played: The hero music piping out of the tiny speakers. The voice over started:

"On the next The President Factor. Reyes all but admits defeat."

William sat up on the recliner like Rikki-Tikki-Tavi.

"In a clip taken in the Humvee, Adhemar was caught saying, 'They're so far ahead of us, it's embarrassing.'" The picture froze on Adhemar's face. Nothing about London or protestors. Anyone watching would conclude he was referring to Beau.

The announcer came back in: *"Is the Democratic hopeful throwing in the towel? Find out on The President Factor. The reality show that shows reality. Political reality! Thursday at 9. Only on BCD!"*

William snapped his head to the White House model in front of him and yelled to no one in particular—yet to everyone in earshot, "Holy Christ! We better make a miniature Beau!"

⋅🫏⋅ TWENTY-SEVEN ⋅🐘⋅

While Adhemar was snuggled up to one of William's "Here we go" tee shirts, nodding off on his way home in William's Benz, ZeeBee was waking up in Sam's arms.

Sam had been staring at the ceiling for the past hour, trying to justify what he was about to do. *Just a little wife tapping*, the president had said. *Just find out how they are approaching the game, Sam. If they're saying anything that might embarrass this administration, I need to know before it hits TV.*

Hating himself for asking, but knowing he needed to get something, however small, to take back to the president, Sam began what he considered a flanking move.

"What did you think of the first show?" he asked with feigned casualness.

ZeeBee tensed up. *That's the type of question your boss asks when he thinks you've blown it.*

"How did we come across?" she lobbed back at him.

"In control."

ZeeBee visibly relaxed. "Excellent."

Sensing an opening, Sam continued, "You guys figure out a solution?"

Too savvy to slip, ZeeBee deflected, "Maybe."

For a brief moment, Sam thought he had an in. He nibbled her ear, whispered, "Give me a hint."

"You know I can't discuss it, honey."

Denied.

"Come on."

"I can't."

"You don't trust me?" Sam chided, pretending to be insulted. "What? You think I'm gonna tell the other team? Give them a leg up? That's absurd."

ZeeBee sat up. "It's not that. I'm—I can't. We all agreed not to talk to our families, so even though I know you can keep a secret…" She drifted off to soften her reply.

"I took an oath, remember?" Sam said, hand over heart.

"Which only applies to matters of state. Which all of this, at present, is not," ZeeBee replied, jumping out of bed, ending the discussion. "And I gotta get back to the set. Plus I need more crackers."

Sam winked. "I took care of it. Check out the pantry."

ZeeBee trotted down the stairs. Sam followed, allowing himself a small smile in anticipation.

"Sam!" ZeeBee shrieked from the pantry where a gigantic stack of Hale and Hearty Oysterettes boxes towered. Sam rounded the corner.

"You've stockpiled my crackers!" ZeeBee sputtered. "Why?"

"You don't know?"

She gave him a confused look. "Hale and Hearty is going out of business? Oyster crackers are endangered?"

"Nothing jumped out at you when you returned to the U.S.? Nothing at the airport? On the way home? You guys didn't see anything?"

"Wasn't looking out the window."

Sam abruptly turned and walked toward the front door.

"Call Adhemar. We're going to the Giant."

Growing up in New York City, Adhemar was conditioned to film sets popping up overnight. Colorful notices about moving cars to make room for production vehicles were taped to light poles and string-tied to trees three days beforehand as was required by New York City law. But if you were out of town, you didn't see them and you could come back to find Tom Cruise running up the stairs to your next door neighbor's brownstone as you were getting out of your cab from the airport. And of course, being a New Yorker, you'd ignore him and probably get annoyed that you had to dodge the giant crane set up in front of *your* brownstone while cursing all the Haddad's trailers that had now taken up every parking spot for blocks that you also missed because you were reading *The New York Times* you grabbed out of the terminal, being someone who still liked to leaf through a paper instead of swiping an iPad.

Thus Adhemar didn't think it strange to see something on the streets of DC like a scene from *War of the Worlds* with police barricades and hundreds of people standing in a line to get into the Giant Foods store on Wisconsin Avenue when he got out of William's redirected Benz. He was annoyed, though, that his trip home would be delayed. ZeeBee had been short on the phone about Adhemar meeting her and Sam at the food store "immediately if not sooner." Sam was saying something in the background lines of "Ya just gotta see it."

Once the Secret Service flashed their badges at the traffic cop guarding the entrance, the barricades were moved aside, and the driver brought Adhemar to the front of the store.

Adhemar rolled down the window. "What are we shooting?"

Sam and ZeeBee stood next to an Army sergeant armed with an M16 who was allowing people into the store one at a time. "No one, I hope," ZeeBee said, coming over to the car.

"Ha. That armed soldier looks exactly like the guys we left in Chad. Remarkable."

"That's because he's real, Adhemar," ZeeBee said in a whisper.

Adhemar blanched. "What's going on, Zee?"

"We haven't gone inside yet. We waited for you. Sam says it's been chaos."

Inside the store, ZeeBee and Adhemar moved as though the floor were as unstable as the scene surrounding them. People raced past, pushing shopping carts like TV show competitors trying to grab the most items in a race against time.

Sam explained, "It started this morning, right after the White House admitted to the wheat crisis. There's a fungus, UG99, now just called UGG, that took only two weeks to wipe out our entire flippin' wheat crop. The FDA figured it hitched a ride in the cuffs of a bunch of churchers returning from Kenya."

Wheat crisis? Heart pounding, Adhemar flashed back to the video he saw in Chad. *Why hadn't he paid attention? Did this mean his radar was off? How. Did. He. Miss. This!*

"We have no more wheat?" he stammered.

"Zero."

"The administration knew about this for two weeks and did nothing?"

"The White House attempted to misdirect people into thinking they should avoid wheat products. They put out a bunch of overt campaigns the last two days while you guys were out of the country."

Oh God. With a sinking feeling Adhemar remembered the Flipboard story he so easily dismissed about the kids in Kansas. The three started down the bread aisle. It was bare. Secret Service walked ahead and behind. Alert. This wasn't any ordinary shopping trip. Instead of weekly specials, immense end-of-aisle displays depicted giant loaves of bread, stacks of pancakes, and piles of donuts with a simulated black mold-like substance creeping up their sides.

Sam stood under a sign depicting two powdered donuts covered in green powder mold. "The government's campaign includes stuff like these beauties. Went up in a flash. Gotta wonder who the printing company was!"

ZeeBee approached the display with caution as though it were real. "Ya-uck. Disgusting or not, you're not going to convince millions of lunch box-packing moms to change their habits overnight," ZeeBee said with a shudder.

Sam nodded. "That is correct. The *bread is bad* campaign didn't work."

"Duh!" ZeeBee said.

"But then once people figured out wheat was toast—" He winced. "They grabbed anything and everything made with flour."

"Will it spread to other things like vegetables?" Adhemar asked. *God, this stuff looks really, really gross.*

"No. It only attacks wheat."

"We're now a nation forced into a gluten-free diet. What's the president doing about it?" Adhemar asked.

Sam pursed his lips. "God knows."

At that exact moment, in the real Oval Office, the president sat behind the real Resolute desk—an iPad propped open in front of him. Skype was up. The president scrolled through his contacts and stopped on a photo of the president of Russia: Vladimir Chernobyl. He started a video call.

Ringing. Ringing.

Chernobyl answered, his face filling the screen, "Hello, Mr. President."

The shot was so close-up, the president could see that Chernobyl had missed shaving a small patch on his right cheek. He touched his own cheek and automatically moved back from his own device's camera. "Hello, President Chernobyl. Thank you for taking my call."

"*Da.*"

The president cleared his throat. For an hour, he'd been rehearsing his approach with Chief of Staff Roger Smithy, who'd coached him to smile a lot.

"Chernobyl likes happy times now," Roger stressed when the president segued into a serious face, as he was apt to do, considering the situation. He hadn't spoken with the Russian president in months. And when they did talk, they kept things light. Chernobyl probably thought he was calling to place a bet on the Washington Capitals, who were at that precise moment in the second period of an exhibition game with the Russian national team—because yet again, the NHL was on strike and the players had bolted to Europe to get in some ice time. The Russians were winning. It was a good time to call.

Roger was sitting on the other side of the iPad, out of camera range, gesturing to the president to smile, smile, smile.

The President took the cue, beamed at the iPad and began the international game of small talk. "How's the weather in Moscow?"

Roger gave a thumbs-up.

"Good, good." Chernobyl smiled back. "You?"

"Typical Washington summer," the President said, pretending to wipe his brow. Chernobyl chuckled.

Roger threw the okay sign. Perfect. The president cut to the chase. "President Chernobyl, I'm sure you know that we have a crisis of magnanimous proportions. Our wheat crop, every last shaft, has been hit with blight. Rotted. On the ground." He gave a goofy grin. Paused. Waited. Chernobyl's face was a mask.

"Gone," the president said in a dramatic whisper.

Pause. No response from Chernobyl.

The president cleared his throat again. This was not the way he imagined it going. "I'm calling on our friendship over the years."

Chernobyl shrugged.

Undeterred, the president continued, "I'm calling on our friendship to help us weather this disaster. It will throw off the U.S. economy, which is central to the international economy—

your economy. Plus you are the only ones who haven't been hit by the blasted fucking stem rot."

Chernobyl raised an eyebrow. "Hmmm. Might it be fair to say, Mr. President, that it is more central to the health and wellbeing of every American?"

"That too," the president snapped back, impatient. "Bottom line, Chernobyl, we need you to sell us some wheat." The Hail Mary pass.

"No." Chernobyl tossed it off as though he were passing on a barista's query about milk in his café mocha.

"No?"

"No." Matter-of-fact.

The president felt his face stiffen. Roger was now on his feet, gesturing wildly, making an Alfred E. Newman *What, Me Worry* face.

The President took the direction and relaxed. Smiled at Chernobyl. "Buddy?"

"No."

"I can help you with those pesky sanctions." He forced a laugh. *We're old friends here.*

"No." More matter-of-factness.

"Why not?"

"Why should I help you? You're going to stop us from invading Finland."

An hour later, Sam trudged along Constitution Avenue. After getting an urgent text from the president, he'd abruptly left ZeeBee and Adhemar in the cookie aisle, or rather now the *defunct* cookie aisle. He was sweating. The humidity in DC is well documented. Heck, the entire place was built on a swamp. He'd been walking around for half an hour, zigzagging back and forth in his undercover best to lose any tail that might have been following. Up ahead, the presidential limo was parked within sight of the Lincoln Memorial, one of Sam's favorite places to take out of town guests. Secret Service out front and behind.

Without enthusiasm, Sam continued toward the limo. One of the agents opened the back door. Sam hopped inside and, exhausted, flopped on the seat next to the president. The president was sipping a Coke.

"Next time, can you pick me up? It's still a hundred degrees out there," Sam whined.

"Did you take evasive measures like I asked, Sam? Don't want to anyone to see us meeting," the president shot back.

"I did, but I work for you, Mr. President," Sam said with a sigh. "It's okay for me to come to the White House. I do it all the time." He was starting to think the president was losing it.

The president opened his window and threw his Coke can out, then watched one of the agents retrieve it. It was something he did when things were not going his way. Almost as if he thought could throw his problems out the window. They'd been going through a lot of cans recently.

Sam was on alert now.

"The game's changed, Sam," the president said, popping open another Coke.

"Now what?"

"It's the real deal. Reality, I'm talking, Sam. What's going on right here in DC. Right on my watch. And it's got to stop."

Okay, where is he going with this? "Mr. President?"

"Forget getting the poop on the game, Sam. This is bigger than that. Your country needs you. I need you, Sam."

Sam's eyes started to glaze over. He'd heard this before. "How so, sir?"

"Chernobyl turned me down. The commie bastard turned me down. No wheat for you! What is he? The Soup Nazi? He's the Wheat Nazi, that's what he is. Millions of god-fearing American school children can't have their PB&J

for lunch because of that fucking TV show! Chernobyl is watching that show and hates us because of it! Reyes is completely to blame. It was his idea to do that fucking show and now it's come back to bite—me! Not him. Oh no, not yet, but it will bite him."

The president was starting to spit. Sam was still unfazed.

"But before that happens, you've gotta get him to help me outta this mess, Sam. He'll be able to come up with something. He's a clever son-of-a-bitch." The president had worked himself up into a full frenzy.

"You said that before, sir," Sam said calmly.

"Well. He is!" The president pounded on the armrest between them.

Sam didn't flinch. "He's not going to discuss anything with me. And ZeeBee isn't planning on sharing anything anytime soon."

The president clutched Sam's arm. "Then you'll have to find a way."

Sam shook his head.

"It's your job," the president spat out.

"I'm not comfortable—"

The president interrupted, "Just do it. That's an order from…"

Sam mouthed the words along with the president…

"…your commander in chief."

Grabbing a Coke for himself, Sam got out of the limo. He continued down Constitution to the Lincoln Memorial and on to the larger-than-life statues of the Korean Memorial. Soldiers in full battle gear advancing through a field, eerily lit by small lights at their feet pointing to their agonizing faces. Sam stepped off the path and walked among them, dwarfed. The guards noticed, but didn't stop him. He'd been here many times. His hall pass was a CIA ID.

The Korean Memorial was Sam's place to lose himself. That night he needed to step away from the man he was: the husband to ZeeBee. He took out his phone and called an old classmate, Army Colonel Marty Bauer, who had moved over to the Naval Hospital when they closed Walter Reed. He'd been deployed many times.

"Marty, it's me. Do you still have that backpack you brought back from Chad? Excellent. I need to borrow it."

ꕔꕔ TWENTY-EIGHT ꖕ

The next morning, in his *The President Factor* Oval Office, Adhemar watched Harrison nod, eyes half closed, on the opposite couch. It was 7:00 a.m. He was killing time waiting for ZeeBee to come by to take him to breakfast with Sam—and wondering why he had agreed to it in the first place. ZeeBee had called at 6:00 a.m. to cajole him into the breakfast meeting, which wasn't easy. He was feeling the pressure to finish their presentation for Thursday night and was still a wee bit jet-lagged. When ZeeBee rang and asked to meet at the Old Ebbit Grill, he initially said no.

She was persistent. "Do you have any food in your place?"

"Not really, but *The President Factor* said they were going to cater in for us."

"Sam wants to see you."

"I saw him last night. He looked good."

"He looked like crap this morning. And he said it was important."

"All of us?"

"No, just you and me. I'll pick you up," ZeeBee sweetened the pot.

After a moment's wariness—Sam worked for the president and the president was a Republican, and this was the home stretch on the first challenge—Adhemar agreed. Sam was ZeeBee's husband and he trusted him.

While waiting for ZeeBee, Adhemar sorted through a pile of packages William Williams had just messengered over, conveniently forgetting or just ignoring his protest the night before. Pinky was off to the craft services cart to pick up their breakfast.

"Harrison, what do you think of these?" Adhemar said, shaking open one of the black Father of Modern Politics tee shirts.

Harrison, a big fan of HBO and Showtime historical series, loved big, dramatic sets. When Adhemar tapped him to be his chief of staff, the first thing flashing into Harrison's mind was an image of himself, Adhemar and ZeeBee on a barge. A very colorful barge. A barge like the ones Henry VIII and his entourage used to travel on from palace to palace. On Harrison's imagined barge with the flags waving and the breeze blowing, the three of them sat in throne-like chairs. He saw them gliding up to a picturesque dock in front of the White House on Inauguration Day. Tucked into another corner of Harrison's brain, the knowledge that DC was built on a swamp and that most likely at one point in history barges actually ran on Pennsylvania Avenue probably helped fuel the conceit. He re-ran the images often.

Now through his half-closed eyes, he saw William's black tee shirt and *wham*—he added another layer: they were now wearing the tee shirts on the barge. Like those dream sequences in which today's images are juxtaposed with god knows what—this made sense. Not normally a superstitious person, Harrison was toying with the idea that his ability to adjust the barge scenario with current events meant a victory in November. At the very least, he thought it would keep him positive in the face of bad polling data—something that so far, thank god, he did not have to test.

His sixteenth-century thoughts were interrupted when ZeeBee trotted in, proudly wearing her Chad backpack and popping crackers. She zeroed in on the tee shirt. "Father of modern politics?"

A moment's pause. *Was there a whiff of mockery here?*

"I can picture that, ZeeBee," Harrison said.

"Me too," she said looking closer. "*Here we go*? Adhemar, when did you say that?"

"I honestly don't know, but it's catchy."

ZeeBee swung her backpack around, rummaged inside and pulled out what appeared to be a large brown cookie. "Look what I picked up outside." She tossed it to Harrison.

"What's this?"

"What we'll all be eating if the president doesn't stop the madness."

Harrison unwrapped the cookie and sniffed it. "Smells like dirt."

"It is. Mixed with oil and sugar."

He recoiled. "Yuck. Where'd you get it?"

"In Adams Morgan. From a group who can now be part of the American dream." She tossed one across to Adhemar. It fell short and hit the floor. *Whack*! They stared at it.

"That thing didn't even bounce!" Harrison said. "People really eat them?"

"They do when there's nothing else to eat," Adhemar said soberly.

"Are we heading in that direction?"

"No. But at the moment, it's a little like fat camp out there. And a cookie is a cookie."

Pinky returned with a tray piled high with bacon, eggs and fruit. Boy, it smelled good. Adhemar spun ZeeBee around and propelled her towards the door. "ZeeBee, let's go before I change my mind."

Located around the corner from the White House, the Old Ebbit Grill was popular with staffers and political power players despite the draw it also had with tourists. Its multiple rooms were decorated with gas lamps, paintings and murals by named artists, polished mahogany and stuffed game trophies, including a pair of what ZeeBee kept calling a gemsbok or something that sounded like that. It also boasted the best raw bar in town. A Washington institution, both ZeeBee and Adhemar were regulars, as were their Secret Service escorts.

"I'm bummed we won't be able to get some bread pudding with this flour shortage," Agent Kraatz commented as they pulled up to the restaurant. As always, he got out first and scanned the street. *Uh-oh.*

He quickly shut the door behind him. A young woman was approaching with a baby carriage. Jury-rigged to the top of the carriage was some sort of signage. Agent Kraatz sprinted up to stop her, then relaxed when he read the sign: Will trade toys for flour. He spotted a few Thomas the Tank engines. His kids would have fits if he tried to get rid of Thomas. The woman was clearly desperate!

Watching the action from inside the Explorer, ZeeBee winced.

Inside the restaurant, Sam had commandeered two booths in the Old Bar. He'd already ordered a selection of food, including grilled asparagus, fruit and two orders of the restaurant's signature breakfast dish: Eggs Chesapeake. Similar to Eggs Benedict, the chef used crab cakes instead of Canadian bacon. Yum. ZeeBee slung her now ever-present backpack onto the leather seat and scooted in next to him. Adhemar pulled up a chair opposite them.

The crew piled into the other booth. *The President Factor* had given them strict instructions not to tape anything inside the restaurant, citing national security. They kept looking around, trying to figure out who was meeting with whom that the White House did not want caught on camera, not realizing it was CIA agent Sam. To them, he was just ZeeBee's husband, who did something for State.

The three dug in. Food first, discussion after. ZeeBee paused after devouring her eggs. "I'm still feeling a little like Marie Antoinette. Sam, did you see that woman with the baby carriage?"

"Yeah, she stopped outside the window and glared at me as though I personally started the whole thing. I mean, what can I do?"

"I think the question is, what's the president doing? Sam? Or can't you discuss?" Adhemar said, nodding towards the next booth and the camera crew.

Sam's smiled to himself—this was perfect. Adhemar was opening the discussion right where he wanted it. He grabbed an asparagus spear off ZeeBee's plate, gnawed on it a bit, and then leaned in, head down. Copying Sam's lead and feeling a little like spies themselves, ZeeBee and Adhemar followed suit. Adhemar enjoyed the playacting.

Sam whispered, "Here's the situation. The only country with wheat is Russia, and Chernobyl is refusing to trade with us. He thinks we're going against him with the Finland thing."

"You're making that up. There is no Finland thing," Adhemar whispered back, still leaning dangerously close to his plate.

"Tell that to Chernobyl. He can't differentiate between the Sunday morning talks shows and *The President Factor*," Sam hissed.

"That's ridiculous," Adhemar said, leaning back in his seat, pulling out of his spy position.

Recognizing he'd lost an advantage, Sam replied in a normal tone. "Ridiculous or not, that's his perception." He thought he had them when they were mimicking his posture. That usually worked. Not this time. ZeeBee and Adhemar were too smart. He speared a piece of grilled pineapple and pointed it at Adhemar. "You could figure a way around this."

"Of course I could," Adhemar said rather smugly.

Sam saw another opening. He slapped the table. "Great! I'll set up a meeting with the president."

ZeeBee sat back in the booth and hooted. Adhemar merely smiled. Sam read Adhemar's expression and tried another tack. "Adhemar, the American people need you."

"Don't bring out that card, Sam. Please. Here's an idea: Get Beau to help." Adhemar winked across the table to ZeeBee.

Sam snorted. "Right."

ZeeBee said, "Honestly, Sam, this isn't Adhemar's fight." *What's gotten into him?*

Sam's eyes went from Adhemar to a distant point somewhere behind Adhemar. He refocused and spoke slowly, "Adhemar, just so we're clear. You're refusing to meet with the president to help him solve this crisis?"

"That is correct."

"Crap. Can I call upon our friendship?"

"Sam, you know I can't."

Sam sighed. "Okay, then." He reached over to pick up another of piece of asparagus off ZeeBee's plate. As his fingers connected with the green stick, his hand knocked the creamer over. Cream splattered ZeeBee's sleeve. "Oh God, I'm sorry, Zee."

"That's okay." She leaned over and kissed him. "Don't fret. I still love you, secret agent man." She stood up. "That's why God invented ladies' rooms. Be right back."

As she walked away, Sam offered Adhemar his hand. "Thanks for meeting with me anyway, Adhemar. You can imagine the pressure I'm under." Getting a nod from Adhemar, he continued, "Can I get a few moments with ZeeBee? I need to apologize for the creamer. She may be smiling, but that's her favorite suit."

"Absolutely," Adhemar said, getting up. "I'll be in the car." He squeezed Sam's shoulder—no hard feelings here—and left.

The camera crew followed Adhemar as Sam expected. He sat still for a moment and then deliberately rubbed his eyes.

A man in a nondescript suit appeared with a leather gym bag. He quickly opened it, pulled out a backpack identical to ZeeBee's and rapidly transferred the contents. *Done.* He shoved ZeeBee's now empty pack into the gym bag and tossed the new one back on the booth.

"It's live," he whispered to Sam.

Sam didn't touch the backpack. He sat frozen in the booth and waited for his wife to return.

He had tears in his eyes.

TWENTY-NINE

On 42nd Street, thirty or so people jockeyed for position outside the giant windows of BCD's street-side studios.

It was 8:00 a.m. Inside, just out of view of the folks on the street, Wink Goodenoff was in the middle of a standoff with *Wake-Up America's* producers.

"I'm not going to comment on any footage from *The President Factor* until I get something that's more balanced," Wink said with the authority he had as show anchor for more than a decade.

Ziggy Brown, the more senior of the producers was not moved in the least by Wink's stand. "That's all we got, Wink. This is what they sent over and this is what you're going to comment on. Just read the prompter. Period."

"It's completely biased."

"I wouldn't go that far."

"Who's the political analyst here, Ziggy? You or me?"

Ziggy snorted. "Wink, sweetheart, this is an early morning talk show. Not *Meet The Press*."

"It's a news show. And, remember, I was the first to interview Senator Reyes after his *Russia from my porch* speech on the Senate floor. He came to me first. You were certainly happy with those ratings, were you not? I got them for you. Me!"

Ziggy shrugged.

"I have a degree in poli-sci, goddammit. And I'm not going to be part of any political agenda the network or whomever is controlling the clips from *The President Factor* has," Wink said in what he thought would be the final word. "My journalistic integrity is at stake here, not yours. I'm not running them." *Dad would be proud.*

"Okay," Ziggy said. "You're fired."

Moments later the crew was clipping a pair of lavaliere microphones—lavs for short—to the shirt of Harry Jones, the show's new anchor. Thirty-five and looking not a day older, Harry came to *Wake-Up America* after being one of BCD's embedded journalists in Afghanistan. He returned to the States, and when offered the chance to deliver the international news roundup every weekday morning, he grabbed it. He was just as startled to see Wink herded off by two armed security guards as when the show producers whisked him into the green room for a quick make-over comprised of changing his tie to the one Wink had been wearing only moments earlier.

"I think they are going to notice I'm not Wink," he joked to the network representative from the sixteenth floor who suddenly appeared in the room.

"Just read the prompter and you'll be fine," the network suit said, handing him a few notes.

"Are we going to even mention Wink is off the set?" Harry was concerned about his audience. One didn't toss to a car commercial and then disappear. It just wasn't done.

"No."

"Have you prepped the guests?"

"We have. They don't know Wink is gone, they just know that you, our international news correspondent, will be handling their interview. It will make sense. We'll spin the Wink-thing later."

Harry blanched at the cavalier toss. *Wink-thing? Hell, the guy had just been fired!* He scanned the notes.

So it happened, when *Wake-Up America* came back from an extended commercial break, Harry Jones was sitting on the bright lime green couch between two clearly agitated guests. On his right, a good-looking forty-five-year-old Latino perched on the edge, his jiggling legs betraying his fake poise. On Harry's left, a feisty young woman kept flashing her breasts at the cameraman in a vain attempt to get attention.

In BCD's control room, the Chyron operator was tapping out the guests' lower thirds: Hernando Gonzalez, President, Hispanics United for Change and Lois Smith, President, Stop Immigration Now. They had also added the organization's acronym SIN to her title.

The red tally light over the camera came on. Harry scanned the teleprompter. "It's creating a lot of buzz," he began. "This past Thursday night, almost every American TV was tuned to the premiere of *The President Factor*. And as you know, we promised we'd do play-by-play analysis as the show unfolds. This groundbreaking reality show is an exclusive production of BCD television, and that's why we can bring you some of the compelling footage as soon as humanly possible after it is shot. Here's a sneak peek at show number two."

The footage rolled:

CHAD. Adhemar was giving his *"I am not the Hispanic candidate"* speech while holding the Sudanese child.

Back on set, Harry read off the prompter, "We just played a clip from this Thursday's *The President Factor*. This morning I have two politicos who have the most to say—" Harry started to stumble as he read the rest: "—on Adhemar's position."

Oh crap, he thought, *they've given Adhemar a* **position** *on being Hispanic.* He continued, "To start us off is Lois Smith, the leader of SIN. Lois?"

Lois licked her lips. "Thanks, Harry. Goodness. Senator Reyes is just plain scary when he is doin' his planning. I almost couldn't breathe when he talked about opening our borders to an influx of refugees from God knows where."

"I didn't hear him say that, Lois," Harry said.

"Well, Harry, I believe he said, *I will bring a better life to all Americans*." She folded her arms defensively. "He said that when he was looking directly...directly at that clearly unwashed little boy in his arms."

While shocked at Lois's remarks, Harry had heard worse when he was in Afghanistan. But those remarks never made it to network TV. They were live! "To be fair, Lois, what the Senator said was that with God's help, the little boy might someday be an American."

"Exactly. And when would that someday happen? Huh? As soon as he takes office, that's when. That's when they'll start arriving."

Hernando waved his hands trying to get Harry's attention. "I agree with Lois, Harry. He turned his back on his race when he said he was not the Hispanic candidate. He is not a man to be trusted."

Thankfully, Harry had declined a beverage from the PA a few minutes earlier when he saw it came in a coffee mug with a photo of Wink's eight-year-old daughter and "World's Best Dad" on it. A good thing because he would have spit it across the room after Hernando's statement.

"I never thought I'd see the day when the two of you would be on the same side," Harry choked out.

"We're on the side of keeping America safe from terrorists, Harry," Lois said with self-importance.

Hernando nodded.

"Terrorists?" Harry snapped, getting his rhythm back. "Where do you see terrorists, Lois?"

"What's going on in Africa—wherever the heck the Senator is down there—puts that child in some sort of danger. I saw refugee tents in the background. Someone drove those people to those tents. Once all those people in all those tents come here, the terrorists will follow. When they hit our shores, Lady Liberty better duck and cover."

Oh, good God! What the hell is she talking about? Harry quickly looked to the teleprompter, hoping that someone had anticipated this turn of events—because clearly the producers knew what direction these guys were going in. *Someone surely has prepared a succinct rebuttal.* The teleprompter was not rolling.

Harry scanned beyond the lights and saw a network exec leaning forward, waiting for his response. Good God, it was Buzz! Knowing this was his make or break moment, and not wanting to become a *Harry-thing*, Harry knew what he had to do.

"Let's take a quick break. When we get back, we'll examine the question: Is Senator Reyes advocating opening our shores to terrorists?"

Buzz gave him a thumbs-up.

Harry wanted to throw up.

Forty-seven floors above the *Wake-Up America* studios, Makki sat in her office, watching the show. She felt the same way Harry did.

▰ THIRTY ▰

U nlike that practical joke told in high schools at the beginning of the year where everyone swears there is a swimming pool under the basketball court until some poor freshman is duped into bringing his swimming suit to school—the bowling alley under the White House Portico is indeed real. The proposal to recreate it for *The President Factor* came from Trammel Washington, who had on occasion knocked down a few pins on the real one.

The producers were not initially sold and argued the teams would be too busy to bowl, plus the cost of construction could not be justified if the room never appeared on camera. Still, Trammel pressed and all but guaranteed it would be used. "We're recreating the damn thing down to those 1980s bowling pins on the walls," the network's CFO quipped when the proposal had reached his desk months before. "By God, someone sure better put on some bowling shoes and throw a few." The CFO, having been one of the people who green-lit the building of the set with real barbed wire for the disastrous reality show *Sue The Neighbors* that never saw the light of day, was understandably skittish around construction budgets. Trammel pointed out that this set did not include live cattle as the other one had. Plus he had some inside intel on the candidates and could with a clear conscience reassure said CFO that one of the candidates and his running mate not only owned their own bowling balls, bags and shoes, but had matching turquoise bowling shirts. The only thing that might stop them from using the faux White House lanes would be if they were too busy preparing their presentations to take the time to throw a few frames. In other words, the bowling lanes would have their network moment, guaranteed.

On the morning Harry Jones became the morning anchor, Beau and Mike were in the bowling alley, decked out in their turquoise shirts. They'd procured one for Hawke as well. Though it was not an exact match, it was close enough for the three to appear as a team. Yancey, however, was in street clothes. The camera crew was taking bets on who would throw the most gutter balls and had set up a camera to record the action at the foul line.

Beau was approaching the lane, his Brunswick marbled ball in hand, staring down thirty feet of bird's eye maple. Mike and Hawke perched on retro 1980s orange plastic-metal chairs at a mini scorer's table, alternating between watching. Beau handle a seven–ten split and catching the action on the flat screen TV mounted to the wall across from the lane. *Wake-Up America* was on.

Beau picked up the spare with a "gotcha," a saying that was beginning to wear on the two at the scorer's table who were far better bowlers but somewhat intimidated by the cameras. This adversely affected their game.

Then, on the TV, Harry Jones tossed away his journalistic integrity. Mike leaped up. "They're crucifying Reyes," he said, rubbing his hands together in a bad imitation of Uriah Heep.

Beau dried his fingers on the little puffs of air coming out of the ball return. "For now. They'll be after us soon. We just haven't given them anything to sink their teeth into yet. Just turn the darned thing off."

Sitting along the wall, Yancey was playing with the remote control. He obliged. "With all the rooms to choose to replicate, they decided on this one? Couldn't they have given us the Blue Room?" He drawled out *blue* to sound like *ba-loo*.

"You're still not going to bowl?" Hawke said. "We just started a new game. There's a bunch of shoes over there. I'm sure we can find a pair that would fit you," he said, looking at Yancey's Ted Baker Derby lace-up shoes.

"No. I'd like to able to continue to say that I've never bowled," Yancey said, hoping his remarks would make it to a tease for the show, or maybe a radio spot. He'd like a following.

Beau stopped drying his hands and nodded to Mike. "You're up, Number Two."

Mike winced at the name.

"We should just have a bowl-a-thon to decide the winner," Hawke said, slapping the table. "Let's get 'em down here."

Mike was poking around the balls on the rack, subconsciously trying his thumb in each ball, smarting from Beau's number-two remark. He equated it with Hertz commercials, lost basketball tournaments and a childhood memory of the woman next door and her constant chirping encouragement to her dog through her screen door when she let him out to poop in the backyard. He started to pout.

Beau watched Mike fuss with the bowling balls. Annoyed and anxious to keep an approaching cameraman from reaching Mike while he was in what Beau had dubbed his *pissy mood*, Beau yelled, "Just pick one up, already! We're not keeping score."

"I'm keeping score," Mike yelled back.

"I didn't ask you to keep score."

"You always have to keep score. Or why play?"

"For the fun of the sport, dumbass," Yancey said and then slapped his hand over his mouth, horrified. "I am so sorry, Congressman. I didn't mean any disrespect."

Mike took it well. "That's okay, Yancey. We're all on the same team. Ain't that right, Beau?"

"Yes we are, gentlemen. We are on the winning team," Beau pronounced.

Mike found his ball, went to the line and threw a gutter ball. He looked at his thumb as though it were the reason he whiffed and then trudged back and flopped into his seat.

"You have another ball," Hawke pointed out.

"I don't want to play anymore. I'm worried about the game." Mike ran his fingers through his hair. Nervous tension. *Am I the only one concerned about the pending presentation?*

Exasperation showed in Beau's face. *What the hell is this defeatist attitude? We can't let the public see this.* He quickly jumped in front of the camera. "I told you we're not keeping score!"

"I'm worried about the other game, Beau. *The President Factor*! Lord, we don't have a clue what to do! We're down here, pretending to have fun, when in two days we're gonna get in front of that camera with our pants around our ankles." Mike had given up trying to hide his fears. "That, fellas, will be something they can sink their teeth into."

Beau relaxed. This he could deflect. "I'm not *pretending* to have fun. I *am* havin' fun. Hawke, you havin' fun?" Beau said with flair.

Hawke got up, grabbed the first ball in line, unconcerned. He threw the ball and knocked down eight pins. Another split. "I'm havin' fun. Come on, Number Two—lighten up."

That was too much to bear. Mike shot up and stormed out of the room.

Yancey leaned forward, suddenly interested in the goings on. "You do have a plan? Please tell me you have a plan."

Hawke threw his second ball and picked up the split. Beau applauded.

Hawke spun around. "Yancey. Do you think Beau would be the Republican nominee for president of the United States if all he did was go bowling when faced with a crisis?"

"Some presidents have been known to freeze—" Yancey started to say.

"He was thinking! He didn't want to panic the school kids," Beau interrupted. He couldn't abide anyone voicing any criticism of his hero.

"Sure," Yancey said dripping sarcasm. "Can one of you unfreeze the plan so you don't panic me?"

Beau shook his head as though he were sitting in that classroom with the school kids and had to explain why they weren't going to have cookies for lunch.

"We're not quite there yet. But things are falling into place," Beau said. "My plan is rapidly taking shape."

If the president would freaking call me with it, that is.

THIRTY-ONE

Before heading to his Sit Room to finalize his plan with the team, Adhemar was backstage in one of the dressing rooms, getting made up. Paper collar around his neck, Maxine, the makeup artist, buzzed around, applying foundation.

ZeeBee poked her head in, caught her reflection in the mirrors and instinctively raised her chin. "It's really blowing up, Adhemar."

Adhemar felt Maxine slow down a little, her makeup sponge pausing in its forward motion inches away from his brow. Watching the sponge hover, Adhemar thought, *Hmmm, interesting reaction.* Although there were no cameras in the dressing rooms, Maxine was part of *The President Factor* crew and Adhemar didn't know if everyone—or anyone for that matter—had to sign nondisclosure paperwork.

Looking to throw focus off ZeeBee and back on him, Adhemar leaned forward and squinted at his reflection in the mirror. "I hate that we have to go through all this. I didn't wear makeup when we were in Chad."

ZeeBee clued into Adhemar's redirection. "That's because you wanted to look like the troops. And troops don't wear makeup. Or even comb their hair," she explained.

Adhemar started touching the makeup under his eye. Maxine cleared her throat. "We don't want to be all shiny and such on camera, do we?"

"Would it make a difference?" Adhemar said, still touching under his eyes.

"Remember Nixon?" Maxine replied deadpan.

Adhemar stopped touching.

ZeeBee tossed her backpack on an empty chair and whispered in Adhemar's ear, "I'm spooked."

"Maxine? Can you give us a few?" Adhemar asked.

Maxine reluctantly left, giving Adhemar even more reason to doubt the existence of nondisclosure agreements.

ZeeBee spat it out, "Sam desperately wants you to counsel the president on the wheat crisis."

"I already told him no."

"I know. I was there, but when I came back from the ladies room, he was almost desperate."

This was new territory. Adhemar and ZeeBee kept a Chinese wall between them regarding Sam's CIA duties at the White House. Adhemar wanted to be able to say with honesty that he was not privy to anything that went on behind the scenes with the president. This could break the wall if they weren't careful. He chose his words. "How involved is he?"

ZeeBee stared at him.

"Okay. I know nothing. We are not having this conversation," Adhemar said.

ZeeBee nodded. "It sounds dire."

"It is dire."

ZeeBee moved her backpack off the chair and sat down. "Adhemar, what would *we* do? If we had to? It's really nasty out there."

Adhemar picked up a makeup brush and tapped it on the counter, collecting his thoughts. Powder dusted up. "Well, yeah. That's not good. If Chernobyl thinks *The President Factor* is real, it could go down in history as causing a major famine. Forget being the father of modern politics, I'll be the father of starvation."

"You could come up with a solution, like that!" she declared, snapping her fingers.

Adhemar smiled at her snap. "I could."

"You always do."

"I do." Adhemar tapped some more. Although he hated the term, Adhemar secretly considered himself to be an out-of-the-box thinker, once quipping to a *Washington Post* reporter, "What exactly is *in* the box?" when they'd challenged him to come up with an alternative to sequestration. After a few more taps he had it!

"The press has been crappy. Consistently misinterpreting what I've been saying on this show…controlling the spin. And the producers have fucked us with their edits. Yes?"

ZeeBee nodded.

"Let's fuck *them!* We'll hijack the crisis and use it for our own purposes."

"Brilliant," ZeeBee shouted, without having a clue what Adhemar meant but secure in her faith that whatever Adhemar came up with, it was sure to be good for their polling.

Adhemar jumped up and was now pacing. ZeeBee grew excited. A pacing Adhemar was a thinking Adhemar.

"We'll call Chernobyl. Didn't he study method acting at the Vakhtangov Theatre in Moscow?"

"Yes."

Pace. Pace.

"Good. Good. First I'll say we knew all along he was kidding with the president and congratulate him on his Stanislavski technique. Then I'll invite him to make a cameo appearance on the show. He could appear on the screens in our Sit Room, which will earn him his SAG card. That's the lure. He'll wet his pants for that."

Pace. Pace.

He snapped his fingers, continued with enthusiasm. "Then—then we'll mock up shots of him standing on a humongous pile of flour, being offloaded on the Fulton Ferry Landing. Right across from the site of the World Trade Center."

"Brilliant." ZeeBee could now say it without blind faith. It *was* brilliant.

"Then we call a presser and announce everything!" Adhemar said. But then stopped pacing.

Uh-oh.

"We need a slogan. A hashtag."

They stared at each other.

"The chicken in every pot is chicken Kiev!" ZeeBee said the proverbial first thing that came into her mind. Besides being ridiculous, it was way too long for a hashtag.

Nope. Couldn't even shorten it.

She tried again, "Russian wheat can't be beat?" ZeeBee knew that wasn't going to do either, but her creative process was to throw stuff out there and take it hostage.

Adhemar pondered. And paced.

ZeeBee continued. "Wheat, beat, meat? That's a lot of food. Wheat, bread? Anything with bread, Adhemar?"

Adhemar stopped pacing. Tipped his head and said, "Got bread?"

"Yes. Yes. Yes!" ZeeBee danced around the dressing room, jumping over her backpack.

Adhemar opened the door and shouted down the hall, "Maxine, come on in, I'm ready for you." After settling in the makeup chair, he adjusted his paper collar and winked in the mirror at ZeeBee. "Zee, you should freshen up yourself, we're going to be in front of a lot more than *The President Factor* cameras in about an hour!"

Forty-five minutes later, now made up to perfection, Adhemar and ZeeBee strutted into their Sit Room to brief the rest of the team before they made the call to Chernobyl. Big grins. Confident they were about to score with their wheat crisis bit. Harrison and Pinky missed their entrance. They were focused on the TV screens before them, where President Chernobyl was about to be interviewed on CNN.

ZeeBee and Adhemar pulled up short.

On the TV, an animation played out: CNN–*Live*.

The shot changed to a double box: Chernobyl in one, Anderson Cooper in the other.

Cooper looked up from shuffling papers on his desk. "*Well! President Vladimir Chernobyl finds he has a SAG card this evening.*"

ZeeBee blurted out, "We just..."

Adhemar grabbed her arm and gave a jerk, stopping her. Cameras were rolling and he didn't want to share their plan.

On the TV, Chernobyl smiled. "*Da. Anderson that is true. I'm joining The President Factor as a political advisor. Of sorts.*"

Adhemar started. This was more than coincidence. "What the...?"

On the TV, Cooper continued, "*This doesn't have anything to do with your selling the U.S. ten million metric tons of wheat, does it? Tit for tat?*"

"*What are you saying about tits? I'm not providing prostitutes, Cooper. Wheat! Wheat! Just saw a need that we, as a friend of the United States, could fulfill,*" Chernobyl sputtered.

"*Ah. We have a photo, don't we? Yes,*" Cooper said, quickly changing the tone of the interview. A shot of Chernobyl standing on a stack of hundreds of bags of flour came on the screen.

Along the bottom of the screen was #GotBread?

"Son-of-a-bitch. Turn it off," Adhemar said evenly.

Harrison protested, "Adhemar. This is solving—"

Adhemar grabbed a pad and wrote: We Have a Leak. He passed it to Harrison and Pinky out of camera sight, tossed his head in the direction of the door and marched out. The rest quickly followed.

Adhemar had taken note earlier that the cameramen would leave their cameras outside the bathrooms for obvious reasons, so he led the team into the men's room.

ZeeBee eyed the urinals, clearly uncomfortable. Adhemar slammed the door shut behind everyone and looked in the stalls. After he determined the room was clear, he locked the door and spat out, "That was my idea. My fucking solution."

"We were just discussing it," ZeeBee added. "Right down to the SAG card. And the hashtag."

Pinky took it in. "Anyone else hear you? Cameramen? Anyone?"

ZeeBee and Adhemar shook their heads.

"When and where were you talking about it?"

"The dressing room. A few minutes ago." Adhemar's eyes shot to his military advisor. "What are you thinking, Pinky?" Adhemar asked.

"Espionage, Adhemar. Plain and simple. You were bugged."

"This is outrageous," ZeeBee said.

"Outrageous or not, it obviously happened," Adhemar said. "We've gotta find that bug."

The group went to the dressing room. Maxine was gone. Adhemar locked the door. They didn't talk and quietly tossed the room, systematically examining everything. Pinky started walking a grid pattern, checking the walls and floors. Mike took the chairs, upending them, tossing cushions. Harrison tackled the lights, unscrewing the bulbs around the make up mirrors and looking in each socket. ZeeBee removed everything from Maxine's makeup case and examined every lipstick, eye shadow, powder and eyeliner. She flipped the make up brushes, sending powder into the air. Nothing.

They leaned against the walls, perplexed. Adhemar rummaged through Maxine's makeup case, pulled out a lipstick and wrote on the mirror: We've Looked at Everything!!!"

Pinky shook his head and pointed to ZeeBee's backpack. No one had examined it because…it was ZeeBee's!

ZeeBee gagged.

They approached it as though it were a bomb. Pinky reached in his pocket and pulled out a small wand-like device and ran it over the backpack. It beeped.

They all jumped back. Pinky quickly turned the wand off.

Adhemar gave Pinky that wide-eyed look that said *What the heck?* He wrote on the mirror: You had that all along?

Pinky shrugged, sheepish. He wrote back, Sorry. Forgot.

ZeeBee reached for the backpack, but Adhemar stopped her and used the lipstick again: Don't talk.

The group nodded. Agreed.

Adhemar continued writing: Z, has that been out of your sight?

ZeeBee shook her head no, then it came to her. She grabbed the lipstick: Only today at breakfast. Went to bathroom—remember?

ZeeBee leaned against the counter, stunned. The group backed off. She met their eyes, blinking rapidly.

Adhemar took the lipstick out of her hand and wrote: We all have a job to do, Z.

Pinky moved Adhemar out of the way and cleaned off the mirror with some makeup remover from Maxine's kit. Moments later, they headed back to the men's room.

They left the backpack in the dressing room.

No one sits on a public bathroom floor unless they are drunk, an extra in a crime movie, or a victim in real life. Yuck. Yet inside the men's room, ZeeBee had slid down to the floor like someone shot her. She felt as if she, herself, had betrayed everyone. She couldn't meet their eyes. "I'll resign," she said in a low voice.

Adhemar pulled her to her feet. "ZeeBee. We don't blame you." He looked to the rest of his team.

"No, we don't," Pinky quickly said. "Let's face it. Are we surprised that this president engineered this?"

"No," Adhemar quickly replied.

"No," ZeeBee meekly said.

"Who knows what kind of pressure he put on Sam? Let's not forget Sam is CIA and has to do the President's bidding, so it was out of his hands," Pinky continued. "I know what it's like to have to follow orders."

Harrison had pulled at his hair so hard it stood up. All he needed was eyeliner and he could play backup for Green Day. "The president of the Untied States bugged us," he said with surprise and annoyance in his voice. "Can he do that?"

"The courts ruled he can if it's in the national interest," Adhemar said.

"Cheating is in the national interest?"

"He will say he bugged us to get Adhemar's take on the wheat crisis, and with the uproar that is going on outside right now, no one will take him on," Pinky said. "That's bad enough. The fact that the bug is still live shows the intent to get information on our plans for the challenge."

"I never thought of that," Adhemar said.

"Someone was and still is on the other end of that microphone taking notes. Once you stopped talking about Chernobyl, they could have pulled the plug and turned it off."

"But they didn't," ZeeBee said.

"No they didn't," Pinky replied.

"So they're keeping it active to get insider information on what we're going to present," Adhemar said. "If we weren't sitting in this effing bathroom, we'd be back in the Sit Room right now going over our presentation."

"And handing it right to Beau," ZeeBee said. "We can't do that!"

"Just leave the fucking backpack in the dressing room," Harrison said. "They have to know we figured it out by now."

The whole thing disgusted Adhemar. While he admitted to himself that he was a little over the top when he proposed *The President Factor*, he truly did believe there needed to be more transparency in government. Now it was corrupted by a clandestine move on the part of the president and Beau. This sickened him. And because it concerned Sam, a CIA operative, he couldn't talk to the press about it. There had to be some way he could take advantage of the situation. He started pacing.

"We have to turn this back on them."

ZeeBee perked up. Here was a challenge. If she could turn this around, she wouldn't feel so bad about Sam. At least not at the moment.

Pinky mentally started going through his West Point intelligence training.

Harrison imagined wrapping the straps of the backpack around Beau's neck.

They stayed in the men's room for half an hour.

When the idea came, it was obvious. And so simple.

🐴 THIRTY-TWO 🐘

Two hours after leaving the men's room, Adhemar and his team were huddled in a cherry red vinyl booth in the back corner of the Eighteenth Street Diner miles away from *The President Factor* set. The now infamous backpack was smack in the middle of a speckled yellow Formica table. The diner was not a complete throwback to the '50s like Johnny Rockets, but it had that *We've been here a long time and we're proud of it* feel.

The perfect location for an all-American counterplot.

As if they were of a collective mind, the group had ordered three servings of French fries with gravy, a house specialty that could once again be served with the wheat crisis over, along with grilled Danish—another house specialty, taking comfort in the American-ness of their choices. They did, after all, represent the Democratic Party.

Their server, Patty, with food balanced up her arm to her shoulder, attempted to move the backpack to make way for the fries. She had only touched the strap of the darn thing when the entire group shouted, "Noooo!"

Not expecting the visceral reaction, Patty recoiled, rearing back at an impossible ninety-degree angle, causing a busboy pushing a cart with a teetering load of coffee cups to zigzag around her. Patty'd been zigzagging around the diner herself for five years, carrying a lot more than three plates of

French fries, which was why she didn't spill a drop of gravy during the maneuver.

She did, however, wonder what was in the backpack. Later that night she told her son that the group's reaction made her think it was drugs or snakes and that she was half-expecting something to happen. Like maybe she was on a hidden camera show?

After she sprang back to an upright position, Patty gingerly passed the still steaming plates of fries across the backpack, keeping an eye on it in case it started to travel by itself. It didn't. No snakes.

The group awkwardly balanced the plates on the edges of the table. Half on, half off. They lacked Patty's internal gyro, making it a bit risky. Pinky gave up trying to free a hand to pick up his fork and just raised his plate to his mouth and bit off a gravy-coated French fry.

"Don't drop anything and make a mess," Patty admonished, watching them. When she realized no one was going to pop out like on that hidden camera show to interview her, she turned her back on the group. "Your Danish will be right out," she tossed dismissively as she walked away.

Adhemar waited until Patty was out of earshot. Then, with purpose, leaned over and spoke directly to the spot on the backpack they had identified as containing the bug—thanks to Pinky's wand-thing. "Sorry to drag you all out here, but someone outside of our camera crew taped the conversation about Chernobyl I had with ZeeBee in the dressing room. Obviously with a hidden mic."

"Obviously," Harrison said.

"And then they fed that information to the president."

"Check."

The next part was a little hard to say with a straight face. Adhemar plunged in, "While I don't imagine the president would be interested in our solution to *The President Factor*

Finland challenge, there is no telling if that same person might be tempted to pass info to Beau and his team."

"Roger that," Pinky chimed in.

"That's why we're here at the diner. We know we're safe here. No hidden mics."

Harrison started choking on a French fry. ZeeBee gave him a stern look and passed over a glass of water.

Adhemar waited until Harrison's choking subsided. He didn't know how sensitive the mic in the backpack was and didn't want Harrison's coughs to drown out what he was about to say. "Okay. Let's review our presentation for tomorrow. I'm confident we will win this phase of the competition. Our solution is best for the American people. And best for the world," Adhemar said, working hard to keep a smile off his face and in his voice.

"It's brilliant, Adhemar. They'll be stunned," Harrison said, continuing the game.

By agreement, ZeeBee contributed nothing to the ruse outside of ordering food to establish her presence at the diner. In her gut she knew Adhemar was right. Sam had no choice but to do what the president ordered. They all believed the extent of his involvement ended with gathering intel on how to solve the wheat crisis, but if Sam was forced to listen to the recordings, ZeeBee could only say things she knew were true. Sam was very good at reading her. And they couldn't put Sam in the compromising position of deciding whether or not to tell the president that ZeeBee was making stuff up.

So an uncharacteristically mute ZeeBee nibbled on her fries, leaned back against the red vinyl booth and listened to her team spin the web.

"Let's begin with the broad strokes. Pinky start us off," Adhemar said.

Pinky snuggled up to the backpack and spoke, "We took a hard look at Helsinki. Specifically its architecture…"

☙ THIRTY-THREE ☙

And on the other end…

After ZeeBee left the Old Ebbit Grill with the bugged backpack earlier that morning, Sam had sped over to the White House to set up a post in the real Sit Room. He and the president then listened as ZeeBee and Adhemar came up with the plan to get the Russian president over to their side. Once Adhemar and ZeeBee wrapped it up, Sam told the president he wouldn't listen any further.

"I want plausible deniability, Mr. President. For the sake of my marriage. Solving the wheat crisis is important for the welfare of Americans. Solving *The President Factor* challenge isn't." He stood there, giving his commander in chief the opportunity to show his metal.

The president liked the idea of plausible deniability. *After the WMD fiasco, anything was possible. And if the recordings leaked and he wound up in front of a congressional hearing—?* He shuddered. He did, however, promise Beau he would come up with a plan, but the fucking wheat crisis took all of his attention. So, he reasoned, his dedication to the country kept him from formulating a plan for Beau. *It wasn't his fault he hadn't come up with something, was it? His patriotism was the reason he had to resort to getting a little help from the opposing team. Besides, Adhemar was a brilliant strategist. It was his obligation to explore all the options.*

Sam broke into his thoughts. "We either shut this monitoring down or I boogie out of here, Mr. President. I can't hang around while this is happening."

"Can you set something up to automatically record whatever they say? I don't want to listen either, but can we record everything they say through tomorrow morning? This way neither of us knows what we will be passing on to Beau."

"I can do that, but there is no *we* involved in this part. It will be files that *you* will be passing on to Beau, sir. I want nothing to do with this."

"Technicality."

"An important technicality, Mr. President. Or I can't help you. I am so uncomfortable with this entire thing. You know that."

"Can't or won't?"

"Both."

The president knew when he was outplayed. "Oh, all right. Make it snappy. I've got to call Chernobyl and beat Reyes to the announcement, Sam. Chop, chop."

Sam set to work.

"How do I get this stuff to Beau anyway?" the president asked. "Use one of my little drive-thingies?"

"You can't just hand a USB drive with the White House seal on it to Beau without causing suspicion," Sam snapped. He passed over a thumb drive disguised as a pack of gum. "I'll send someone to pick it up tomorrow morning, then figure out some way to get it to Beau."

"Wow," the president said. "They really make things like this at Langley?"

"Nope. I bought it at the Spy Museum as a joke a while back."

"This isn't a joke, Sam."

"I beg to differ, Mr. President," Sam said, ending the conversation.

The next day, Beau was in the East Wing of the National Gallery. Mike stood next to him, mesmerized by a gigantic Calder mobile. He'd bought a few mobiles over the years for his kids, and his dad had given him a memorable one with silver sailboats during the craze that swept the nation when he was in grammar school, but he hadn't appreciated mobiles as an art form until he saw the bright red-orange Calder hanging above. It was at least thirty feet across! And magnificent. It dominated the massive sun-drenched room.

"Jesus, Beau. I'm sure glad you dragged me over here," Mike whispered in awe. "I wonder if they have it rigged to move? That would be cool."

Beau shrugged. It was his first time inside the modern wing himself, but he wasn't interested in the art that surrounded him. They were there because Sam told him to choose a public place for the hand-off of the backpack recordings. Public and artsy, Sam said. Something about the president wanting to expand Beau's appeal to more upscale viewers and trend setters, having seen his own numbers rise when he engineered a *candid* shot with his family at the MoMA. Beau didn't really care where he got the recordings and recognized when someone else was calling the shots.

Despite his false bravado the past few days, Beau was worried he would be standing in front of millions of *The President Factor* viewers, bullshitting his way through some cockamammie plan he and his team could slap together in a day. When the president's call came in, it was better than he expected. Somehow he'd managed to bug the other team!

The president had prepped Beau on what he was sending over. "I'm not gonna deliver you a win on a silver platter. You're only going getting the raw recordings. I have not listened to them."

Beau wandered the first floor of the National Gallery's modern wing, killing time. Sam had instructed him to spend half an hour there and then go to the cafeteria and buy a pack of gum at noon. He brought Mike with him as a cover of sorts. They strolled through the traveling exhibit of Andy Warhol's pop art on loan from the Albright-Knox Art Gallery and paused in front of the iconic Marilyn Monroe portrait. Up close, he marveled at Warhol's brushwork. He briefly entertained the idea that more secrets might be embedded in microdots on the surface of the painting.

At 11:45, he grabbed Mike and went through the sparkly tunnel resembling an entrance to a spaceship that connected the modern wing with the main gallery. It took them past tables of art books, calendars, stuffed *Scream* dolls. They stopped at the snack counter. Drinks, cookies, candy and gum. The guy behind the counter was the man with the leather gym bag from the Old Ebbit.

Beau made a purchase and left. Grinning.

⇐ THIRTY-FOUR ⇒

I t was finally Thursday night. Everyone connected with the show was in DC for the second installment of *The President Factor*. The candidates were poised to present their solutions to the world.

Makki, Buzz and the rest of the network executives, plus a cadre of high-profile guests, milled about the back of the control room. A bevy of black-tied busboys rushed around, clearing up the remnants of a catered dinner. A pile of oyster shells littered a bed of ice sculpted into a replica of the White House. A three-foot high cake made in the shape of the network logo had been consumed down to the cardboard tray it stood on as though everyone thought flour was going to be scarce again. Insane. And wonderful. The blowout you'd expect for the network's number one show.

Yes. Number one. *The President Factor* was number one *with a bullet*. When the dust had settled and the Nielson numbers came in for the premiere, the show had swept across all demographics, even households with children.

Thursday night was expected to be another champagne evening for the network.

Thirty minutes before air, two more high-profile guests arrived. Two tall men in black tie. Look-alikes. Makki gauged them to be in their sixties. The chatter in the room died and the majority of the network folks tried not to stare but sneaked quick looks anyway. Buzz immediately rushed to their side, then caught Makki's eye with an *I need you here* look. As she made her way to the trio, she snagged a glass of champagne, thinking, *This doesn't bode well.*

"Makki, I'd like you to meet the Rich Uncles, Bill and Gil," Buzz said in measured tones, watching her reaction.

Makki immediately stiffened. The Rich Uncles were ultra-right-wing billionaires, not a song and dance team despite the capitalization of their group title in every paper she'd ever read. *Why were they here?* She put on a smile, all business. "Hello. I think we may be able to rustle up some food for you, if you'd like."

"That would be most kind," Gil, the elder of the two, replied.

As she turned to flag down a waiter, Makki casually mentioned, "I have a little housekeeping to take care of before the show starts." She flashed the three another big smile. "Buzz? Can you spare a few minutes?"

She walked away from the group and headed for the hallway, hoping Buzz would follow. He did. Once there, she leaned in. "The Rich Uncles? The Rich Uncles?" she shrilled. "What are those two doing here?"

"That's above your pay grade, Makki. Please keep it down." Buzz took stock of the hallway in case they were going to have it out in semi-public.

"No. Tell me, or I get Trammel in here," Makki threatened. "How can you think inviting them tonight won't hit the press? We can't be on one side or the other politically with this show. You know that."

Buzz pursed his lips. "Okay, but this is not for public consumption. Nor can you trade on it."

"*What?*"

"Trade on it. The network is up on the blocks. The Rich Uncles are in the final stretches of buying us."

"What the fuck, Buzz!"

"It's true, Makki."

Realization hit Makki hard. It all made sense now. The leaning towards Beau. The slamming of Adhemar in the promos. "Jesus Christ, Buzz. They haven't even bought us yet."

"I was instructed to back Beau now, before they buy, so later it can't be said that they are pulling the strings," Buzz admitted with a shrug. He'd been known to side-step crappy decisions when it suited him, which is how he had survived and made it to the top of the network. He was doing it again.

"What about our news programming?" Makki wailed. She put out a hand to steady herself against the wall. Head spinning. "This could get worse than Disney and that pedophile story on ABC."

"Oh now, that's a bit of an exaggeration, don't you think?"

She looked pointedly at him, then shifted gears. "What the fuck is up with their names? Bill and Gil?"

"I don't know. They're not even related. You're either with me or against me on this, Makki. Besides, I see a promotion in your future if this show continues to get the ratings."

"Oh, don't try to buy me off," Makki snapped.

"From what? Calling a press conference? Nobody will come. Stuff like this isn't news. People don't care."

"They should. The Rich Uncles are only buying us to further their political views."

"And who are you? The moral compass of the media? Grow up."

Before she could answer, Buzz put a finger to Makki's lips. "Don't throw your career away."

▪ THIRTY-FIVE ▪

Show time.

Adhemar, ZeeBee, Harrison and Pinky marched down the hall that would take them to the left side of *The President Factor's* Roosevelt Room. The hall was lit for drama. Light spilled over the top of the sets, wooden braces holding up the sides casting long shadows. A stray Klieg light here and there. Craft services, with its folding tables piled high with chips, yogurt, fruit, drinks, cookies, stale bagels and the customary gigantic bowl of mini candy bars, was along the way. Director chairs were stacked in a corner. Apple boxes— those little wooden step-like things one saw everywhere on film sets—piled up along one wall. Sitting on the back of a golf cart moving in front of the group, a cameraman recorded a shot that resembled those *We are your hometown news team* promos every local TV station did during sweeps. Missing were the wet cobblestone streets and the overhead God light.

Unexpectedly and completely out of character, Adhemar waved to the camera.

ZeeBee carried two bags of Oysterette crackers. One was open—being raided. A black leather Ben Sherman Notation Range Messenger bag she'd picked up in Los Angeles was slung over her shoulder. Harrison clicked the top of his Montblanc pen in time to the rat-ta-tat of her Christian Louboutin red-bottomed stilettos. Pinky's medals shined. Adhemar was Adhemar—'cause that's all that was necessary.

They were confident, determined and buttoned up.

Ambling along the opposite hall towards the right side of the Roosevelt Room with their own golf-cart-riding cameraman and much the same staged setting was Beau and his team. Their brown suits (Beau had bought one for Yancey despite his protests) blended into the shadows. They started to pick up the pace after falling a bit behind schedule when Mike stopped at craft services for a banana—which he was now eating. Yancey tried to discourage him but lost. The shot the cameraman got resembled a group of undertakers, one of whom was apparently hungry, heading to a funeral. Their expressions, however, clashed with this scenario—all three looked like cats that had swallowed the proverbial canary.

Hours earlier Beau had choreographed their entire presentation. Not knowing what to expect from the recordings after the warning he received from the president, he was delighted to find Reyes's entire plan all laid out. All that he had to do was pull some props and decide who was going to handle which part.

"This is pure theatre, boys," he said, gathering them into a quasi-huddle in their Oval Office. They'd pushed the couches back to the wall and removed the coffee table. Beau loved any chance to reenact his football glory days.

"It's TV, Beau," Mike said.

"He's speaking metaphorically, Mr. Future Vice President," Yancey gently corrected. After his *dumbass* remark at the bowling lanes, Yancey was vigilant in choosing how he addressed Mike.

"Just testing y'all," Mike shot back, recovering. "*Joo!*"

"Pay attention," Pinky hissed. "Beau, take us through the play."

Beau beamed, ecstatic that Pinky had picked up on the football theme. "Hut-hut," he barked, dragging them into a circle. Pulling out his iPad, he launched the sketchpad and began to draw the layout of the Roosevelt Room with the federal-style table and everyone's respective seats. He laid out the how, when and where they would move—creating drawings that resembled football plays—*Xs*, arrows and all.

They rehearsed for half an hour. When Beau deemed they were ready, he added a few audible cues to take them through their routine.

"I feel like I'm performing on Broadway in *Jersey Boys*, Beau," Yancey said, humming "Walk Like A Man" after Beau added what he termed a *spin around*.

"Perception, Yancey, is the name of politics. I know it's a cliché, but we *will* be a machine out there. We'll practice until we can do this eyes closed. I don't want us stepping on each others' lines or running into each other."

"I'm going to say it again for the record. I think this idea is crazy," Yancey said.

"You are wrong, Yancey. This is a well-thought-out solution," Beau said.

"That we didn't come up with," Yancey pointed out.

"The idea itself, no, we didn't think of it."

"Not even close."

"Agreed. But we brought it to life. We didn't actually create it, but I'd say we sure as heck own it," Beau said.

"Here, here," Mike shouted.

Beau's exercise, plus the confidence that they were about to blindside Adhemar, gave the group a bit of a swagger as they sauntered down the hall towards the Roosevelt Room.

Hawke swung an Army issue briefcase.

Beau was whistling.

Trammel Washington waited on the Roosevelt Room set at the head of the conference table. He'd been kept in the dark, as he should have been, regarding the solutions the teams were about to present. He was excited. And nervous. He hadn't gotten over the last time the producers threw him on live TV and the battle with Beau's brother, Benny, over the mic. He hoped the candidates would not throw too many curve balls.

The floor director gave Trammel his cue and the tally light came on. He began:

"Good evening. This is *The President Factor*. Tonight, we're live as we wind up phase one of the most watched reality show in the history of reality shows."

The *Alice in Wonderland* doors opened on either side of the set and the two teams entered. As they took their seats, Trammel continued, "As everyone knows, presidential candidates Senator Adhemar Reyes and Governor Beau Simpson were given a crisis situation *slash* challenge last week. They, along with teams comprised of their vice presidents, chiefs of staff and chairmen of the Joint Chiefs, had seven days to come up with a solution. Tonight they will present these solutions to me...the American public...and the world."

Trammel rather liked saying that.

He looked to Beau, then Adhemar. "Candidates?"

Adhemar spoke first. "Ready."

"Ready," Beau echoed.

Trammel spoke with the just right amount of gravity. "Your first task was to take on this crisis situation: You were informed that Russia was amassing troops on the border of Finland. Posturing to strike. The government of Finland has asked for support from the United States in the form of two thousand troops. If you were the president of the United States, what would you do? But before we get to your solutions, let's take a look at how you got there."

Compared to the promos and teases, the presentations were straightforward. Both teams were shown starting in their

Sit Rooms where they discussed options. Viewers googled *Seven Days to the Rhine* to keep up with Adhemar's thought process, gasped when Adhemar said, "That is essentially an act of war," then relaxed when he continued with, "We don't want to go there." It was quite a ride. When the team finally settled on going to Chad, a contingent of military families watching together in Rockville, Maryland, stood up and applauded. Heady stuff.

Beau's decision to go to Helsinki found viewers with DVRs replaying the sequence, thinking they had missed something. *Surely there was something more to the decision to go to Helsinki than getting there before Adhemar? There had to be. Didn't we just find out Adhemar went to Chad? We must have missed something.*

They hadn't.

In the studio, watching the video, Beau winced. *Goldarnit, I knew we'd look bad here.*

The first clips ended, and the show cut back to Trammel. "There you have the two candidates' initial reactions to the challenge. The first steps in the plans. Candidates, any comments?"

Adhemar looked around at his team. They shrugged. "Not from us. I think you've done a good job of presenting our process, Trammel."

"Governor?" Trammel said.

"Ah, Mr. Speaker, a lot of my planning went on inside... my head. So we didn't discuss our plans...out loud."

Mike nodded, thinking: *So that's what was going on.*

"Okay. Shall we move on to what you learned from your field trips?"

Beau was getting nervous. Suppose they showed Reyes talking through his solution! He jumped in, "Ah Mr. Speaker, y'all aren't going to give away the ending now, are you?"

"Absolutely not, Governor. We're just showing a little of your trips. Giving people context."

Adhemar was glad Beau spoke up. He too wanted a surprise ending.

Again, the video was straightforward. Viewers saw Adhemar and his team in Chad and got a chance to put all of the quotes used in the teases into context. It was like Candy Crawley had jumped in to set the record straight. Again.

In the control room, Makki gave a silent cheer.

When they showed footage from Helsinki, millions of viewers continued to wonder why Beau went there, but the Republican contingent was energized by his sweeping hand gestures.

A group of Young Republicans camped out at their favorite bar in the District, slapped each other on the back with comments like: "Keep it close to the vest, Beau" and "Now there's a commander-in-chief."

The show so far had done its appointed task, keeping viewers glued to their sets.

Time for a commercial break.

ᵚ THIRTY-SIX ᵚ

B ack from the break, Trammel summed it up: "It was
a busy week for our candidates and their teams. We
saw some heartbreaking scenes from Chad and—"
Trammel struggled to find words—"some beautiful
shots from atop the Helsinki Olympic Tower."

"It *was* beautiful," Mike blurted out. Yancey rolled his
eyes. All was caught on camera.

Trammel continued, "Now, what we've all been waiting
for. It's time for the candidates to present their solutions."
He pulled out a silver dollar and held it up to the camera.
"A coin will determine who presents first," he said, tossing
it into the air.

Beau suddenly jumped up and snatched it mid-toss,
elbowing Trammel out of the way in the process. The Speaker
was upstaged again. Regaining his footing, Trammel cursed
the producers under his breath for going live but chided
himself for not seeing it coming. At the end of the day Beau
was Benny's brother.

Smugly nodding at Beau's gymnastics, Mike nudged
Hawke and whispered, "He's still got it."

After dancing back to his seat, Beau flipped the coin
across the table to Adhemar. "Ah, Senator Reyes? Y'all don't
mind if I go first do you?" he asked casually. *Please, please,*

please let me go first, Beau prayed. His entire plan hinged on presenting first.

"Any particular reason you want to go first, Governor?" Adhemar replied innocently.

Uh-oh. Hawke and Mike looked at each other.

Adhemar continued. "Not that I object, of course. Just wondering."

"No, no particular reason," Beau stammered.

"Actually—" Mike started to speak. Hawke kicked him under the table.

Beau recovered. "Just being gentlemanly, Senator. Give you the opportunity to close, seeing as y'all were the person who proposed the game to Congress. I figure that should give you home court advantage." He winked to camera. "For the first round."

"Well, I sure do appreciate it, Governor, and I'll take advantage of it, I'm sure. Okay with you, Mr. Speaker?" Adhemar asked as gracious as can be.

"Nothing in the rules states otherwise," Trammel said. "Governor Simpson, you're first, then. Tell the American people how you would handle this crisis that could ultimately shift the power in the Baltic Sea." Trammel waved his hand, giving them the floor.

Snap. Snap. Pinky unlocked his briefcase. Like Pavlov's dogs, the rest of the team shot out of their chairs at the sound, thanks to Beau's training.

Yancey stepped around the table, passing out high-gloss brochures with images of smiling Fins on the front. "Don't open just yet," he sang out.

He pivoted to join Beau, Pinky and Mike now marching in step towards a TV screen on the wall behind the now seated Trammel. They assembled two by two, facing the TV. Then in perfect unison, performed Beau's *spin around* to face the camera.

From Trammel on down, no one's eyes left the maneuvers. Pinky snickered to Adhemar, "They're like my grandmother's drill team."

Beau started, "Speaker Washington, fellow Americans. This situation called for a deep understanding of the psyche of the Finnish people."

Mike stepped forward and with a flourish announced, "We present…Operation Celluloid."

On the TV: *A slick edited montage showcased Hollywood films that had been shot in Finland. They all featured the neoclassical buildings of Helsinki.*

Beau had chosen the *William Tell Overture* for the video despite Hawke's insistence he couldn't listen to it without silently adding the words from the *Lone Ranger*. Beau dismissed Hawke's comments. He shouldn't have. At the appropriate point in the music, three quarters of the viewers silently mouthed *Hi Ho, Silver*—a reaction that would set the tone for the Republican's entire presentation.

The video showcased shots from a series of films: Reds, then Gorky Park and The Jackal. Title cards identified the movies for anyone who didn't recognize the footage.

Besides being shot in Finland, Beau had chosen the films for either their title value or star value. Maybe some people wouldn't recognize *Reds,* he figured, but who didn't know Warren Beatty! As it played out, Mike tried not to look in Adhemar's direction. Beau had warned his group to not make eye contact with their rivals until they had finished their presentation. "Y'all all don't want to be distracted by the panic I'm sure is going to spread through Adhemar's team, boys," he cautioned.

"I don't think I've ever witnessed anyone seeing their life flash before them, but I believe we're going to witness that once we start," Hawke added.

Despite Beau's direction, Mike did a quick take. Adhemar sat with a blank look on his face. Mike looked back to the TV to make sure their video was playing. All was as it should be. *But was it?* Adhemar was not reacting. Mike took another quick look. Adhemar caught his eye and, unfazed, raised his eyebrows.

Back on the TV, the title card for White Nights appeared. Hawke whispered, "That's my favorite."

The clip from White Nights ended with a tap dance routine by Baryshnikov and Hines.

Ta-da.

On cue, Beau stepped in front of the TV. "For many years, the people of Finland have welcomed the movie industry into their cities and their hearts."

Yancey stepped forward. "A history deeply rooted. A tradition of sorts. Passed down from father to son. Mother to daughter."

Mike stepped into the formation alongside Yancey and Beau. "For generation upon generation, the people of Finland have profited from their country's resemblance to Russia. They have embraced this. Renting their buildings for movie sets. Many have also acted in these films. As extras mostly, but nevertheless—their names were in the credits."

"Impressing their friends," Hawke said, stepping up to complete the mini formation. "A perfect example of Finns profiting from the Russian experience." His step was so military in nature he started to salute Trammel but caught himself as his hand passed his eyebrow. He deflected the action by rubbing his forehead. People around the world replayed it on their DVRs and noticed Hawke wincing at that moment, causing a million or so tweets to go out with the Twitter hashtag #Hawkebraintumor. It would take a week for the speculation to die down.

"Word," Mike said.

"Based upon this rich history…" Beau paused, milking the moment. "Based upon this rich history, we feel that the people of Finland would not mind in the least if Russia invaded their country."

Trammel gasped and then covered his mouth, embarrassed.

Mike sneaked another look at Adhemar, expecting to see fury on the senator's face. To his surprise, Adhemar sat with a smile. *That's odd.*

Beau was now almost boasting, pride in his voice. *Here it comes.* "We have designed a handout that we calculate will cost the American taxpayer only three hundred thousand dollars to print and distribute to every household in Finland. That is far cheaper than any military option of providing any number of troops."

He held up the brochure Mike had passed out. "Speaker Trammel, could you kindly read the handout for the people at home?" he said, now openly smirking at Adhemar. "Senator Reyes. You may want to follow along."

Trammel opened his brochure scanned the contents and quickly folded it shut. Stunned. *Surely they are not serious.* "One moment, folks," he said, taking a couple of steps over to Beau. With a fake smile he patted Beau on the shoulder, opened the brochure and said quietly, "Governor, did someone mix up your printing?"

Beau looked at the inside of the brochure. "No, Mr. Speaker, that's our printing." He chuckled, "Did you think it belonged to Senator Reyes? If so, you are mistaken. It's my—ah—our presentation."

Eyes widening, Trammel stared openly at Beau. "You are planning on passing this out to the people of Finland?"

"We'll drop them from the sky!" Beau corrected.

Trammel looked as though someone had just told him his cat had died. He shook his head and haltingly read from the brochure, "You are cordially invited to a private showing of *The Russians Are Coming, The Russians Are Coming*."

Beau said, "That is correct. We have negotiated a fair price for a nation-wide showing of this movie for every man woman and child in Finland."

"Another bargain. Way cheaper than military action," Yancey interjected.

"This comedic look at an American community faced with a Russian invasion will belay the fears of the Finnish people," Beau continued.

Pinky spread his arms in a welcoming gesture. "Getting invaded by the Russians is not something to worry about!"

"It's going to be fun," Yancey added.

Beau went off-book to take a final dig at Adhemar: "The Finns will be able to make money off it! Or at least get their SAG cards," he said with a smirk. Adding the reference to the Chernobyl caper was a brilliant touch he thought. *We've beaten you at your own game.*

Finished with their presentation, Beau's team stood tall. All four were now smirking at Adhemar.

Trammel staggered back to his position at the top of the table and gripped the edge to keep himself from sinking into the image that flashed in his mind: the melting Wicked Witch from the *Wizard of Oz*. He took a moment to compose himself. "Let's hope they don't bomb us," he said under his breath. Letting out a big whoosh of air, he straightened up and faced the camera.

"Okey-dokey. Moving on. Senator Reyes, it'll be your turn right after this break."

Under his breath Trammel muttered, "*God help me.*"

THIRTY-SEVEN

The world media community was as stunned as Trammel but only momentarily. After a pause to replay Beau's presentation to make sure they had heard it correctly, they sprang into action and posted, blogged and tweeted:

Governor Simpson advocates going to the movies for nations threatened by invasion.

Presidential candidate shuns European allies.

Simpson joins the staff at *The Onion*?

Someone started a new Twitter hashtag: #WTFBeau. It went viral in seconds.

Dave Reynolds choked on his blini and caviar.

On NPR, they broke into their regularly scheduled programming with, "Just now on live TV, Governor Beau Simpson made history as the most clueless presidential candidate this country has ever known."

On CNN, a crawl: Breaking News: Gov Simpson thumbs nose at Finland.

On FOX, a crawl: Breaking News: Gov Simpson scores in first round on *The President Factor*.

In the East Wing of the White House, the president poured himself a double shot of Petron, wishing he had listened to the recordings from the backpack. *How had this gone so wrong?* Picking up a phone, he called for his driver.

At the Republican National Committee—pandemonium. *Where did Beau get that idea?*

Where indeed.

On the set, oblivious to everything, Beau and his team high-fived each other to the shock of the entire crew.

Once the commercial break was over, Adhemar and his team took the floor. Unlike their opponents, they stayed seated. "Mr. Speaker, Governor Simpson has stunned us with his presentation," Adhemar said in all seriousness.

Mike nudged Beau. "Gotcha!"

Adhemar suppressed a smile, careful not to acknowledge what he had pulled off. *Mamá*, he thought, *I listened. I watched out for everything.*

He continued, "Not only has Governor Simpson insulted the Finnish people and proposed to put them in grave danger, he has sorely underestimated the might of the Russian military. This is a scenario we would never propose. Never consider. This idea would never be on the table in the Reyes White House." Adhemar deliberately looked at Beau. "At any point."

Beau was confused. "Huh?" He glared at Yancey as though Yancey were responsible. Reading Beau's look, and realizing he was about to become a scapegoat for the entire campaign, Yancey jumped up. "That is not true! You—"

Hawke quickly bounded over to clap a hand across Yancey's mouth. "Continue, Senator Reyes. He's just tired."

"Not a problem, General Warford. I understand," Adhemar said benevolently, smiling at Hawke like a parent whose son had just wrecked the car taking the dog to the vet after witnessing a hit and run on Fido. *Actions like that are okay with me.*

Hawke forced Yancey into his seat, then forced himself to smile back at Adhemar.

Adhemar continued, "To tackle this grave problem, we explored many options, each one having its merits and drawbacks. We knew we needed to design something that would not put our current military operations in jeopardy."

Adhemar nodded to ZeeBee. *You're up.*

"We met with the leaders of England and Ireland," ZeeBee said.

Beau asked Mike, "When did they do that?"

"Dunno."

Now on the TV, a video of the paper milling process: large canisters marked chlorine fill a warehouse.

Adhemar continued—it was his show. "For years the paper milling industry has used chlorine products and vast quantities of water to process paper. Without going into specifics, every environmental agency in the world recognizes the damage this causes to our environment and to the American people."

The screen showed water flowing out of a plant into a stream. Dead fish floated by.

"England has developed a process to tackle this deadly combination. The solution is a closed-loop system that eliminates chlorine and reuses water. The process is oxygen based. The project is called H2-OH."

On the TV: A colorful H2-OH! logo animated on.

ZeeBee added, "It is the number one priority of the UK."

Beau faked falling asleep. "This presentation needs some oxygen!" he said.

Mike snickered.

Trammel glared. "Gentlemen. Senator Reyes has the floor."

"Thank you, Mr. Speaker. To continue, I met with the leaders of England and Ireland and designed an agreement whereby the United States will enact stricter control over papermaking pollution to restrict the use of chlorine products. We will institute H2-OH in the U.S. The industry has run wild for too long. With our commitment toward a greener world, both these countries have jointly agreed to be the peacekeepers in Chad," Adhemar said.

Trammel put up his hand to clarify. "England and Ireland working together?"

"Correct. We stopped there on our way back from Chad and secured their consent."

Beau couldn't resist another comment: "Who does he think he is? Brendan Behan?" It fell flat.

Ignoring him, Adhemar wrapped up. "Together, they agreed to deploy troops to Chad to replace the two thousand American military we will be sending to Finland."

Visibly relieved, Trammel nodded. "There you have it, America. Two candidates. Two solutions."

Mike started clapping. Once he noticed he was the only one doing so, he sheepishly stopped, but not before the cameramen had captured the looks of amusement on Adhemar's team. These contrasted sharply with the *for God's sakes, stop it* looks from Beau and Hawke. Yancey was staring straight ahead, stunned at the turn of events.

Trammel continued, "To recap, Republican candidate Beau Simpson's plan is to drop leaflets from a plane—perhaps a crop duster?—on the entire population of Finland, inviting them to multiple screenings across the country of *The Russians are Coming, The Russians are Coming.* At these events the Finns will be told to welcome the Russian invasion with open arms."

"I wouldn't exactly call it an invasion," Beau protested.

"I would," Trammel snapped. "Basically, it's suck up and deal 'cause the U.S. says it's going to be fun."

Catching activity on Beau's side of the table out of the corner of his eye, he put out a hand to stop any more comments.

He nodded towards Adhemar with respect. "The Democratic candidate, Adhemar Reyes, presented a plan to clean up water pollution in the U.S. from paper mill run-off, which will in turn guarantee a deployment of two thousand British and Irish troops to Chad. This will allow the U.S. to move two thousand troops to Finland to fulfill the request of Finnish government. A critical part of the challenge."

Beau interrupted, "With our plan we don't need to deploy troops. The Finns will not mind—"

"Quit while you're ahead, Governor," Trammel said, effectively shutting Beau down.

"When we come back, I'll give the teams their next challenge."

The President Factor then went to break.

⇐ THIRTY-EIGHT ⇒

As Americans ran to the bathroom, called their friends tweeted and grabbed a few more beers from the fridge, waiting for *The President Factor* to return, the presidential limo pulled up to ZeeBee and Sam's townhouse, double-parked alongside Sam's BMW and essentially blocked the street. The little presidential flags fluttered in the slight breeze. A Secret Service agent jumped out the front door of the limo and stood uneasily at the rear bumper. He disliked the impromptu trips the President made.

Inside, the President was riveted to his iPad, watching the commercial break. Like the Super Bowl, *The President Factor* was the primo place for advertising. The cost of a thirty-second spot was more than $2 million. In the ad that the President was watching, two little kids dressed to look like Adhemar and Beau raced across a wheat field towards a box of cookies.

Sensing that the limo had stopped, the President peered out the window. "Are we here?"

"We are, sir," the driver said.

"Hit it," the President said.

The limo's horn squeaked out the first few bars of "Hail to the Chief."

The President peered out again. No movement outside. "Again. Can you make it louder?"

The driver adjusted a knob on the dashboard and the horn blared the familiar tune.

After ten seconds or so the townhouse's front door whipped open and Sam flew down the stairs. The Secret Service agent quickly opened the door to the backseat and Sam tumbled in. His CIA training took over and he slunk down, even though the windows were so darkly tinted that no one could see in.

"I thought you didn't want this to be obvious," Sam snapped at the president.

"When one is obvious, they become invisible. If I avoided you, it would raise suspicion," the President said. He spoke slowly, using the tone he took with his thirteen-year-old daughter when she wanted to go shopping alone without Secret Service protection. Just the right amount of lecture and condescension. She usually ignored him. He never picked up on it.

Sam was not affected by the president's attitude either. "You've never come to my house before, so how would avoiding me here raise suspicions?"

"Do I detect a note of sarcasm, Sam?"

"That would be correct, Mr. President."

"Considering your position right now, I don't think that is advisable."

With that, Sam sat up. "My position?"

"Your position on this debacle."

"Debacle? You're referring to the obscene display of stupidity by Beau Simpson a few minutes ago before millions of people world-wide?"

"You exaggerate," the president said.

Methinks not.

"I do not *exaggerate*," Sam replied, not even considering applying the word exaggerate to Beau's performance. "We know the world is watching, Mr. President."

"Yes. Anyway," the president said, moving on. "You are in no position to criticize anyone. This thing is entirely your fault. Why, you and your wife conspired to bring down the Republican candidate—"

"I quit," Sam snapped. He made a move to exit the limo but couldn't get a grip on the door handle. The next day he would tell ZeeBee how bummed he was that his inability to open the door at that moment spoiled this grand gesture. He finally gained control, opened the door and got out. On the sidewalk, he paused, then leaned in and spoke softly to the President, "You're not the only one who has things taped, sir."

Closing the door, Sam headed back to his house without a backward glance.

Inside the limo, the president seethed. He opened the window and shouted, "Sam! Come back here. That is an order! Sam!"

Sam continued up his stairs. As he hit the top step, he heard the theme song for *The President Factor* playing from the president's iPad. Entering the house, he sped into the kitchen, snagged a beer and was headed into the living room to watch his wife take no prisoners on prime time TV when he changed his mind. He ran into the hall, grabbed his jacket, patted the pockets and grinned. He looked out the door. The presidential limo was gone. He ran down the steps, jumped into his Beamer and sped away.

On *The President Factor* set, the teams were in place. ZeeBee passed around her bag of Oysterettes. Everyone on her team took a few. She held out the package to Beau.

He snarled, turned his head. *We're not friends here, missy!*

Trammel had regained his poise. "Welcome back to *The President Factor*, coming to you live on the BCD network." Smiling, he slapped two new files on the table. Adhemar's presentation had rejuvenated him.

Same action as before. Different scenario.

"Candidates. Palestine has just launched a nuclear attack on Israel," he said soberly.

Beau jumped up. "Holy Crap!"

"It's the game, Beau," ZeeBee said.

"He knew that," Mike countered.

"This is getting tiresome," ZeeBee said.

Yancey slid over to Mike. "Now that…is *déjà vu.*"

Finding himself in a position to capture the moment, Adhemar stood. The camera zoomed in for a close up. "ZeeBee. Harrison. General Bauer," he said, being the leader once again.

The three stood up. Adhemar picked up the top file and led them from the room with a purpose.

Beau scrambled to imitate Adhemar, but his team had started out of the room without him. He picked up his file. "Guys. Hold up!" After throwing one of his *trust me* smiles at the camera, he hurried after them, thinking, *We should have rehearsed this as well!*

The cameras swiveled around to Trammel. He waited until the *Alice in Wonderland* door closed behind Beau. "What will the candidates do? Find out next week. I'm Speaker of the House Trammel Washington. You've been watching *The President Factor.*"

The control room erupted.

People rushed Makki and Buzz. "Killer scenario," a junior exec gushed. "Did you know about that?"

"No. The challenges come from Speaker Trammel," Buzz said, moving past the guy to all but hug the approaching Uncles. Lots of back-slapping.

"Brilliant, brilliant," Gil said, then leaned in to Buzz and whispered, "We need to talk." Bill was right behind him; he thrust his hand at Makki. "We're looking forward to working with you both. This reality show business has so many possibilities."

Makki looked at Bill's outstretched hand.

Would it become her future or her past?

⇸ THIRTY-NINE ⇻

As soon as his team cleared the door into the hallway Adhemar turned and gave them high-fives.

"One down," he said.

The camera crew was up ahead, sprinting down the hallway to position themselves in the Sit Room. Adhemar was pleased, for it gave him a chance to celebrate out of camera range. Spying the craft service table, he trotted over and grabbed a few mini candy bars. He passed them out. "Fuel up."

"Did you see their faces?" Harrison asked.

"All of America saw their faces," ZeeBee pointed out. "That went so much better than I imagined."

"All of the *world* saw their faces. What are we polling, Harrison?" Adhemar asked, biting into a Snickers.

Harrison pulled out his iPhone. Scanned Flipboard. "We are at…" He double-checked the screen. "We're at a… Holy god! A ninety-five percent approval rating."

"We're gonna ride that straight through to November," Adhemar declared.

"Damn straight," Pinky added.

The candidates' Sit Rooms had been prepped for the new challenge. On one of the screens: a map of Israel. On the next: the same map with a highlighted red area around the Gaza Strip, overlaid with a chart entitled Death Toll. That number was constantly inching upward. Black silhouettes of men, women and children completed the chart. On a third screen: a map of the West Bank, labeled Palestine. On the last screen: A photo of a stern-looking Palestinian man in military uniform, identified as Said Abu. Next to him: a series of international phone numbers related to aid organizations.

The scene was set.

Adhemar burst through the door, eager to tackle the crisis. Despite the win, he knew this was not the time for the team to rest on their laurels. He paused for a moment to take in the info on the screens, and then playing to the camera, he slapped his hands together. "Okay. Scenario number two, folks. Let's see what we've got."

ZeeBee walked over to the screen with the photo of Said Abu. "This guy is one of the senior members of Hamas right now."

Pinky moved to the screen depicting carnage. "What the hell happened to the Patriots we sold Israel? Didn't they deploy?" he demanded.

Adhemar smiled, "You know how the Patriot missile got its name?"

"Something to do with defending the country?" Harrison answered.

"Nope. It stands for Phased Array Tracking Radar to Intercept On Target. So we have to assume that they didn't intercept Palestine's missiles for one reason or another. We can't delve too deeply into what might have gone wrong because that's a given in this scenario. So I'm not sure if that is significant right now, Pinky," Adhemar said curtly.

"Don't they have their own nukes?" Pinky kept pushing.

Annoyed, Adhemar made a slashing sign across his throat and opened his eyes wide, tilting his head towards the cameras. Ohhhhhh!

"I'm not going to go there. As I see it, we have two options. Retaliation or negotiation," Adhemar continued, deflecting what might have been the outing of Israel's nuclear program for the world to speculate on.

"Well, they are an MNNA," ZeeBee added.

"Major Non-NATO Ally. We are obligated to do something."

Sitting on a shelf below one of the screens, a bright red phone rang.

"Has that always been there?" ZeeBee asked.

"I don't know. But this is the first time I've noticed it," Adhemar replied.

"Me too," Pinky said.

Yancey said, "It's been here. I saw it before and didn't think it was real. I guess it works."

They gathered around it.

"Is no one going to mention the irony of them propping this set with a phone of that color?" Harrison asked.

Inside the control room, *The President Factor's* closing animation was playing on the AIR monitor. After that, the credits would roll and the second episode would be over.

Sitting at the switcher next to Bob Henderson, the show's director, was Trammel Washington. He'd rushed to the control room as soon as the floor director gave him the cue he was *out* so he could watch the action coming from the candidate Sit Rooms. Sitting on Bob's other side was Makki.

The three were immobile, staring at the console in front of them, where the name Said Abu flashed next to a phone icon. That phone icon was affixed to Adhemar's now-ringing red phone.

"Is it really him?" Bob squeaked out.

"Who the hell knows? This wasn't in the script," Trammel

snapped. "Where the fuck would he get this number?"

"I'll bet someone tweeted it," Trammel said.

"Tweeted? The phone number for *The President Factor*…
the exact number for the Reyes Situation Room…was
tweeted?" Makki all but shouted. She spun around in her chair
and glared at the crew. They all shook their heads.

Abu's name continued to flash on the console.

"What if he was watching the show and decided to call
in?" Bob said.

"The head of Hamas, Bob? Just decided to call in?"
Makki said, dripping sarcasm.

"It could happen. Do you think he thinks this is—" Bob
jumped out of his chair, voice going up a notch, "Jesus Christ!
What if it is him and he thinks this is for real!"

Makki gave Bob an *Are you really saying that?* look. "I
believe he would know if he nuked Israel, don't you think?"

Back in Adhemar's Sit Room the red phone rang again.
Taking a deep breath, Adhemar punched the speaker button.

"Senator Reyes here."

"Senator Reyes. This is Said Abu." A deep male voice
boomed from the enhanced speakers. *Loud and clear.*

Harrison quickly hit the mute button. "Is that an actor?
What does our contract say about role actors—I thought it
was just us and whoever we brought in."

Adhemar, aware of the cameras, said nothing. His stare
was closed, contemplative, stone-walled.

Pinky leaned over the phone and punched the video
call button. A video feed of Said Abu popped up on the
screen above the phone. They jumped back in unison, all
but Adhemar, as though they had been put through one of
Beau's drills.

ZeeBee turned her head. "Oh yeah, it's him," she said,
putting the speaker back on.

On the screen, Abu smiled. "Senator Reyes, first let me

congratulate you on winning."

Adhemar pulled himself together. "We haven't officially won yet, Mr. Abu."

"We both know that isn't true, Senator," Abu replied.

Adhemar allowed himself a smile in return.

Abu continued, "This is a very interesting project you have going. It has me wondering. Finland. Now Israel. Are you planning on defending all your allies? Or would we have a sit-down first?"

"We are exploring all our options at present," Adhemar said, now back in presidential candidate mode. *This is like being in a debate.*

"I am amused to see Palestine recognized as a country. Tell me, are we in the United Nations in this scenario, Senator?"

ZeeBee handed Adhemar the brief. He waved it at the screen.

"I haven't had a chance to look into that yet."

Abu chuckled. "That seems to be our ongoing fate. Tell me, are we on camera right now?"

"Ye—" Harrison started to answer. Adhemar grabbed his arm. "Since you are watching the show, I'm sure you can see that we are not live right now, Mr. Abu. The closing animation is playing, is it not?"

Abu left the screen. Adhemar and his team looked at each other.

And…*he's back*!

"Yes, you are correct. Excellent. Senator Reyes, the reason I am calling—you have heard of RFID chips, yes?"

"Radio Frequency ID? Yes. The chips embedded in passports, drivers licenses and IDs that contain all sorts of private information."

"This information can be picked up by a reader from almost ten feet away, yes?"

"That is common knowledge, Mr. Abu."

"Thank you, Senator Reyes. But now the U.S. and other countries have encoded their RFID data because a few—shall we say entrepreneurs?—have made their own readers. This I know as well. So, I would like to have the schematics and codes for the equipment that is used to track and read these secure RFIDs. And, of course, the encryption software," Abu chuckled. "That will make it easier to find people, will it not? In my country and yours."

"And you could make your own fake IDs. Passports and such as well?" Adhemar said.

"That is another use, of course." Abu flashed a smile. "So I'd like to have it."

"I'm sure you would, but I don't see how I could be instrumental in getting it to you. Even if I wanted to. Which I don't."

"I'm not so sure, Senator."

"Oh?"

"This little game you are playing. What do you call them? Real life shows?"

"Reality shows."

"Yes. Yes. A reality show. Soon I will know what to expect from the next president. Yes?"

Adhemar shrugged. "These things are not real."

Abu's friendly tone disappeared. "Then why are you playing them? No matter. Here is my reality. I need those plans."

"I won't give them to you," Adhemar matched his tone.

"I will call back in an hour," Abu threatened.

"My answer will not change," Adhemar said deliberately.

Abu smiled an icy smile. "Then, Senator Reyes, maybe I *will* bomb Israel."

The video transmission ended.

🫏 FORTY 🐘

In the control room, Makki grabbed Bob by the shoulders. "Did you record all of that?" she shouted. *Buzz is going to wet his pants. I'm golden*, she thought. *I'll need a new dress for the Emmys.*

"Absolutely," Bob answered, voice trembling.

Meanwhile, over in his Sit Room, Adhemar was the antithesis of trembling. Indeed, he was stoic. He sat at the head of the table, his team on either side, munching on mini candy bars and Oysterettes. They were unusually quiet. Adhemar had chosen his course of action.

The door burst open and Makki and Trammel stormed in. They came to an abrupt halt when they saw the tableau.

"That was phenomenal. What are you thinking?" Trammel screamed at Adhemar, forgetting the cameras were still rolling. He had lost all sense of decorum after witnessing the exchange with Abu.

"We're a tic behind a nuclear holocaust is what I'm thinking," Adhemar replied, deadly serious.

Makki wasn't listening. "Effing great TV. Gonna blow the top off the ratings next week. We'll grab some of this to tease the show—" She paused. "Boom! This may be bigger than Ed Sullivan and the Beatles!"

"Makki! Abu was fucking serious. Get a grip," Adhemar said sharply, then immediately felt guilty.

ZeeBee, Pinky and Harrison all looked back and forth from Adhemar to Makki. *Who is this woman? And how does Adhemar know her?*

Trammel sank down in a chair. He'd been so caught up in the game that he forgot his real job. "Jesus Christ. You're right." His eyes met Adhemar's. "Holy crap, now what?" he said soberly.

Makki watched Adhemar, now suddenly guarded.

Adhemar was matter-of-fact, "I have no choice but to drop out of the game."

"You can't quit," Makki shot back. *Ohmygod. He can't do this to me!* Visions of her fabulous office flashed in her head. The Emmy was fading away fast. *No! This show has to continue.*

"I can. First we came close to causing a famine with Chernobyl thinking this show is for real, and now we're a trigger for the annihilation of an entire country?" As Adhemar spoke, he picked up steam. He knew this was right.

"You have to finish the game. If you quit—you lose," Trammel stated the obvious. Plus, as a fellow Democrat, even though he knew the voters still had to go to the polls in November, he sure as hell didn't want Adhemar's name anywhere near the word "loser" in print or mouthed on any talk show or newscast.

"The game has to continue," Makki said with deliberation. She walked over and stood dangerously close to Adhemar. *Cameras be damned.* She put her arms on his shoulders, leaned up and whispered in his ear. "Sweetie. You don't want to stop this show. Do you? We can figure out a way to see each other that won't jeopardize it."

She felt him lean in to her, and for a split second she thought he was entertaining her suggestion, but he shook her off. "I can't play with people's lives."

"What do you think you'll be doing if you get elected?" she shot back.

"I won't be playing, then," Adhemar said.

"You'll regret this. You are going to lose." She paused for effect. "You'll lose *everything* if you quit. Everything, Adhemar."

Adhemar looked at the beautiful, sexy women who had invaded his thoughts for the past week. That morning he'd resigned himself to knowing that if he saw her, he would find a way to get her alone.

Not anymore.

For the second time in less than a week, he had to ask himself, *What were you thinking?* And it made him sad.

He stepped back. No woman could compete with Adhemar's commitment to the American people.

Makki was exceptional at reading body language, having gotten into it after someone turned her on to the old TV show *Lie to Me*. Watching Adhemar, she knew she'd lost. She folded her arms. Time to take control of the situation. Her job depended on it. "You signed a contract, Senator Reyes." Makki's tone was cold.

"Try to enforce it, Miss Alden," Adhemar said quietly, "The contract states that I will appear in *The President Factor*. In a few minutes there will be no more *'The President Factor.'*"

Yancey was stretched out on the couch in Beau's Oval Office, oblivious to all that was happening on the other side of the studio. He'd pretty much admitted to himself that Beau was not going to win this game. Controlled indifference was his position now.

Mike and Hawke circled from him to the president's desk and back like pieces in Pong.

Beau was on the phone, pacing in front of a Federal-style mirror on the wall across from Yancey, checking himself out of the corner of his eye. Maybe he remembered reading the pizza descriptions at YoGo Pizza because *That's how Kennedy must have looked during the Bay of Pigs!* was going through his mind. *Yep, Beau. You look very presidential.*

Yancey watched the posturing and snickered. Beau had been on hold with the White House for more than ten minutes. "You're not going to get anything there, Beau," he drawled.

"Shut up, Yancey." Beau snapped. He abruptly made a face at Yancey and spoke into the phone, "Yes. I'm ready."

Pause.

"Hello, Mr. President! It's Beau Simpson. Yes, I am calling from my own Oval Office." He saluted himself in the mirror. "Yes, sir. It is a mite intimidating. Yes, it surely is. Well now, I'm callin' 'cause I was hoping to get some advice on this Palestine nukin'—"

Click.

"Hello? Mr. President? Hello?" Beau stared at the phone.

A knock on the door. After a brief second the door opened and Adhemar stood in the doorway.

"You can't be in here!" Mike blustered.

Adhemar didn't bother to acknowledge Mike's presence. He strode directly to Beau. "Beau. I'm out of the game."

Beau quickly snapped his phone shut. Barked out a laugh. "What kind of a trick is this?"

"I don't play tricks, Beau."

"Oh, really. How about—"

"I wouldn't go there, Governor," Adhemar said quietly.

Beau broke eye contact. "What's the matter? This one a little too complicated for you, Senator?" Beau said, trying to control appearances.

"Exactly," Adhemar answered, letting it go. Turning his back on the group, he left the room.

Mike did a little jig. "You win, Beau! You win."

Yancey bounded off the couch, reenergized, and grabbed Pinky in a bear hug.

The door opened once more.

Harrison marched in with the camouflage backpack, interrupting the celebration. He tossed it towards Beau. "You might need this," he said with obvious disdain.

Beau sidestepped the toss and the backpack crashed to the floor.

FORTY-ONE

Trammel leaned against the wall opposite Adhemar's Sit Room. He was patient. He knew he was witnessing history in the making. He was back in Speaker of the House mode.

Adhemar stepped out. "Call up the network, Mr. Speaker, I need to go live."

"Absolutely," Trammel said, nodding and pushing away from the wall. "Where do you want to do this?"

"My Oval Office."

"Excellent choice, Senator. I'll meet you in there. Give us about half an hour."

Adhemar reached out and grabbed his arm. "Wait. Call Ruben Santiago from *Deportes*. I'd like him to be here."

As Trammel sped away, Adhemar saw Sam coming down the hallway. He stiffened and started to turn away.

Sam put out his hand in a *stop* motion and shouted, "Adhemar, wait. I quit."

"Whoa!" Adhemar was truly shocked.

"It's all good. Here, I have something for you." Sam reached into his jacket, pulled out a pack of gum and handed it to him. "Another one of those pesky open microphones caught the president trying to strong-arm a CIA agent into gathering information that would help the Republican candidate win

The President Factor," he deadpanned. "The agent, of course, declined to participate. It's all on there."

Adhemar took the gum, puzzled until he identified it as a thumb drive. "Damn. Thank you."

"Think you'll have to use it?" Sam asked.

Adhemar shook his head. "The only thing this will be used for is leverage to get your job back. I'm trusting the American people to do the right thing this November."

He threw his arm around Sam.

"Come on in, I'm about to do you one better."

The scene was set in Adhemar's Oval Office.

Besides calling the network brass to arrange to break into their prime time programming and giving Santiago a shout—which shocked the hell out of the sports journalist, seeing as he had slammed Adhemar twenty-five years earlier with his *Do your homework, Gringo*! comment—Trammel had also called a press conference. Twenty or so members of the press milled around behind *The President Factor's* cameras—the bulk of which were pointed towards a lectern set up to the left of the Resolute desk. A myriad of microphones—network mic flags positioned for optimal exposure—clustered at the front. One rogue camera pointed to the *Alice in Wonderland* door on the left. More than one person in the room had commented on the door's resemblance to the scenes in the Disney movie and posted comments on their blogs about the eerie resemblance under titles like: Has Reyes Fallen Down the Rabbit Hole? to It was a very un-ending to *The President Factor*. This reaction prompted the set designers to start patting themselves on the back; even though they hadn't planned it that way, they would take credit—of course.

A few reporters brought their photogs with them. Since this was the first time that *The President Factor* set had been open to outsiders, lots of photos/videos were taken and tweeted.

Hard to tell the difference between 1600 and this set, tweeted the reporter from *The Washington Times.*

This access alone had attracted most of those present. *The Washington Post* sent a junior reporter from its Style section, as did the *New York Times.* Their stories would catapult them over to a hard news beat the next day.

The bloggers from various outlets were essentially the only ones who gave their readers live notification. One blogger from TPF Insider posted: *Set seems smaller in person.* These reports and tweets sparked a web sensation that quickly had the country in its grip. The news outlets that hadn't sent anyone over thinking it was just a publicity stunt were kicking themselves the next day. A few heads rolled.

Santiago texted his editor: *Not sure why I'm here.*

Trammel enjoyed the spotlight, posing for picture after picture as he waited for Adhemar. He reckoned this would be the last time he'd be photographed on any of *The President Factor* sets. He greatly preferred this setting to his seat on the Floor; this was much more relaxed. He DVR'd himself whenever he appeared on TV and had noticed that his jaw was set hard when he was on C-SPAN, especially when sitting behind the president. His wife was constantly telling him he looked like Arnold Schwarzenegger in *Total Recall* when he did that. Not particularly flattering. She also mentioned that she thought his swagger on *The President Factor* was sexy. It was hard to ignore a comment like that.

And so Trammel posed. He'd buy thirty papers the next day and casually leave them in the bedroom open to his pictures for months afterwards. And cash in.

The door opened and Harrison entered. The set-up resembled actual presidential press conferences where the chief of staff comes in first and sets the tone. It was carefully orchestrated to great effect. Harrison looked spiffy in another Thom Browne suit, shirt and tie. There would be an immediate run on all three pieces, causing the designer's website to crash under the weight of thirty thousand fans looking for store locations.

Trammel wondered how Harrison managed to procure a new outfit, unaware that the entire Reyes team had stocked their green room with a plethora of choices that morning, thinking they might have to boogie out of there and onto another transport if the situation warranted.

Harrison walked to the lectern. "Ladies and gentlemen. Senator Adhemar Reyes," he said with proper authority.

The cameras spun around to the Wonder door as Adhemar arrived followed by the balance of his team. His white shirt glowed, twenty-four carat gold cufflinks peeking out from his perfectly tailored suit jacket. ZeeBee wore her favorite suit—back from the cleaners after the Old Ebbit sauce-spilling episode. It was her way of throwing a middle finger at Beau and the president. Pinky was all polished medals and erect military bearing.

Adhemar deliberately walked past the lectern to sit at the Resolute desk. The room was abuzz. He waited for the commotion to die down and the studio cameras to get set. He had all the time in the world—the world was waiting for him.

He acknowledged Ruben Santiago with a deliberate nod in his direction. The cameras picked it up and the director quickly cut to a shot of Ruben sitting in the front row, making him the most important journalist in the room. He would get a promotion the next day.

Adhemar's tone matched his serious expression. "My fellow Americans, a few minutes ago," he said, pausing for a beat, "I made a decision to drop out of The President Factor."

The roomful of reporters took a collective breath.

He continued, "To walk away from the very thing I was so sure this country needed. I made that decision knowing some of you might see it as a defeat. Might see it as a sign of weakness. A sign that I cannot lead. This is not correct."

He paused to give weight to what would become a refrain.

"A few minutes ago, I realized the true reality. The fate of this great country cannot be decided by two men playing games. It cannot be decided by a TV producer spinning our words, nor can it be decided by someone halfway across the world who thinks he can force me to play chicken with people's lives."

He paused again. The photogs took their shots. The junior reporters saw their bylines on the front page.

"A few minutes ago...I received a phone call from Said Abu."

The world gasped.

⊨ FORTY-TWO ⊨

On January 20, standing on the balcony of the Capitol Building in Washington, DC, at precisely 12:05 p.m. Senator Adhemar Reyes (D-NY) took the oath of office as President of the United States. Vice President Zeniba St. George, stood behind him and to the left with her husband, Sam, her baby bump barely visible under her chic, fitted winter coat. Next to Sam, Marisol Reyes stood proud.

As Adhemar raised his hand to take the oath, ZeeBee tossed some crackers into her mouth.

Millions stood in the cold to watch the ceremony.

Millions watched on TV and mobile devices.

Dave Reynolds was the network anchor that day, giving the play-by-play. Trying hard to contain his glee, he started his introduction, "Today, the man known as the father of modern politics…"

ACKNOWLEDGMENTS

A huge thank you to Hannah Gordon and Marti Gorman at City of Light Publishing for believing in *The President Factor* and in me.

A debt of gratitude to Catherine Adams of Inkslinger Editing, LLC, for her expertise, comments and discerning eye on the first edition of this book.

Cheers to my friends and former colleagues at NY1 News.

A shout out to Rob LoFrisco for his eleventh hour help.

And a thank-you to my brother, Tom, for providing a view from the other side.